D1157652

RUMORS FROM SHANGHAI

A Novel

Amy Sommers

EARNSHAW BOOKS

Rumors from Shanghai

By Amy Sommers

ISBN-13: 978-988-8552-77-1

Cover design: Alex Britton

Author photo © Chuck Berryman

FICTION

EB132

Published by Earnshaw Books Ltd. (Hong Kong)

For Keven J. Davis

Imagine a man with such an abundance of wit and grace that after spending time with him, you came away with the impression that you were somehow witty and charming. Imagine a man who downplayed his abilities with self-deprecating jokes, but in the conduct of his profession, demonstrated the keenest intellect and insight. Imagine a man with a wicked wit, who mocked the absurdities of the pompous or self-important, but who would reveal a tender compassion toward the vulnerabilities of others. He was outstanding in everything he did, and modest to a fault. In fact, his greatest fault was in failing to realize how fabulous he was.

1

Early September 1940

And now, here he was. Muddy water churning below, aching blue sky blazing above as the launch ferried its passengers toward the row of imposing modern stone buildings known as the Bund. The conclusion to Tolt Gross's journey was mere yards away, yet in a sense it was only beginning. Weeks after setting out from Seattle, months after arguing, agonizing and negotiating, after risking alienating his closest allies and greatest supporters, he was about to set foot on the shore of his new home.

The merry-go-round of life was poised to spin him past the stand holding the brass ring, and he was going to prove his mettle by grasping it; showing that he was as able as his friends believed, and immeasurably better than his doubters claimed. Halfway around the world, in an utterly foreign place subjected to military occupation, where he would be under the direction of a man who loathed him, he would hold a position of status and responsibility in a society nominally part of China, and in reality governed by Whites. Could someone like him thrive? This city promised to be a testing ground. It offered him a chance of a lifetime. It was a place where all things were possible.

Shanghai.

He had heard it was a place where skyscrapers soared and nightlife pulsed. That it simmered with a bouillabaisse of people from around the world. That it had been hived off from China by the English, the French, the Americans, various other countries, and most recently, the Japanese. That it hummed, unmindful of the world-wide Depression of the past decade, the war in Europe, even Japan's invasion three years earlier. It remained a thriving, unstoppable engine of commerce.

He would manage a business stretching from the United States to Asia. The starting gun had sounded. Nothing stood in his path. Those law firms back home that wouldn't hire him? The professors who refused to meet with him? The people who questioned how a man like him could coax a horse to carry him over high hedges, could wield an *epée*, could discuss serious topics? He was here to stake his claim.

As the launch carried its passengers from the massive steamer ship to land, it passed a Japanese destroyer, its deck crowded with sailors arrayed for the raising of the flag. Tolt watched the center of the flag unfurled, protruding against the white background punctuated by red rays, the bulge of red resembling a heart filled with blood. He shook his shoulders, wondering why, on a beautiful sunny day, his mind had conjured such a thought. Japan was bogged down in China: Shanghai had seen no major fighting for almost three years. Call it stagnation, call it stasis, but the Japanese weren't advancing. And after all, the British military were here. So were the U.S. Fourth Marines. Life continued.

Beyond the Japanese destroyer, the Union Jack jauntily billowed atop a building with twin domes. He overheard a passenger next to him telling his friend it was the Shanghai Club, housing the longest bar in the world. That image made Tolt smile, but he reminded himself he wasn't here as a tourist. He had a job: righting the good ship Snow Drift Flour Asia; ensuring that it resumed its role as a money-maker, and ideally, expanded beyond its current markets. Despite war in many quarters, here in Shanghai, the waters of commerce were as calm as in the States, with potentially greater catches swimming beneath the surface. His task was to help American business haul them in.

Disembarking, the nails at the bottom of Tolt's shoes tapped a staccato beat as they struck the brass plates sheathing the gangway steps. A drumroll of welcome. He tried to take it all in: the murky odors rising from the river, the blanket of muggy heat, the mass of humanity arrayed on the quay; what he smelled, heard and saw made him feel like he was spinning on a carnival ride.

The Seattle waterfront he had departed from was Lilliputian in comparison to Shanghai's. Here, the river promenade teamed with crowds, vessels of all sizes and types bunched against the bank, the landward-side flanked by stately buildings arrayed like jagged teeth against the sky.

"Be looking for a fellow with a Snow Drift Flour sign; get a move on!" his companion, a young man of medium height with a stocky build, growled. "The sooner we're on shore, the sooner he can get us to the hotel and away from this humid hell."

With both fists clutching his hand luggage, Tolt called over his shoulder, "Hold the phone, son. These stilts are moving as fast as they can."

"I can think of any number of times your legs have moved you faster than they are at the moment," Ronnie wheezed. "Just last night..."

Over the hubbub, Tolt heard a voice calling. "Tolt! Tolt! Over here!"

He scanned the surging crowd. An eager arm made longer by the closed pink parasol it waved caught his eye. "Diana!" he called out, waving back. Catching sight of the two men standing adjacent to the parasol waver, he yelled, "Tak! Quentin!"

"For Pete's sakes, Gross, you can't just stop! The sooner you're down this gangway, the sooner you and your Tea Tones will be reunited. That's the real reason you wanted to come, after all. All this nonsense about your wanting to help run…"

Tolt let the words hit his back but reach no further. His ears were focused on what lay ahead. He could hear Diana saying, "… through the customs inspection. Quick as you can! We'll wait for you at the exit."

Once past customs, he found himself facing a rope cordon outside of which stood a quartet of smiling faces. "Well," he said, taking them in, "if I had known such a warm reception awaited, I'd have come sooner!"

Hands lifted the rope, reaching to pull him into the surging scrum. One pair belonged to Saburo "Tak" Takematsu, a tall, slim fellow with a lock of black hair falling below the brim of his straw hat, almost obscuring his eyes. "Good to see you, Tolt-san!

"I've got chilled champagne waiting in the car to toast your arrival!" said Quentin Wang beside him. His build was more muscular than Tak's, and he wore his hair pompadour-style, combed back from a wide forehead. Thick straight eyebrows rose above deep-set eyes, the corners of which were crinkling with his smile.

"You won't have to ask me twice!" Tolt said, wiping his brow with his handkerchief.

Diana, bearer of the parasol-cum-flag, was now using it as intended to shield her fashionably pale skin from the sun. She laughed and the movement of her head set her glossy bobbed hair swinging below her chic straw hat. Tolt had forgotten the vibrancy she emanated. It hit him full-on.

"I knew we would somehow lure you here," she crowed. "Not getting a job in Seattle was a good thing after all!"

The fourth person in their group, another young woman,

looked over Tak's shoulder at a young Japanese sailor standing nearby, who was watching them. She lightly touched Tak on his arm and said something to him. Amid his friends' exuberance, Tolt couldn't hear but the wariness that then overtook both Tak's and the woman's faces was striking. Tak shook his head, almost as if shaking off the effects of a spell, then resumed smiling at Tolt.

"My manners! Please allow me to introduce my sister, Sumiko," he said, as the woman stepped forward.

Sumiko was slim in form, as was Diana, but more athletic looking. Despite the crush of the crowd, she managed to bow in Tolt's direction. Instead of bobbed hair, she wore hers pulled back into a low, heavy bun at the nape of her neck. A traditional look, but when she stood upright, the thick row of straight bangs across her forehead struck Tolt as quite modern.

"How do you do," Sumiko said with a reserved smile.

"It's a pleasure finally to meet Tak's sister. Who turns out to look like she could be Diana Wang's twin!" Tolt gave a chuckle, and then bowed. "Thank you, Sumiko-san, for coming to greet me on such a hot day."

"A hot day!" Diana laughed, as Tolt rose from his bow. "Mister, you don't know. According to our calendar, this is already fall!"

Diana linked arms and tilted her head to touch Sumiko's. "Remember in Seattle how Tak used to tell us that he had a sister who was my twin? "

Sumiko smiled again. "After hearing about you for so long, it's a pleasure to meet. She offered him a flat rod that had the approximate shape, albeit shorter and a bit thicker, of a ruler. "Perhaps you would like to use this?" She spread the bamboo edges of the rod and Tolt realized it was a fan.

"You don't say!" Tolt asked. "See here, Sumiko-san, will I get a ribbing from Quentin and Tak if I start using one of these?"

"A ribbing? I'm afraid I don't understand. This is a fan, not a rib."

Tolt chuckled. "I'm too used to using slang with your brother." He switched to Japanese, "I mean, if a man here starts carrying a fan will his friends tease him?"

"You know better than to ask that," Tak said. "We'll tease you no matter what!"

"Ah, my brother told me your Japanese is good!" Sumiko observed. "In Shanghai, when the weather is hot, everyone uses a fan, even men."

An older Chinese man standing a little to the side of the group gave a discreet cough. He was holding a white sign: Snow Drift Flour. This was Mr. Li, who had already taken Ronnie's valise. He introduced himself to Tolt; as Mr. Li's hands were full, Tolt smiled a warm greeting, rather than shaking hands.Looking past Mr. Li, he observed that Ronnie appeared none too happy. Their location on the globe had changed, but would much else?

"My manners this time!" Tolt said. "Saburo Takematsu and Quentin Wang, you'll recall Ronald Planter from our law school days. Ronnie, I don't believe you've had the pleasure of meeting Quentin's sister, Diana. And of course, Sumiko-san — Tak's sister Sumiko Takematsu."

"Charmed," Ronnie, his normally pale complexion flushed a blotchy red, answered in a dry tone suggesting that he was anything but. Dabbing at his neck with a perspiration-soaked handkerchief, he drawled, "Would love to chat, but this heat is murder."

The Takematsus and Wangs made polite bows toward Ronnie, who was already turning away.

"You go on, man," Tolt called after Ronnie's retreating back. "I'll meet you at the hotel."

Ronnie waved the back of his hand in a fashion suggesting

he had heard Tolt. Mr. Li nodded, but Tolt noticed the expression on his face had turned worried. Tolt wondered whether he was anticipating difficulty checking in a Negro traveler. There was no time to inquire, however, as Mr. Li, trailed by a string of luggage porters, was already scurrying after Ronnie.

Tak and Quentin used their shoulders to part a path from the quay to the car, and Tolt made his way behind them, his face bearing a wide grin. This was going to be swell.

Three days later, as Mr. Li swung open the doors and entered the reception area of Snow Drift's office, followed by Ronnie and Tolt, silence descended. The space was large, commensurate with the company's established status, with the wall of one side punctuated by a bank of large windows overlooking the Bund and the river. The dark wood on the window frames and on the floor gleamed against the glossy white walls. Etchings of Snow Drift mills in the United States and China were interspersed with framed news articles extolling important events in the company's history.

Apart from a junior staff member sitting at the reception desk and an occasional visitor waiting for an appointment, the room was normally empty. On this morning, however, it was filled with several dozen men in attire ranging from overalls to office wear.

Seeing the ranks of those waiting, Ronnie let out a low whistle. "Sweet Lord," he said in a voice he thought was under his breath, but really wasn't. "What are all these mongrel types doing here anyway?"

Tolt cringed. Mr. Li turned to face Ronnie, answering in pidgin-tinged English, "They belong managers and section leaders Snow Drift Shanghai. Welcome Planter."

"I see," Ronnie answered, taking off his straw hat and twirling it around his finger. "All well and good, Li. But it's not expected

7

that I'll go round greeting each one, is it? I mean, it's not like my first day on the job is a bloody wedding or something!"

Mr. Li nodded in agreement. "You like say few words, chop-chop, then we go your office?"

"What's to say? It's Monday, time to work." Ronnie inclined his head towards Tolt. "You're the one who's supposed to speak the local lingo. Lay some Ching-chong-Chinaman on 'em, then let's get to it."

Tolt nodded, appalled by Ronnie's behavior, but hoping to minimize the slight to their colleagues. Stepping into the room, he took off his hat, and addressed them in Chinese.

"Colleagues, our company's new general manager, Mr. Planter, has asked me to thank you on his behalf. He appreciates your kindness and the respect you have shown to his family by coming personally to welcome him to Shanghai. He wishes to thank you for your efforts on Snow Drift's behalf, and he looks forward to working together."

A shiver of energy vibrated through the men in the room. What was this? A Westerner, and a dark-skinned one no less, speaking to them in Chinese? How strange. And his Chinese actually seemed quite good. It was perhaps even better than that of some of the local workers, whose mother tongue was Shanghainese and who spoke only the barest smattering of the Mandarin dialect from the north.

Tolt stepped back behind Ronnie, who inclined his head, signaling they were done, then started across the room towards the corridor that he presumed would lead to the offices. Mr. Li spoke a few words in Shanghainese to the group, indicating they were free to return to their posts at the mill, warehouse or office, as the case might be. The local employees surged into the center of the room, filling the space previously occupied by Ronnie, Tolt and Mr. Li, murmuring over the just-witnessed novelty.

The corridor bisected the space, with offices on the corridor's right facing Bund-side and those on the left with no exterior windows. As Ronnie made his way down the hall, he opened a few doors, soon ascertaining that any space worthy of his occupancy would be on the right-hand side. The next door revealed a handsome office furnished with modern amenities, but it was the third that caused Ronnie to walk into the room. If the prior spaces had been generous in dimension, this one was positively palatial. It looked like two offices had been combined into one, with a formal seating area on one side of the room and a desk and visitor chairs on the other.

Mr. Li caught up, saying, "Yes, this Mr. Planter room. Is satisfactory? If you no like, we change."

Ronnie grinned and plopped down on the chair behind the large mahogany desk. "Mr. Planter likee just fine. Fine and dandy. Hell, this is even larger than my Pop's office!" He tossed his hat on the desk and gestured to Li and Tolt to seat themselves.

"So, Li, what's a fella got to know to run this place?"

Mr. Li took a small notebook from inside his suit jacket. "I prepared list. Very complete. Perhaps discuss now?"

" Hmm...how many pages?"

Mr. Li flipped through his notebook. "Eight. Plus two more pages of duties optional. You choose. Do, no do."

Ronnie looked at this watch. "Ten pages? Hell, the president of the Chamber has asked me to tiffin."

Tolt raised his eyebrows. "What's that?"

"What the Brits call lunch." Ronnie grinned, appearing pleased to know something that Tolt didn't. "Ten pages to review, we won't be done 'til supper. What categories are on the list anyway?"

"Categories?"

Ronnie waved his hand in a circular motion. "You know, day-to-day vs. major decisions, operational vs strategic, internal vs outward-facing."

Tolt was transfixed by Ronnie's combination of boorish indifference and to-the-point incisiveness. Before Mr. Li could respond, a soft knock sounded, and a young woman entered, bearing a tray on which were arranged three cups of tea and three cups of coffee. She raised a cup of tea, looking at Ronnie with a questioning expression. He shook his head, "No thanks. It's coffee for this Yank." She nodded and put one of the coffees down on the desk before him, then served Li and Tolt their choices and withdrew.

Ronnie took a sip. "Not bad at all." He put the cup down on the desk. "Where were we? Yes, duties. Look, Li, here's the plan: I'm here as GM. My job is to make sure Snow Drift has strong ties to the business community and to keep my ear to the ground for strategic opportunities to grow the business. For the day-to-day — the operational stuff — that's Tolt. On that long list, you take anything that's not strategic or doesn't involve dealing with the community, and you bring Tolt up to speed."

Mr. Li nodded. Tolt felt his spirits soar. The prospect of daily service under Ronnie's close supervision had induced dread. Now, with a free hand to oversee operations, he would be spared that torment. Mr. Li cleared his throat. "Mr. Planter, with Japan situation ..."

"What situation?" Ronnie interrupted.

Mr. Li appeared uncomfortable. "Well, the war..."

Ronnie waved his hand. "Oh, that. Yes, we heard all about it. In '37 things round here sounded dicey, but look now." Ronnie swung his chair around and pointed down at the Bund teaming with people, and the river full of vessels. "It's business as usual!"

"Yes, business general good, but Snow Drift...well, business not so easy before. Situation tricky. Customs clearance, distribution in China middle. Employees Japanese suspect do sabotage…"

Ronnie swung his chair back round. "Sabotage! What sort of racket are you running, Li? No Commie unionizing types on the payroll, are there?"

"No, sir!" Mr. Li assured Ronnie. "Nothing like. Just Japanese… well, sometime they get idea. How make calm? Needs big guy, top man show we serious. Give Japanese face."

Ronnie raised his chin in Tolt's direction. "Well, son, guess this is where we're going to see what you're made of." Turning back to Mr. Li, he continued, "Mr. Li, Pop thinks the sun rises and sets on Tolt here." Regarding Tolt with a challenging expression, Ronnie added, "He's the one who's supposed to know about dealing with you Asiatics. Let's see how he does."

Turning again to Mr. Li, he added, "You get into a jam, then you give me a shout." Ronnie stood and stretched. "Gentlemen, I've got to get ready to head out to meet Mr. Franklin at the American Club." It occurred to Tolt that when it came to sizing up the local power players, Ronnie was showing more initiative than he would have expected.

Tolt and Li also rose and moved towards the door. The sound of Ronnie's voice stopped them in their stride. "One more thing."

They turned to face him. "Gross, remember: when I say you're responsible for making sure things run right, the emphasis is on 'right.' Anything goes wrong, it's my ass that will be on the line with the old man. As far as you and me are concerned, it's your ass on the line first. We clear?"

Tolt nodded and left Ronnie's office with Li. For the umpteenth time, Tolt wondered whether the job would prove worth the fraying of his relationship with his grandfather, the person he loved most, and who had given him the opportunities that made success in this job a possibility.

2

LATE SEPTEMBER 1940

THE CURSES OF two rickshaw drivers who had nearly collided brought Tolt back to the task at hand: getting to work on a bright September morning with his limbs intact. Every sort of conveyance from autos, to rickshaws, motorcycles, trams and occasional donkey carts filled the roads. One could not be too careful. Once safely across the street, Tolt resumed his reverie.

The welcome his friends had arranged the day he alighted on the Bund had set the tone for the days and weeks since. The Wang and Takematsu siblings offered a ready-made group of chums, who devised a succession of pleasurable outings that made him feel at home. And with each, he found the clench in his belly, prompted by the fear that he would be barred entry because of his skin color, had eased. Was it being in the company of the all-powerful Wangs that made his skin color a non-issue? Or that in Shanghai all that mattered was how many Mexican silver dollars you had in your pocket? Who cared? Dissipation of the belly clench made him feel light as the proverbial feather. Hell, the city already felt so much like home, he was prepared to claim rebirth as a Shanghainese. Tolt grinned at that thought, then whistling, he skipped up the steps of the McBain Building.

Office hours started at 9:00, but Ronnie didn't make an appearance until closer to 11:00. Following a night of carousing, he would often bypass the office, heading directly to lunch. On such days, it was more like 3:00 before he made appeared. Either way, he was mostly out of Tolt's hair, leaving him free to devote mornings to reviewing overnight cables, reports on shipping snafus, commodities trading reports and weather predictions for the coming season — data likely to impact pricing and availability of future crops. It was like a crossword puzzle with tricky, but not impossible, clues.

The best part was working with his local colleagues. Initially bemused at the prospect of working for a Negro, they had speculated about whether Tolt would be a continuation of prior Western managers uninterested in their viewpoint, or something even worse. They had only ever used either English or pidgin to communicate with the Americans. While exchanges weren't nuanced, expectations were well understood: do what the Americans demand, don't contradict; but it didn't take long for their misgivings to begin to ease. Communicating with the boss in Mandarin opened new vistas. Not Shanghainese, of course, but still better than bewildering English. And having a boss curious as to their perspective on the China market? A novelty indeed, but an enjoyable one. For Tolt's part, he found them all engaging and astute.

True to Ronnie's word, he was content to leave the day-to-day management operations to Tolt. This was an arrangement that he, Tolt and the local staff all found satisfactory. In the weeks since their arrival, however, Ronnie had identified one strategic project he wanted Snow Drift to pursue. At the beginning of the current week, he had dropped off a report at Tolt's office, asking him to take a look. Tolt spent the previous day reviewing it, and now sat jotting down some notes.

Around eleven, Ronnie popped his head in the doorway. "Have you finished yet?"

"As a matter of fact, I have."

"Well?" Ronnie entered.

"I can see why you're interested. I don't know though — might need further evaluation before recommending to your father."

"What do you mean, 'further evaluation'?" The tone of Ronnie's voice shifted from friendliness to petulance.

"It just strikes me as risky. We've been here, what — less than a month? Do we have enough market knowledge to recommend such a significant investment?"

"Haven't you listened to anything I've told you? Building a bigger, more modern mill in Shanghai is a no-brainer." Ronnie used his right forefinger to press back the fingers on his left hand as he enumerated. "First, the Chinese district around Kiangwan has some of the cheapest land to be found; the price is down significantly from five years ago. And, now that the Japs are in charge, they're bringing some order to bear in this loony country. Any investments made today are going to be worth many times what we put in." He shook his head. "For Pete's sake, Japan's the first Oriental country to industrialize and modernize. Even a simpleton can see they're going to be calling the shots. Not the Brits, not the French and certainly not the Chinese. A can't-lose deal if ever I've seen one."

"Perhaps." Tolt rubbed at some shreds of eraser scattered on his notes. "But the counterpoints are that this war — or whatever it is — has already been underway for three plus years. China's not showing signs of crying 'uncle' yet."

Ronnie's face took on a closed quality, as he gazed out the office window behind Tolt.

"And," Tolt continued, "given the steps that Roosevelt is taking to tighten the noose on exports of aircraft fuel and scrap metal, who's to say things between Japan and America couldn't get dicey? My sources say now's the time to stay liquid in China."

"Your sources. Right," Ronnie scoffed. "You mean those Chink compradore wet smacks you run with." He looked at Tolt, "They're not exactly Swan, Culbertson and Fitz, are they? I mean Swan, they're the most successful brokers in town. And in case you didn't notice from that report I gave you, *they* are the experts recommending this Kiangwan site. There's a reason I feel so confident about making this proposal!"

"Sure, and they're also the same Swan, Culbertson and Fitz who stand to earn a commission if Snow Drift Flour buys the land they're brokering," answered Tolt.

Ronnie scowled. "Why my father thought you should be the assistant GM instead of actually being my valet, is a mystery."

With that pronouncement, Ronnie left, slamming the door behind him. Tolt shook his head with a rueful smile. Life in Shanghai might be grand, but being tied to Ronnie, it couldn't be called perfect.

For lunch, some days he had a tray of delicious noodles brought up from a neighboring restaurant. Other days, he met business associates for multi-course meals at Chinese restaurants. Occasionally, he would lunch with Quentin, Tak or Diana, usually soda shop fare at the Chocolate Shop or Jimmy's Kitchen. One of them might send a note over by messenger to suggest where to lunch, other times they would drop by unannounced.

A little before noon Diana poked her head inside the doorway. "Hungry?" she inquired.

"Always!" Tolt grinned.

"I have a fitting at the tailor's at two, so mind if we just go down the street for noodles?"

"You know me; never met a noodle I didn't like."

Once they found an open table at the noodle shop and placed their orders, the two started to catch up. In just a few minutes, the waiter swooped in to deliver bowls of fragrant soup noodles. Tolt and Diana sniffed with appreciation, then leaned over their bowls with their chopsticks to begin slurping up the mouthfuls of deliciousness.

Diana picked up a bottle of dark, fragrant vinegar on the table and passed it to Tolt.

"You know me well. Don't even need to ask, and there it is."

"Well, sour is your favorite flavor, isn't it?" Diana asked with a smile.

"It's my personality that's so sweet, needs a bit of sour to offset it."

"Quentin always seems to like adding a lot of sugar to his coffee. According to your reasoning, does this mean his personality is sour?" she asked. She lifted chopsticks full of noodles high to drain off the excess broth before sliding them into her mouth.

Tolt laughed as he added a dash of vinegar to his bowl. He took another bite, savoring the increased tang.

Placing her chopsticks across the top of her bowl, Diana said, "I'm curious about Ronnie."

His mouth full of noodles, Tolt raised his eyebrows. "Before you arrived, you remember writing to tell us Ronnie's father offered you the job here?"

Tolt nodded.

"You said your grandfather was arguing with you, didn't want you to come because you had to tell people in Seattle you would be Ronnie's personal servant."

Tolt nodded again, his face troubled.

"You said your grandfather was in a rage, forbidding you from coming, but Mr. Planter senior wasn't giving up. You never told us, though, *why* he was insisting that you tell people that story."

Tolt shook his head. "As long as I've known Mr. Planter, he's always been top notch. Nicest guy you could ever meet. Will talk about anything. But on this one, I couldn't get an answer out of him. He just got all red in the face and told me this was the way it had to be if I was going to take the job as assistant manager."

"Did your grandfather ask him why?"

Tolt shook his head, blowing out his breath with a loud 'whoosh.' "No siree! That was part of what had Papa so worked up. He and Mr. Planter are buddies. Hell, back when Planter landed at Yesler's dock with only a quarter in his pocket, Papa fronted him his first meal on credit. Planter knows Papa takes pride in his family's not having to work as domestic help. No way Papa was going to support such a story, much less swallow his pride and be seen as begging a White man, even one who's his close friend, to explain the condition."

"Well, someone had to be behind the idea." She paused for a moment, took a swallow of tea. "Is Ronnie honoring the promise his father made?"

"Well, as a matter of fact, this morning was the first time since we arrived that he's made me wonder about that." Tolt filled Diana in on the Kiangwan land that Ronnie wanted Snow Drift to purchase.

"Is this a project you want to support?" Diana asked in a cautious tone.

"Not really. What with the hostilities with Japan unresolved, my first reaction is that putting money into a big capital-intensive project in Shanghai isn't a swell scheme. That said, here we are slurping on noodles as if nothing's amiss, so maybe I'm a worrying old granny."

Diana took a snowy white handkerchief from her handbag and wiped her hands to remove any traces of oil. "Our family has holdings in Kiangwan. It's land Papa acquired a few years back when Chiang Kai-shek first decided to create a Chinese alternative to the foreign-concession areas."

Tolt cocked his head with interest.

"Back then, the possibility of Japan's invading seemed remote," she said. "In '31 they tried, but then backed off. The next few years, they'd make noises, but nothing serious came of it, so investment continued. After '37, when they did invade, well, Papa decided not to undertake any projects in Kiangwan."

Diana paused while the waiter swooped in to refill their teacups. "The situation isn't likely to improve any time soon. Last year, my father and Quentin asked a broker our family does business with, to try to sell the property. But, even at a deep discount, we've not received any offers."

"That doesn't sound good. You know which broker your family is using?"

"Swan," Diana replied with a look straight in Tolt's eyes.

"Swan? What in the...?" Tolt exclaimed, shaking his head. The waiter dropped in again, this time to remove their empty bowls. After he had given the table a cursory wipe with a dingy rag, Tolt continued. "Here's the thing. If I object on the grounds of your family's experience, Ronnie's bound to dismiss me as being influenced by my friends, not by the facts."

"Well, if it's facts you need, Papa had an analysis of the Kiangwan market prepared after we had no luck finding any buyers. His reason was similar to yours: he needed objective evidence to show the other members of the family why the land wasn't selling. I saw the report in his office at home. It's pretty nifty, all sorts of statistics on how prices have declined, investment has dropped off, with few new projects in the works. I can ask for a copy."

"Now you're cooking! Which firm did the report? Anyone we'd have heard of?"

"Swan," Diana replied again, this time with a smile in her eyes.

"What? Some kiss-off! The most reputable brokerage in Shanghai talking out one side of their mouth to Snow Drift Flour about how Kiangwan's where it's at, and out the other to the Wang family about how the place is dead. Unbelievable."

"Unbelievable? This is Shanghai. Everything is believable. If you want to succeed, never forget that everything is believable, but nothing is trustworthy."

"Words to live by! Embroidered onto my dressing gown, that's where I'm putting 'em!"

Diana laughed. As they gathered their things to make the table available to one of the customers waiting at the front of the restaurant, Tolt signed the chit the waiter handed him.

"Well, just be careful of that Ronnie," she said. "The father may have good intentions, but from everything you've told me, the son is tricky."

They walked along the sidewalk back towards Tolt's office.

"Say, Quentin was making noise about getting folks together to play golf this weekend." Tolt adjusted the brim of his hat to block the bright afternoon sun. "You heard anything from Tak about whether he and Sumiko can go?"

"No, I've not seen Tak and Sumiko this week." Diana reached into her purse and stopped in front of an old lady seated on a stool selling jasmine buds strung on thread. Selecting a string, she handed over some coins and as they resumed their stroll, she sniffed the fragrant buds. A short way along, a familiar figure emerged through the crowd.

"Tak!" Tolt called out.

Diana looked up and waved. Tak acknowledged them, but not with his usual broad smile. They noticed he wasn't alone. As Diana and Tolt approached within speaking distance, Tolt said in English, "Hey there, buddy! How's the world treating you today?"

Tak gave a small bow, sort of a cross between a Japanese bow and a Western nod of the head. In Japanese, he replied, "May I introduce you to Captain Hajime Takeda?"

The other man stood erect, which coupled with the bright, inquisitive expression in his eyes, made him seem a bit like a bird. Not a trilling happy bird, more like a watchful hawk. Takeda gave a full bow. Tolt bowed in return, and uttered appropriate niceties in Japanese. Diana stood at his side, as if frozen.

Takeda listened to Tolt, then looked at Tak. "Most unusual!"

"He speaks fluent Japanese, so you may speak to him yourself, if you wish," replied Tak in a tone that was polite, but with a hint of dryness.

"Is that so? Doubly unusual." Turning to Tolt, he spoke in a slow way, as if speaking to a small child, repeating again in Japanese, "It is a pleasure to meet you."

Tolt bowed again, and replied in a natural fashion. "It is indeed a pleasure to meet you."

At this, Takeda laughed and looked at Tak, "Ah, I see you have not exaggerated! So unusual for an American, and much more so one who is not of Asian descent."

"You are too polite to a poor foreigner!" Tolt answered with a friendly smile.

Takeda bowed again towards Tolt, this time a degree deeper. Throughout the exchange, Diana retained her stolid demeanor, making only the most minimal nod to acknowledge Takeda's existence.

Tak broke the awkwardness. "Will you excuse us? I'm afraid we're late for an appointment."

Reverting to English, Tolt answered, "Yes, of course! I'll follow up with you later, Tak-san!" Then he called out in Japanese,

"Good-bye, Captain Takeda."

He and Diana resumed their walk back to Tolt's office, where Diana had left her rickshaw boy. She looked down at her wristwatch. "Oh, time is getting on. Let's walk faster, as I need to be at the tailor's soon."

"Wow, that guy is something!" Tolt said. "What's his deal?"

Picking up her pace, Diana frowned, her voice vibrating with distaste. "He... he is the officer who was responsible for planning the aerial campaign when Japan invaded in '37. Thousands and thousands of Chinese civilians died in those attacks. Because of him." Her jaw clenched. "Poor Tak and Sumiko. He also happens to be their cousin. No way for *them* to avoid knowing him."

Tolt was astonished. But Diana wasn't done yet. She twirled her string of jasmine buds ever faster, with a stony expression in her eyes. "And, as if that's not bad enough, he insists he is the man who Sumiko must marry."

3

OCTOBER 1940

SUN STREAMED into the dining room where Tolt was tucking into a hearty breakfast the Number One boy had set on the gleaming table before him. He grinned at the thought of his having a staff to care for him, his clothing and the sleek apartment he occupied: besides the Number One boy, a cook, a wash amah, and a chauffeur. Like living at Papa's hotel, but without the guests! As he sipped his coffee and looked around the open plan living and dining room, it occurred to him that his apartment in the new French architect-designed Gascoigne Apartments resembled nothing so much as the film set of a Fred Astaire picture.

Soon Tolt, attired in golf togs and armed with his driver, was tootling west on Avenue Joffre. He strummed his fingers on the car's armrest, filled with nervous energy at the prospect of meeting Mr. Wang, about whom he had long heard. Since their law school days in Seattle, Quentin had recounted many stories about his father in which Mr. Wang was always decisive and dynamic. He valued the proprieties of traditional Chinese society, including his duties and responsibilities as leader of a family, while embracing the opportunities which Shanghai's modern and international environment offered for business. The stories Quentin shared often involved his father's exploits in overcoming an impediment to a business transaction by finding an imaginative solution to a seemingly intractable problem, one which frequently embodied application of traditional Chinese ethics or social values.

As the car pulled up on the gravel drive in front of the clubhouse, Tolt stepped out into the balmy air, marveling once again that early October in Shanghai felt as warm as Seattle in July. He spied Quentin and his father standing on the stone patio before the clubhouse's main entrance. The resemblance that Mr. Wang bore to the actor John Gilbert was striking. Both wore their hair parted in the center and sleekly combed back, with dark straight eyebrows paralleled by a trim dark mustache. Mr. Wang's build was slimmer in cast than Quentin's muscular frame, but there was definitely a commonality in the confident way each man carried himself. In the pictures Quentin had shown Tolt of his family, his father had worn either a traditional long Chinese gown or formal Western suit, but today he was kitted out in golf attire, albeit quite formally, wearing a suit of tan tweed with plus fours, rather than the more casual version of plus fours paired with a sweater vest that Quentin wore.

Quentin did the honors, and Mr. Wang reached out to shake Tolt's hand with a warm smile. Tolt replied how long he had desired to meet "Elder Uncle" Wang, an honorific that made Mr. Wang smile even more broadly.

As they entered the clubhouse, Diana bounded over to them, holding hands with Sumiko, and exclaimed, "Ah, here you are, and now that we are all together, we shall have some fun!" Sumiko smiled as she greeted Tolt with a polite bow.

Tolt was delighted and surprised at Diana's being there, so much so that he was surprised at his own reaction. Trying to cover his befuddlement, he took in Sumiko's golf ensemble and asked, "Sumiko-san, I didn't know you play golf?"

"Oh yes! I started learning when I was at school in

Switzerland." She beamed. "I love it. Any chance I get, I play."

"And wait 'til you see her. She's so good!" interjected Diana.

Sumiko playfully slapped her friend's arm. "Don't say that, it's bad luck!"

"Never!" laughed Diana.

"No golf for you today, Miss Wang?" Tolt asked with a grin.

"Not my game, thanks," she said, returning the smile. As Mr. Wang and Quentin started to head out to the course, Diana skipped over to her father, tucking her arm into his, and leaning close to him. They led the group through the French doors leading out to the course. "Our cousins are already out at the first tee. Come this way!" she called over her shoulder.

Following a few steps behind, it struck Tolt that he had often observed Diana taking leadership of a group, but her little girl-like gesture in holding on to her father reflected a submissiveness he hadn't previously seen.

With their father's presence, the bustling and attentive service that enveloped Quentin and Diana wherever they went was magnified by a significant factor. Tolt grinned as he observed a man trailed by a bevy of potential caddies approaching them, and he could see from the corner of his eye another fellow who was emerging from another wing of the clubhouse, adjusting his jacket and pulling his shirt cuffs as he hurried over to greet Mr. Wang. The man leading the caddies introduced himself as the course manager and in turn introduced his boss, the club manager. Mr. Wang gave them a polite nod.

Quentin and Diana didn't seem to notice the hubbub, and Tolt thought he detected a glint of humor in Mr. Wang's eye as servers hurried to offer him cool cloths to wipe his brow, a drink, while the course manager extolled the strengths of the different caddies. The presence of four of Quentin's cousins added to the melée. As everyone chatted and proposed who should play with which caddy, the pandemonium escalated to a din. And still, Mr. Wang appeared genial, calm and unaffected. Marveling at Mr. Wang's sangfroid, Tolt wiped his forehead with his handkerchief. In the shower of attention directed at Mr. Wang, no one had thought to offer him so much as a glance. He contemplated whether the combination of heat and noisy racket were likely to induce a migraine.

The caddies assigned, they and the golfers set out for the first hole's tee. The course and club managers made deep bows and excused themselves while the players looked out over the course or consulted their caddy on whether to use a three wood or a driver.

Mr. Wang and the cousins were locked in a vociferous discussion, which sounded like it might be escalating into an outright argument. They were speaking Shanghainese, so Tolt couldn't understand fully, but he gleaned the topic was which foursome should go first. Mr. Wang was adamant it should be his guests, the cousins, and they were equally vociferous that it would be poor form to go before their Uncle Wang. Tolt smiled to himself as he twisted and stretched in preparation for the game.

A touch to the back of his shoulder made him look back. Diana was holding onto the head of one of Sumiko's clubs and had poked him with the handle. When he turned around, she assumed a mock fencing stance and extended the club as if it were her weapon. In her deepest voice, she said, "Sir, I challenge you to a duel!"

Tolt was about to accept, when Mr. Wang called in a sharp tone, "Daughter, be careful! You could injure someone!"

Upon hearing this admonition, he expected Diana to object or make some mocking reply to minimize the concern expressed, but instead, she lowered the club and apologized. "I'm sorry, Father," she said, a contrite look on her face.

Tolt had never seen Diana so chastened and deferential. Intrigued, he moved closer and said in a light tone, "That's all right, I was going to use my best parry move on you. No chance to do me harm!"

Diana looked sober. "I should be more cautious. My father is always concerned about safety, especially when it comes to Quentin and me."

Tolt leaned on the wood club he had planted on the turf like a walking stick. "Is he afraid you're going to be hurt?"

"Or hurt someone else. At least as it relates to me." Diana gave a wry smile.

Perplexed, Tolt frowned. "How's that? You've never struck me as a particularly dangerous type." In a mock serious tone, he added, "Mouthy, sure, but dangerous? Is there another side to you I should be worried about?"

Diana answered in a matter-of-fact voice. "Well, I did almost kill Quentin at birth. And, as he is the only son, his loss would have been a catastrophe for a family like ours. Who would have worshipped the ancestors? No one to carry on the family name. How to continue the family business?"

From the Our House chef, Ping, Tolt knew that peaceful existence in the afterlife required male descendants to feed the ancestors' spirits, but her statement about almost killing her brother pricked his curiosity.

"I'm having trouble grasping how a newborn almost kills. Help me out."

"Well, I was born first, with my umbilical cord wrapped around Quentin's neck. As I came into the world, the cord tightened." Diana formed a ring shape with her forefingers and thumbs, then made the circle smaller.

"By the time Quentin came out, he was blue and wasn't breathing. He almost didn't make it. They weren't able to save our mother. So between losing his wife, and almost losing his heir, the experience left a deep impression on my father. To this day, he worries deeply about our safety."

Diana was as serious as Tolt had ever seen her. "Added to this, he fears my temperament is too flippant, and as a result, I'm likely to come to harm." She started to grin a bit. "And he's probably right!"

Tolt considered how to reply, but before his silence could become awkward, Quentin called out, "Hey, the cousins are going to tee off first. Move back!"

Tolt and Diana followed Mr. Wang, Sumiko and Quentin a short distance behind the Wang cousins. Mr. Wang, Sumiko, Diana and Tolt stood a little to the left of the first foursome, with Quentin in turn a little farther to their left, and bent over his putter, practicing his line.

Tolt admired Quentin's easy touch with the putter, then realized he was being addressed by Mr. Wang. "Tolt, are you by any chance partly of Chinese ancestry?"

Surprised, Tolt answered, "Uncle, that's a question I've not previously considered! To my knowledge, I'm not." He raised his eyebrows and smiled. "I've never thought of myself as looking at all Chinese. Why do you ask?"

One of the caddies presented Mr. Wang with a cup of tea on a tray. He took a sip, then asked, "Have you heard of Eugene Chen?"

Tolt was even more puzzled. "Wasn't he the Foreign Minister in the '20's?"

"Yes, at various times he served as Foreign Minister."

Mr. Wang waved away the caddy who was now proffering him a cool cloth. "Chen grew up in Trinidad and his wife was part French and part African, so their children are a mixture of Chinese, Western and African races. I met Chen's son Percy when he was in Shanghai. A handsome and dashing young man. You and he have similar colored skin. It made me wonder whether you, too, might have some Chinese blood."

Mr. Wang's query, while blunt, didn't strike Tolt as provoked by any malice. Indeed, he didn't sense any anti-Negro feeling in his attitude. Tolt concluded that this was another instance of the Chinese ability to be frank in a way that Americans often found disconcerting, such as when Chinese asked how much money you earned or told you you were fat. It was all about getting to the facts at hand.

In the midst of this exchange, Tolt suddenly saw the head of the driver swung by the first player teeing off, detach itself from the club handle on a trajectory to strike Quentin straight on the forehead. Almost faster than the eye could see, Tolt raised his own driver to block the hurtling projectile, and the 'missile' made a loud cracking noise, then dropped onto the grass with a thud.

Mr. Wang looked down at it and realization of what had occurred registered. His face froze. Sensing the rush of energy around him, Quentin looked up from his putting practice, while Diana covered her mouth to stifle a scream, and Sumiko's expression assumed a look of terror. The Wang cousins turned to see what had become of the missing club head, perceiving with horror the tragedy that had been averted by the narrowest of margins. The demeanor of Quentin's father changed with almost equal rapidity, his confidence gone, his age and frailty revealed. Observing the now-harmless club head on the grass before him, and the expressions of those facing him, Quentin, too, perceived what had just transpired.

Seeking to break the tension, Tolt said, "Well, that's one way to make sure we're all awake!"

Mr. Wang turned to Tolt, reaching both his hands to grasp

Tolt's right, which he shook with great vigor. "Thank you," he said in a voice thick with feeling. He cleared his throat, trying to master his emotions. "My deepest gratitude. I don't know how to thank you for...for preventing a tragedy!"

Seeking to downplay the seriousness of the situation, Tolt replied with a Chinese aphorism, as to who can say whether something that appears a calamity may turn out to be a fortunate event.

Mr. Wang shook his head. "Yes, yes — none of us can say when a misfortune may turn out to be fortunate, but today, I can say for our family it was a beneficial day indeed when you befriended my son."

The lighthearted mood of earlier was gone, replaced by palpable anxiety. Turning to the others, Mr. Wang regained his self-control and said in an encouraging tone, "This has given us all a shock. Shall we return to the clubhouse for some tea?"

Everyone agreed that this seemed wise, so they abandoned the planned round. Striding alongside Tolt, Quentin clapped him on the back, his gesture expressing deep appreciation.

Diana, walking on Tolt's other side, had also recovered her usual good humor. "Well, now that you've saved Quentin's life, Papa can stop worrying about my having almost taken it at our birth!"

"You!" Tolt shook his head and chuckled at Diana's irrepressible spirit.

"The speed of your reaction just now was amazing," said Quentin.

"Well, I guess it's a good thing after all that Papa made me study fencing with that fellow Rupp," Tolt demurred. "Rupp's training and Saint-Georges's 'eye of the cat' strategy have served us well. We'll have to drink a toast to them."

Diana laughed. "Brother, now that Tolt has saved your life,

Papa is in his debt, so Tolt can ask him for any favor he wishes! That's a chit we may need one of these days if we get in a scrape."

"Sister, near as I can tell, you're the one getting in scrapes, and Tolt's the one with the chit, so you'll have to stretch to figure out how you're going to use this to your advantage."

"One of these days, I'm sure I will."

"Who are Rupp and Saint-Georges?" inquired Sumiko.

Tolt started to answer, and then Quentin, interrupted. "Saint-Georges was the Chevalier de Saint-Georges, a fencing master who worked for the French king before the revolution — the best fencer in Europe. Tolt studied fencing with a retired German navy officer named Rupp, who taught him about Saint-Georges. Like our friend here, Saint-Georges was dark-skinned, with a French father and African mother and he was raised in the Caribbean before his father took him back to France."

"Turns out you *were* listening all those times I was droning on!" Tolt joked.

Quentin grinned at his friend. "Of course!" Quentin turned back to Sumiko. "Saint-Georges was also a soldier who fought for his country when it was invaded, a virtuoso violinist, composer and conductor. What in English they call a 'Renaissance man.'"

"Ah, I see."

Looking at Quentin, Tolt asked, "Did I ever tell you what my buddy Jimmy said when Papa's friend Mr. Gayton showed us a picture of Saint-Georges?"

Quentin shook his head.

"Well, Saint-Georges had on a white wig, like gentlemen wore back then. His face was dark and handsome. So I whistled, and said something like, 'Forget Douglas Fairbanks and D'Artagnan. Paul Robeson ought to make a moving picture of the Chevalier!' Jimmy, he just scoffed and said, 'No one would go see it.' When I pressed him to explain why, he said, 'Who could believe a Negro could be a hero? Especially in some war?'" Tolt shook his head. "But I didn't care. To me, Saint-Georges sure looked like a hero."

Quentin clapped his hand on Tolt's shoulder with a warm laugh. "Well, you, my friend, you're a modern version of Saint-Georges. "

"Go on with yourself!" Tolt laughed back, but his heart warmed. Sumiko smiled. "A fencer, soldier, musician. Yes, a Renaissance man sounds right! Perhaps this winter, one of the fancy dress balls will choose a theme where Tolt will have a chance to dress as Saint-Georges."

Diana giggled at that thought. "With or without the powdered wig and short breeches, you'll always be heroic to the Wang family."

Diana's words evoked giddy laughter amongst the friends as they entered the clubhouse, filled with relief at a crisis averted.

4

November 1940

Tolt sat in the entrance hall to the Wang family home reading that day's *North-China Daily News*. The banner headline concerned England's victory over Italy in a naval battle:

Taranto Echoes
BRITAIN ALL SMILES.
First Lord on the Victory

Tolt read how British naval forces had deployed planes to attack the Italian fleet at anchor. An accompanying analysis noted that it constituted the first all-aircraft ship-to-ship naval attack in history.

The British had deployed obsolete biplanes to strike the Italian battle fleet at anchor using aerial torpedoes, succeeding despite the shallow depth of the water. The analysis finished with the question, "Will this devastating attack wrought using the Royal Navy's carrier-launched aircraft, instead of its battleships, mark a beginning? Time will tell whether an era of naval aviation looms ascendant over naval battleships's big guns."

In the gaiety of Shanghai, it was easy to forget that there was indeed a war going on, not just in China, but also in Europe. Engrossed in the news from Italy, Tolt lost track of where he was. Suddenly, he heard the unmistakable clip-clop of high heels and looked up to see Diana descending the stairs, followed by her maid bearing an evening wrap. Wolf-whistling as he stood to greet her, Tolt dropped the newspaper on the bench. Who cared about naval innovations halfway around the world? Diana, wearing a slim, silver-colored silk evening dress covered in metallic paillettes, shimmered under the light of the entryway chandelier.

"With that dress, you glisten like a sockeye salmon making its way upstream!" he remarked.

Diana narrowed her eyes and replied, "You're not comparing me to a fish, are you?"

"Well now, what if I am?" Tolt grinned. "Just the other day, Quentin was telling me how your grandfather loved his carp, gave them names, sang to them, would tell anyone who would listen how beautiful they were. Are you saying you're not as beautiful as your granddad's carp?"

"Hmmm. When you put it like that, it doesn't sound so bad." Diana fiddled with one of the dangling jade earrings peeking from her shiny hair. "But, grandfather didn't start talking about the beauty of his fish until his later years. Before that, he was renowned for the number of concubines he kept! Is this a sign that you're aging before your time, Mr. Gross?"

"Hmmm. Now I'm the one who has to ponder!"

She turned her head to look back at him while he draped the cloak on her shoulders. Tolt felt his pulse quicken.

"You know, this is why we Chinese women are fond of Western men."

"Because we help a lady with her coat?"

"Well, yes, but it's not as simple as that. Hsiao Ch'en could have put on my coat. That's her job, and a Chinese man would have let her do it. A Western man looks at it differently, he thinks he's supposed to do it as a sign of chivalry."

"And?"

"And," Diana said smiling, "Chinese girls like it."

They were heading to *Le Nuage* before meeting their friends. Tolt had overheard Diana mentioning that she wished to try this popular French restaurant, and he used his success in securing a difficult-to-get Saturday night dinner reservation as an enticement for her to dine with him. When Diana asked about the others, Tolt replied that the reservation was only for two (neglecting to reveal that he had not asked for a larger table). Unsure about whether Diana saw him purely as a buddy, Tolt refrained from explaining his desire to spend time alone with her.

"Well, it's a good thing Papa thinks you're the bees' knees, or I'd never be allowed to go out alone with you." Diana pulled up the sleeves to her evening gloves.

"How's that?"

"A proper Chinese girl doesn't go out alone with a young man."

"But every dance club or cabaret our crowd visits contains acres of tables with Chinese girls out alone with their fellows!"

"Yes, but are they properly brought up young ladies?" Diana raised an eyebrow. "And for those who are, I wager their families don't know who they're with or where they are!"

"So, how does proper Diana Wang avoid scandal dining alone with yours truly?"

"Oh, that's easy! I told Papa. After saving Quentin's head, you can do no wrong. The key is making sure there's no gossip. He mentioned to a friend who always goes to *Le Nuage* that I'm doing Papa a favor by taking a business associate of his out when he and Quentin aren't available. That will be the seal of approval!"

Tolt felt a pinprick of guilt at his deception but getting time

alone with Diana warranted the subterfuge. The maitre d'
warmly welcomed them while escorting them to their table and
Diana whispered, "I heard that the food is divine, but the service
is bad. Guess that isn't true."

"Oh, it's true," Tolt grinned back at her. "But they just happen
to like me!"

Diana giggled.

As they took their seats, a waiter hovered, ready to take their
orders. The maitre d' dismissed him curtly and consulted with
Tolt as to what was particularly good and fresh that evening.
Tolt quizzed him knowledgeably about the type and quality of
mushrooms the chef was offering as part of a special fall menu,
which increased the maitre d's degree of deference.

Diana played with the charms on her bracelet as she watched
the exchange, and then noticed that the guests at the adjacent
table had foregone reviewing their menus to overhear the maitre
d's recommendations to Tolt. She smiled.

Finally, it was decided that the foie gras would not be served
with the chanterelles-type mushrooms proposed, as Tolt feared
that the richness of each combined would be overwhelming.
Instead, they would rely on the other courses to get their fill of
the mycological bounty on offer. Diana overheard the adjacent
diners asking their waiter to make the same substitution.

As the maitre d' hurried off to search for the brand of
champagne Tolt had ordered at his recommendation, Diana
asked, "Where did you learn so much about French food? I don't
recall ever eating it in Seattle."

Tolt proceeded to regale her with the tale of Ping's scheme to
master French cooking so as to prove it was less sophisticated
than Chinese cuisine. Diana giggled at the thought of Ping,
displaced from his homeland yet determined to prove the
peerlessness of Chinese cookery. "It sounds like your home was

happy." She took a dainty bite of the smoked salmon.

Tolt finished chewing his own, pondering her observation. "Well, I guess it was, now that you mention it."

"You guess? You didn't know it was happy?"

"Sort of. See, with my folks having died in the flu epidemic, and Papa so sad at losing my dad, his only child, I guess I thought mostly about what we had lost. But, in terms of what we had, Papa made our own little world. He tried to shield us from the worst of American race prejudices."

"It's similar to how we grew up. No mum, but my father focused on making our lives as happy as possible." Diana nibbled at more of the smoked salmon, then continued, "Of course, with the demands of business, Papa couldn't take us to see our mother's relatives in Osaka very often, but he made our life in Shanghai very loving."

"Hold the phone. Do you mean your mother was from Japan?"

Diana laughed. "Yes! My father went to Japan for university. She was the daughter of his professor. It was a bit scandalous that Papa chose his own wife instead of letting his family arrange things, but my mother's father was such a respected scholar, my grandparents overlooked it."

"Wow! That means you and Quentin are half Japanese. In all his stories about the family, he's never mentioned that."

Diana shook her head. "No, that he prefers not to discuss. In fact, he'd probably be irritated if he knew I had told you, but it's something I'm not ashamed of. Sumiko and Tak both know."

"Well, as Quentin's never chosen to share the news with me, I'll keep it under my hat." Tolt grinned, then after swallowing more champagne added, "My Papa may have created his own perfect world for us, but now that I've seen what life in Shanghai offers, Papa's kingdom doesn't hold a candle. These days I do feel like a king!"

"Your life in Seattle seemed pretty nice."

"Sure, it was. It is. But you can't understand what it's like being a Negro in America. That sense of waiting for folks to look down on you, talk mess about you or refuse to give you the time of day. Papa shielded me from the worst of it, but even so, it's always there, lurking. The first weeks you all took me out to these fancy joints, I kept expecting someone to object to a Negro presence. But, seems like all what people care about here is whether you've got coins in your pocket. The rest doesn't matter."

Diana nodded. "I see what you mean, but you realize it's not quite that straightforward even here. Some places don't admit non-Caucasians. We just know which to avoid. The Cathay was notorious; it might be better now, with fewer foreign visitors coming."

She dabbed her mouth with her napkin, then added, "There is a lot of social freedom in Shanghai, but for young women family pressures can be challenging."

"What do you mean? Quentin tells me your family is pretty open-minded, not itching to arrange a marriage for you."

"Marriage? Goodness, so serious! I'm not speaking of myself." Diana took another swallow of champagne, then giggled at its fizziness.

Tolt smiled, but wondered if her reaction meant she had no interest in marriage. The waiter removed their plates and the next course appeared. After he had departed, Diana resumed. "My family *is* quite open-minded, so long as I marry a Chinese, of course."

Tolt felt his stomach jump but tried to remain focused on what she was saying. "But not every girl is so fortunate. Look

37

at Sumiko. She and Tak seem to have modern lives; her parents are quite open-minded. But her wider family? They want her to marry someone she doesn't love."

"Ah yes, that Takeda guy. Does he want the match or is it just that he's going along with the family?"

"Sumiko tells me that he truly wants the match. She says he's a determined person, very focused. And, he has focused on getting her, no matter what."

"Come on, Sumiko is still free and planning to kick up her heels tonight on the dance floor," Tolt responded, trying to lighten the mood. "Let's enjoy our meal and then we'll head over to meet the others." He raised the glass of champagne that the maitre d' had just refilled.

As they clinked glasses, Tolt thought both about how lovely she looked and the requirement that any man she marry be Chinese.

"Let me get this straight. On Saturday we're going to go see dogs race. Dogs with monkey jockeys?" Tolt asked.

Quentin laughed. "The monkeys are just for fun and good publicity photos. After the races is the tea dance! And then we will go to supper."

"Ah yes, the tea dance. If we lose all our money on the hounds, we can still dance our troubles away." Tolt nodded to the portable chess board between them on the lunch table. "Checkmate, by the way, my friend."

"Ai ya! Next time we're playing wu-tzu ch'i."

Chuckling, Tolt replied, "I'll get you chatting while we play that too, and we'll find ourselves back to this same situation!"

The two friends were having lunch with the dual purposes of evaluating the success of the prior weekend and planning amusements for the following Saturday.

"So, who all is going to the Canidrome?"

In a gesture that Tolt thought of as characteristically Chinese, Quentin used the fingers of one hand to fold down the fingers of the other to count, starting from the thumb, instead of the pinky finger as an American typically would. "There is you, Tak, Sumiko, me, and Diana of course."

Tolt interrupted, "That's five. What about the dancing?"

Quentin laughed. "Always in such a hurry! You didn't let me finish. And, because of the dancing, we need another girl, so I'll ask one of my cousins to join us."

"Which one?"

"Oh, I don't know exactly. There are so many; I'll just find out who's free," Quentin replied in a casual tone. Tolt burst out laughing, and no matter how he tried to explain why this struck him as amusing, Quentin didn't see the humor.

After lunch, Ronnie and Tolt both happened to arrive at the office at the same time. A Western Union messenger was handing a telegram to the receptionist. Ronnie snatched the envelope from the messenger's hand as the receptionist was still signing the delivery receipt.

Tolt stood next to Ronnie as he opened the envelope and read aloud the message:

LIKED REPORT RE KIANGWAN OPPORTUNITY FOR SD

Ronnie looked up and beamed at Tolt. "Swell! Dad sounds as keen as I thought he would be." As he resumed reading the telegram, Ronnie's brow began to furrow:

ANALYSIS OF KIANGWAN FOR WANGFU INDUSTRIES CONTRADICTS SWAN'S REPORT FOR SD.

APPRECIATE THOROUGHNESS. AGREE WE SHOULD NOT PROCEED.

KEEP UP GOOD WORK!

"What report for Wangfu Industries? What's the old man on about?"

Fixing his gaze on Tolt, Ronnie's eyes narrowed. "You. You sent him something. What was it? I send him a report to do the project. You send him something telling him not to. You miserable..."

"Look, I told you from the get-go I wasn't keen on the project. We both agreed that gathering more information was useful. You yourself said, 'the more information the better.'"

"Jesus, Tolt," Ronnie spluttered, "Yes, I did, but I didn't know that meant you were back-channeling to prepare a special report contradicting everything Swan said!"

"Hold the phone, son. I didn't have a special report prepared to contradict yours. I got an existing report about Kiangwan. I sent it to your dad and gave you a copy. There was no back-channel."

"Yeah, that's a swell line. Am I supposed to be senile? I've entirely forgotten some report you supposedly gave me just weeks ago. Sure."

Ronnie turned around and stalked down the hall to his office, Tolt behind him. The employees they passed looked worried at the stormy expressions on their managers' faces. Once in his office, Ronnie picked up the overflowing inbox on the desk and tipped it over. Mail and memos cascaded across the desk's surface. A large envelope labeled "Kiangwan Analysis" that had been at the bottom fell on top of the pile.

Ronnie grabbed the envelope, shaking it for emphasis, "Sure. You gave it to me. But, it's like dinging a car and leaving a note at the edge of the windshield where it will be blown away. Your conscience can rest easy, without having to pay the repair bill."

It occurred to Tolt that Ronnie was sometimes cleverer than he gave him credit for. Before he could reply, Ronnie carried on,

"This is easy enough to resolve. Given the value of the Swan name and all the information I provided Dad on their credibility, it's simply a matter of finding out who prepared the D-minus effort you scrounged up and impugning their reliability."

Ronnie gave Tolt a wide smile with an expression that announced, "so there!" He then opened the report, and spied the name of the firm responsible for preparing it: Swan, Cuthbertson & Fitz.

"What the..."

"Ronnie, don't you see? Swan's playing both ends against the middle. They gave you a report saying how top-notch the Kiangwan project was and at the same time, prepared this one showing it's a loser. How can they be trusted?"

Ronnie narrowed his eyes, "You son of a bitch. I..."

Diana Wang sauntered into Ronnie's office, with her bobbed hair swinging under a jaunty red beret, and called out, "Well, hello there, Misters Big Shot. How's the flour business this week?"

Before Tolt could reply, Ronnie spat out, "Peachy. Just peachy."

He spun to leave, but before doing so he turned his head to glare over his shoulder at Tolt. "This you will pay for, Gross. Dearly."

"Was it something I said?" Diana asked with a bemused look.

"No, not at all. We were just debating the pros and cons of a project. Things got heated."

"I'll say! Heated enough for him to take it on the heel and toe." She adjusted her beret and asked, "Got time to go meet Sumiko and Tak with me for tea at the Astor House, or do you need to smooth things out?"

"No, no — tea is fine. Let me get my hat and we'll head over."

As they departed, Tolt wondered what payback Ronnie would devise. Should he have gone along with the Kiangwan scheme? Was he going to end up with the choice of pressing

Ronnie's dinner jacket or heading back to Seattle with his tail between his legs as Ping had warned?

As they walked down the corridor to the elevator, Diana hooked her arm in his and looked up at him with a happy grin.

Thoughts of Ronnie fled.

Saturday afternoon rolled around and found everyone gathered in front of the Canidrome Hotel at the appointed hour. Tolt noted that the cousin selected to accompany them was Irene, whom he had previously found to be quite shy in conversation, but an exuberant dancer. Inwardly he commended Quentin.

The complex's main building was imposing, with strong vertical lines in the masonry exterior walls, emphasizing the height of the central tower overlooking the facility. Beyond the portico outside the entrance where they congregated, Tolt could see expanses of green lawn.

Pointing there, Quentin said, "When the weather's warmer, that's where the tea dances are held. Come autumn, they move indoors."

Tolt observed how sleekly elegant the entire complex seemed. There wasn't a single building or entertainment venue he could think of in Seattle that could hold a candle to it. While he had never been to Los Angeles or San Francisco, the Canidrome seemed like the sort of glamorous pleasure palace that one would expect to find in California. The friends made their way inside to the foyer, where the manager hurried over to greet Quentin with a degree of affability and deference that was noteworthy even in Shanghai. Diana leaned over towards Tolt,

"Quentin loves this," she whispered. "Of course, the attention is not really because of us. Our uncle is one of the key financial backers of the Tung brothers who own the Canidrome."

With bustling ostentatiousness, the assistant manager

paraded the friends through the foyer to the stands, announcing in a loud voice key facts about the facility, such as its square footage, the number of tea rooms, dining rooms, ball rooms and bars, and a listing of all the famous people who patronized the establishment, noting that before the start of the war, Madame Kung, the elder sister of Madame Chiang Kai-shek, had even taken tap dancing lessons from one of the Negro American musicians who used to play at the Canidrome. Tolt and Diana exchanged raised eyebrows at this item, smiling at the picture of a Chinese high society lady learning to tap dance from a traveling American musician.

Once seated, and with their refreshment orders placed, it was time to make their wagers. With the exception of Sumiko, they consulted the racing forms and based their bets on an analysis of the competitors' statistics. Sumiko waved away the form offered to her. After surveying the dogs during a walk-by, she announced her selection and filled in her betting slip. Young boys outfitted in Canidrome uniforms dashed up and down the aisles adjacent to the terraces, collecting all the slips. The starting bell rang. None of the chosen competitors came close to catching the mechanical hare, except Sumiko's. Her dog surged across the finish line as if pulled through the air, beating his competition in resounding fashion. After the race, the dogs sheathed in the colorful racing silks were paraded in front of the viewing stands by their trainers in matching colored jackets. As Sumiko counted her winnings and smiled, her friends clamored to know her secret.

"It was his look," she explained, pointing to the winner passing them by.

"What do you mean?" asked Quentin. "He looked fast?"

"No, not that. His expression; he had a determined look in his eyes."

The others raised their eyebrows and shrugged. Watching the

next group of dogs trot by, they all tried to gauge which looked most determined, while giving glances to Sumiko to see how she was assessing the group.

"Number three. To me he has a determined look," announced Diana.

"No, I disagree, my money is on Number five!" Tolt countered.

"What do you think, Sumiko-san?" asked Quentin.

"Number two. It's going to be Number two," she replied.

"Really?" asked Tak. "He didn't look at all determined to me."

Sumiko nodded. "I agree."

"You agree?" asked Tolt. "But then why are you going to place a bet on him?"

"Because he looks happiest. Did you see how he bounced a little on the pads of his feet as he walked by? I think he enjoys this more than the others and will be the most eager runner of the group, so he will win."

Diana and Tolt were bemused, but adhered to their selections. Tak was busy chatting with Cousin Irene, comparing notes on various dance bands, so didn't place a bet. Quentin added a bet of his own on the same dog as Sumiko, and handed their slips to the waiting boy.

After winning for a second time, Sumiko's eyes twinkled and the others laughed, amazed at her good luck, declaring that henceforth, they were relying on her to make all betting decisions for the group. As the hounds for the last race made their way to the start, they all looked at Sumiko with eager anticipation, awaiting her decision.

She pursed her lips as the last dog took his place. "Well, which is the winner this time?" Tolt asked.

"Hmmm… This race I am not placing a wager," Sumiko said in a meditative tone.

"But it's the last race!" interjected Diana.

"They all looked a bit sullen and unhappy. I just can't imagine which one is going to focus on winning."

This announcement puzzled the others. "Well, as it's the last race of the day, I'm going to take my chances anyway. Number six looked fast to me," declared Diana. The others in the group, except Sumiko, all agreed they too would wager on Number six.

When the gates opened, the hounds bounded out, appearing to gather pace. As they rounded the first corner, they clumped together. The race could go to any of them. Suddenly, the hare stopped 'running,' with the result that the pack overtook it, then devolved into a swirling mass. All bets were called off.

The crowd groaned. Sumiko gave a sly smile, as Tolt exclaimed, "Girl, from now on I am *always* taking your direction when it comes to big decisions!"

"We'll hold you to that!" joked Quentin.

"Fine with me! With Sumiko's insight, we can't go wrong."

Tak placed his hand on Sumiko's shoulder. "What is it you Americans say? My sister, she's an ace!"

"Yes indeedy, my friend," laughed Tolt. Sumiko flushed, gazing down in embarrassment.

"All this excitement's given me an appetite," Tolt added. "What say we head over to the tea dance and get some rations?"

Quentin offered Sumiko his arm, and they led the way to the ballroom. Tolt gazed around at the paneled walls, decorated sconces holding elaborate lights framing an ornate chandelier hanging from the center of the ceiling. One side of the room was dominated by a sizable stage on which a full band was playing a combination of American and Chinese jazz tunes.

Observing Tolt's scrutiny of their surroundings, Quentin said, "This is the Canidrome's smallest ballroom. They have several more, including one twice this size for the evening dances. Plus, there are I don't know how many gambling rooms."

Tolt nodded, thinking of all the other clubs and entertainment establishments in Shanghai and trying to imagine the combined capacity they offered to whirl away life's cares.

After being seated at a large table adjacent to the dance floor with an excellent view of the musicians, the friends ordered afternoon tea and, with great gusto, consumed the cakes, sandwiches and pastries.

Their appetite for food satisfied, the next hunger to be appeased was for dancing. They took to the floor, switching partners amongst the group's members. Tolt had danced with Diana many times, but as he whirled Sumiko around the floor, he realized they had never danced together before. He wondered if dancing with a Colored man was uncomfortable for her.

As if sensing his thoughts, Sumiko said, "I was wondering when I was finally going to get to have you, a real American – as my partner!" She gave a laugh and with a mischievous look added, "Diana has been hoarding your talents!"

"Well, thank you kindly, ma'am, I'm honored," Tolt replied with a grin, and stopped dancing for a moment to give a brief bow, causing the surrounding dancers to swerve to avoid the unexpected roadblock. Sumiko laughed, and as they resumed their travels across the floor, Tolt asked, "In Tokyo do you have anything like this or a horse racetrack?"

"Oh yes! The Tokyo Racecourse. It's a horse racing track that was built a few years ago. Much larger than this; why, it can hold almost a quarter of a million people."

Tolt laughed out loud.

"Why are you laughing? Did I say something incorrect?" Sumiko asked with a puzzled expression.

"Not at all. I'm just laughing because the scale of things in the Orient is so big. Even in a country with a small territory like Japan, there are so many people! In the last census, I think the entire population of the City of Seattle was something like 360,000 people. Most of my hometown could fit into the Tokyo Racecourse. Nuts!"

"Ah, I see."

To avoid an energetic duo who were about to crash into them, Tolt gave Sumiko a deft swing to the left. She followed his lead with ease. "Well, with the situation being what it is, these days, it's not really considered proper in Tokyo to go to the races."

"What situation?"

"Well, this w... I mean, the 'China Incident'."

"What incident?"

"That's what we call the military actions between Japan and China."

"Ah, and here I thought it was supposed to be a war."

Sumiko gave a rueful smile. "We Japanese receive dual messages. On the one hand, the events here are called an 'incident.' Not a war. On the other hand, the streets at home are filled with notices and news broadcasts urging us to make sacrifices for the war effort. For example, in Tokyo I could no longer dress like this." Sumiko looked down at her dress.

Sumiko was wearing a dress that was pretty, but in no way remarkable or risqué. "I'm no fashion expert, but you look proper as far as I can tell."

"Nowadays, notices in big print are posted everywhere, "DRESS PLAINLY AND HONOR YOUR EMPEROR." Women no longer wear Western dresses like this in public." She shook her head. "Even pretty new kimono are not appropriate. Instead we vie to show our patriotism by wearing our oldest, drabbest clothes."

"And what do you think about that?" Tolt asked, releasing Sumiko's waist as the song ended.

She shrugged. "It's..."

Before she could finish, an officer wearing the uniform of His Majesty's Imperial Japanese Navy approached. Tolt noticed that all the surrounding couples, be they Western or Chinese, looked their way with expressions that ranged from suspicion and anxiousness to disdain. The officer stopped in front of Sumiko, clicked his heels and gave a deep bow. Sumiko made a bow that was suitably low in return. The officer ignored Tolt, but Tolt stood his ground, observing their exchange with considerable interest.

Speaking in Japanese, the officer said, "Miss Takematsu, Lieutenant Takahashi at your service." He took a white card from a pocket inside his jacket and using both hands, presented it to Sumiko with another deep bow. Inscribed with the naval crest:

In Solemn Observance of the 2600th Jubilee
of the
Imperial Dynasty of the Empire of Japan
The Commander and Officers
His Imperial Japanese Majesty's Idzu
Request the pleasure of the company of
Miss Sumiko Takematsu
November 23, 1940
At 10 am
R.S.V.P. Wardroom Mess Secretary

Sumiko took the card in two hands, bowed in return, and expressed a few niceties about the honor of receiving the invitation. The lieutenant clicked his heels while bowing, then walked away at a brisk pace.

Tolt offered Sumiko his arm to leave the dance floor, observing, "Well, that was a performance!"

Sumiko's face had lost its liveliness, her expression now

closed-off. She sighed but did not reply. As they reached the table, she handed the card to her brother without a word. Tak read it and frowned.

"You must go, of course."

"Yes, I know."

"Do you want me to go with you?"

"No, thank you." Sumiko paused. Tolt struggled to catch what she whispered to her brother. "How did that lieutenant know to find me here? And why deliver the invitation here, in front of so many people, instead of to our home?"

Tak's reply was easier to catch, "We told the houseboy where we were going this afternoon. He must have delegated the delivery to a trusted officer. Given who he is, it's not surprising that the officer would make every effort to hand the invitation to you himself."

Tolt couldn't hear the rest of what was said, but resolved to find out more when the chance arose.

5

January 1941

The Lunar New Year was approaching, and the Wangs insisted that Tolt stay with them during the first few days of the holiday. Thus it was that the afternoon of New Year's Eve, he arrived at the Wang compound, bearing his suitcase. It held the new suit he had had made at Diana's insistence, new clothing being a must on the first day of the New Year.

The holiday passed in a blur of food, noise and jollity. To Tolt, it resembled an American Christmas but magnified and expanded. How in the world could people make and consume such vast quantities of food? And drink? Each day brought a new round of visits from extended family and friends. It was now midway through the fourth day of the new year, and his head still hurt from the copious amounts of yellow wine that Mr. Wang had insisted he and Quentin enjoy with him the previous evening. This day, the Wangs were hosting visits from various friends. Tolt hoped he could keep up.

Diana approached, accompanied by an older gentleman. "Tolt, this is Mr. Sun. Like you, he's in the flour milling business. Fufeng Flour Mill in Shanghai was the first modern flour mill in China! His father and grandfather started it in 1898."

Tolt inclined his head. "That is some history! Where are you from, Mr. Sun? Ningbo, like so many of Shanghai's best businessmen?"

"No, no, from Anhui. But milling flour involves trade, so being in Shanghai puts our business in the center of things. Miss Wang tells me you work for Snow Drift."

Tolt nodded. Sun gave him an appraising glance and continued. "We understand the owner has sent his son here."

"Yes, Ronnie's grandfather started the company, so he's the third generation. His family wants him to understand all aspects of the business."

"Just like a Chinese family!" Mr. Sun observed with a chuckle.

"I suppose that's so. Have Fufeng and Snow Drift done business before, sir?"

"Yes, from time to time. Mostly when one of us has a supply contract due without sufficient wheat available to fulfill it."

A servant refilled their cups with fresh tea.

"Is most of your wheat domestic, or imported?"

"For the past decade, we've focused on domestic wheat. But since... well, since '37, supplies have been disrupted. We must take wheat where and when we can find it. So if you ever find yourselves holding more than you can use, don't hesitate to let Fufeng know!"

The holiday celebrations drew to a close. Tolt returned to his apartment and prepared to resume daily life, albeit with a tighter waistband. Arriving at the office the first day back, he found a message from Mr. Sun, Fufeng Flour's owner, requesting Tolt take a meeting with his General Manager, Mr. Ch'en, who would be arriving at 11 a.m. to discuss a matter of some importance. Tolt signed a reply, indicating that Mr. Ch'en was most welcome and sent the runner on his way.

Ronnie was walking down the hall towards him, rubbing his head as if it ached. Given the limited outdoor activities during dreary late January holiday period, Tolt figured Ronnie likely had a hangover that had been building over successive days. Observing the runner disappearing, Ronnie asked, "What gives? First morning back at work and already someone's chasing us down?"

"Oh, that was from Fufeng Flour. Over the holidays, I met one of the owners and he sent a message asking if this morning I could meet with their GM about something urgent."

"What's so urgent that he can't come himself?"

"Didn't say. You're welcome to sit in and find out."

"Yeah, I just might do that."

At the appointed time, Ronnie, Tolt and Fufeng's Mr. Ch'en took seats in the conference room and sipped their tea. Tolt assumed the role of interpreter between Mr. Ch'en and Ronnie.

"Mr. Sun sends his regrets for the directness of this request. Just before the holiday, we received two communications. One was from the Japanese military authorities accusing our mill of trading with the free Kuomintang forces; if confirmed, they would turn our mill over to a Japanese owner."

Once Tolt interpreted, Ronnie asked, "Can they do that?"

Mr. Ch'en nodded. "Certainly. They need only tell the Japanese-backed local government to prepare the necessary paperwork, and it will be done. Some local companies have avoided such orders by registering their companies in the International Settlement as foreign businesses."

"I've heard of such arrangements too," Tolt replied. "But the Japanese don't always respect them. Hangfeng Textile Mill tried something similar. They leased their business to a dummy British company and then the dummy company financed the deal by taking a loan from a bank that took shares in the company as collateral. The Japanese didn't buy it and confiscated all the assets."

"Mr. Sun is familiar with the Hangfeng transaction. He

suggests something different; Snow Drift, an actual operating entity, will take the Fufeng assets via lease. Snow Drift is a real business and is foreign-owned. Mr. Sun believes that such a transaction would be treated as genuine." After Tolt finished translating this exchange, he and Ronnie looked at each other, both intrigued.

"What would be the advantage to Snow Drift?" Ronnie asked.

Mr. Ch'en answered, "On this point, Mr. Sun is open to considering your proposals."

Tolt used the pause that followed to pose another question. "You said that before the holiday, you had received two communications. What was the second?"

Mr. Ch'en smiled. "Ah, yes. It was from the government forces in Chungking, for a large order for milled flour. The price is good. However, currently Fufeng does not have sufficient supplies on hand. Mr. Sun requests that Snow Drift sell us the needed flour, and when payment is received from the customer, Fufeng will split the profit with you."

"But I thought you just said that the Japanese were threatening to confiscate Fufeng's mill on grounds that you were dealing with the Chinese government in Chungking?" Tolt exclaimed.

"That is so. Once a foreign-registered company, however, the Japanese would have no power over us. We would like to proceed with both initiatives."

Tolt updated Ronnie, who replied looking at Tolt rather than Mr. Ch'en. "Please thank Mr. Sun for presenting Snow Drift with these opportunities. We will discuss."

After escorting Mr. Ch'en out, Tolt returned to find Ronnie in his chair facing the bank of windows overlooking the Huangpu River. Without turning his head he said, "Well, well, well... 1941 is looking like it's going to be a bang-up year!"

"Sure, if we want to get smack in the middle between the

Chinese and Japanese."

"Come on, Gross. You're supposed to be sympathetic to the Chink side. You're not keen to help supply their army?"

"Of course I'm sympathetic. I hate what Japan is doing in China. But we both know that if Snow Drift starts trading with the Chinese forces, there's a chance the boom could drop on us. Your father didn't hire me to be a swashbuckling pirate."

Ronnie bristled, sitting up in his chair and turning to face Tolt. "No one's asking you to swashbuckle anything," he said. "You may be a sailor on the good ship Snow Drift Shanghai, but it's yours truly who's at the helm. *I'm* the one who's charged with making this business grow."

"Fair enough. But on that point, is the up-side from half the profit enough to justify the risk?"

"Who says we'd be limited to fifty percent of the profit?"

"Well, that was the opening offer. You have different terms to propose?"

"Yes, I do. But that's not to say that I need to show Fufeng all my cards. "

"What are you thinking?"

"I'm thinking about how valuable this deal is to Fufeng. Without it, they're done. So we'll tell them that the time to get the paperwork sorted will take too long for them to be the seller to the Chinese forces. Instead, Snow Drift will sell the flour to the buyers in Chungking. There are sure to be plenty of expenses involved, expenses that will reduce profit. We'll sort those out, and then give them thirty percent. They won't be happy, but what choice do they have?"

Ronnie looked quite pleased with his plan. Tolt started to offer another view, but Ronnie waved his hand. "No more of your doom-and-gloom. I'm going to write this up to the old man and let him know what's cooking. Too sensitive for a telegram. Your job is to find out how long the lawyer can drag out preparing the lease paperwork. Get Smythe's time estimate, then pad it."

The rest of the week passed in a blur. Before the holiday, a shipment of wheat was supposed to have arrived from the States, but storms in the Pacific delayed passage, and now the Snow Drift Shanghai mill was unable to fulfill various pending orders. Tolt scrambled to see which of the orders was the most pressing and whether any domestic wheat could be used in substitution. He informed Ronnie of the lack of wheat to fill existing orders, much less the proposed Fufeng order. Ronnie told him to focus on getting the lawyer's plan for how the Fufeng assets could be put under Snow Drift control, safe from Japanese confiscation.

By late Thursday afternoon, Tolt made his way back from the Snow Drift mill to the office on the Bund, tired, but relieved: the ship had arrived. As he was hanging his hat and coat on the rack in his office, Ronnie came whistling down the hall, twirling his hat on his index finger.

"What gives?" he asked Ronnie.

"Heading out. Big shindig tonight at the American Club." Ronnie stopped and placed his hat on his head. "Got all the details in a letter to Pop typed and posted to make tonight's boat to Hong Kong. From there, it will go to the States via air. "

"Just today I received Smythe's estimated time to arrange the corporate lease. You want to include that in your report?"

"Not to worry. Fufeng cares about time. Pop will care about money. I've given him the whole run-down. Once he reads it, he can send the green light via telegraph and we're set."

Tolt wondered what Ronnie's letter contained, but was unwilling to give Ronnie the chance to refuse to tell him, so he simply said, "The delayed shipment finally arrived. By Monday the broker expects our wheat to clear customs. Then we can get our back orders milled and filled."

"Good."

"But I've checked with the milling team. There still isn't enough wheat on hand to add a new order for Fufeng. How are you thinking to secure that wheat?"

"Within two weeks, a new shipment is arriving at Hong Kong," Ronnie answered as he headed out the door. "Maybe we can get it milled and shipped direct from there."

Tolt had his own plans for the evening. Tak and Sumiko were not yet back from visiting their parents in Tokyo, but he, Quentin and Diana planned to meet for dinner and then maybe visit a jazz club. After the stress of sorting out the backlog of work that had piled up during the holiday break, he was looking forward to some relaxation, and the evening proved the hoped-for diversion. On their way into the club, Quentin ran into a group of old school friends, who urged him to join them at a nearby cabaret.

"Go on, man, it's fine," Tolt reassured him. "I'll be sure to get your sis home at a decent hour."

By the time Tolt and Diana entered the club, the room was quite full. Around the walls were wooden booths separated with high dividers, and in the middle of the room, the band was located on a small raised stand. At an outward facing corner, two booths straddled either side of the corner. The hostess showed Tolt and Diana to the empty one; given the angle, they couldn't see who was on the other side, but even amidst the band's ebullient sound, they immediately recognized one voice: Ronnie's.

"...a nice little deal I've assembled. See, the Chinks just focused on keeping their flour mill out of Jap hands, and selling the shipment to Chungking. Not an easy game, mind you, what with Nip scrutiny and the trade blockades they've got going. But I figured out a way to make it work."

His companion's reply wasn't intelligible to Tolt and Diana, but he must have asked what solution Ronnie had devised, because next they heard Ronnie proclaim, "...smuggle the flour from Hong Kong!"

In an expansive manner, Ronnie continued "...so then I got to thinking, if I'm going to all this trouble to get through the Jap blockade going *into* China, why not see if there's something worthwhile to bring *out* on the back-end?'

This time the reply was audible. "And was there?"

"Oh yessss," Ronnie replied, with a laughing tone to his voice. "Turns out there's plenty of iron ore in China's interior, so a shipment will be brought back to Hong Kong, where we can figure out who will pay the highest price. Should bring quite a tidy sum. And the best part is, Fufeng doesn't need to know anything about that side of the deal. That will be 100% Snow Drift."

They couldn't hear the next question, but Ronnie's answer made them frown. "Not to worry. If it does go sideways, I'm set to lay the whole ball of wax at the feet of that darky Pops has saddled me with."

The increased volume of the soloist's belting tones drowned out the next comments. Tolt felt a wave of distaste. Diana looked at him with an expression combining sympathy and outrage.

"What say we call it a night?" Tolt suggested. Soon they were out in front, waiting for the driver to bring up the car.

Once en route, Tolt fumed. "Iron ore? How the hell is he going to find a way to sell iron ore?"

Diana shook her head. "He's tricky, isn't he? Not nearly as clever as he thinks he is. And *that* is where he can go astray."

"Sure enough. Today, when he told me he had posted a detailed report to his father, I wanted to ask him if he had kept a copy, but he can be so touchy, I decided against it."

"Does he usually keep a copy of letters?"

"Yes, for important ones."

"Well, just now it didn't sound like he was going anywhere soon. Why don't you drop me off, then Hsiao Li can take you down to the office for a look? I'd go with you myself, but it's already almost one and I promised Papa I wouldn't be late."

That late in the evening, and with curfew imposed in the non-Concession areas, traffic was light. Soon Tolt was down in the Bund office and rifling through the letters on Ronnie's desk. Sure enough, Wang had made a facsimile and Ronnie's explanation was detailed. Not only the arrangements with Fufeng were outlined, but the smuggling arrangements, both out of and back into Hong Kong, were also laid out with specificity. This was not a letter one would want to be seen by anyone outside the company.

Suddenly, a conversation from some weeks earlier flashed into his consciousness. Over lunch, Tak and Quentin were debating the pros and cons of sending important correspondence to the States via Hong Kong versus northern China and overland by train to Europe. From a timing perspective, Quentin observed Hong Kong was clearly superior, even if the cost was higher, but Tak had cautioned, "Time isn't everything, the subject also matters. Don't forget: in Hong Kong, letters are subject to censorship." Quentin had agreed, noting the British civil service's thoroughness was helping customs catch smugglers operating in the colony.

Tolt felt sick. What would be the result of the British censors learning of Snow Drift's smuggling plans? And what about Ronnie's plan to pin the operation on Tolt if it went sideways? He looked at his watch. It was now 2:30. The Central Post Office staff would soon be on the job. Maybe there was a chance the letter hadn't gone on the evening ship. It was remote, but still a chance.

He pulled on his coat, planning what he would say to try to retrieve the letter. But how would he convince the Postal Service, known to be rigidly formal in its procedures, that sealed mail bags should be opened? Much less opened for a Westerner? Success seemed remote. Unless. Unless he could enlist someone local, someone with powers of persuasion...

Within thirty minutes, Driver Li had dropped him off at the Wangs' gate and headed around back to park the car. Tolt pondered whether to ring the bell or wait until some sign of life could be seen within the house. He cursed himself for not asking Li to help him rouse someone.

As he stood shifting his feet to warm up in the damp Shanghai winter's night, he noticed that a light in one of the upstairs rooms had come on. Soon the window for that room was cracked open and he could hear Diana's voice calling softly down, with a hint of laughter.

"Whatever do you want at this hour?"

"I'm so sorry to bother you, but... hey, why are you awake anyhow? I haven't yet whistled or thrown any pebbles. Are you clairvoyant?"

"Hsiao Li sent Hsiao Ch'en to tell me you had a message."

"I see. Well, fact is that I need your help."

Soon enough, Diana was slipping out the gate, encased in a heavy black coat. Driver Li realizing his work was likely not done, drove round front to collect them, then started back downtown. Tolt showed her the copy of the letter and explained the danger of it being seen by censors in Hong Kong.

During the drive to the Central Post Office, Tolt and Diana hatched a plan. By the time they arrived, it was almost 4 a.m. Lights were on and people seemed to be at work. Exiting the car, Diana clutched the letter facsimile and grinned. "Wish me luck!"

Tolt sat in the back seat, strumming his fingers on the leather seat and trying to imagine what was going on. The leather was still warm from Diana's occupancy. In between agonizing over Snow Drift's coming ignominy, it also occurred to him that any girl who would sneak out in the middle of the night to help save the day was pretty swell. Unfortunately, anxiety about Ronnie's letter overrode these more pleasant thoughts. Time passed. Tolt looked at his watch. It was now almost five. From the main gate, he finally glimpsed Diana's slim shape. She approached the car, looking drained, her grin no longer present. Tolt groaned and let her in.

Tolt wrinkled his face, asking, "So what happened? No luck?"

"They were pretty stern."

"How stern?"

"I asked for the Commissioner of Posts, but no one was very interested. I had to say it many times, to many people, before I was finally shown into the office of the Assistant Commissioner, who runs the night shift. I showed him the facsimile and said I had to get back the original."

"What did he say?"

"He was cold. Told me it was impossible."

"Then what happened?"

"I started sobbing."

"Sobbing? You?"

"Yes! I had to persuade him it was serious. But the tears didn't move him. I leaned over his desk and whispered to him in Shanghainese, very urgently, that the letter involved an action against the Japanese. I told him I typed it up, and made a terrible mistake sending it via Hong Kong because it most definitely could not be seen by the British censors."

"What did he say?"

"Not much. He still looked like it was impossible, but he did ring a bell and one of his underlings came in."

"And?"

"He asked about the status of yesterday's mail to Hong Kong. The junior said most of it had gone on the *S.S. Chinkiang*, but there were four sacks that had been too late and were sent back. They are to go tonight on the *S.S. Fuchou*."

"What did he do?"

"He told the underling to open the sacks."

"Wow."

"At first, his staff didn't believe him. The man's eyes stood out and he asked the Assistant Commissioner who would break the seals. And then, he said he would do it himself!"

"You don't say!"

"So, there we were: the Assistant Commissioner, his junior and me. We headed down to the basement and there were a dozen other postal staff along with four mail sacks, massive really, all filled with letters and sealed. The Commissioner went round and clipped the strings holding the seals. His staff were stunned. I could hear them whispering to one another that they had never seen such a thing. But once the seals were cut, they turned the mail sacks upside down. Mounds and mounds of letters spilled onto the floor. He had me show them the address and instructed them to help me go through all the sacks." She shook her head at the memory.

Tolt hesitated to ask, but finally drew the courage to pose the question. "So?"

"After twenty minutes of frantic search by all of us squatting amidst piles of letters, one of the postal staff stood up and waved the letter. And here it is!" With that, Diana pulled the letter out from inside her coat and presented it to Tolt.

Relief swept over him and he reached out and wrapped his arms around Diana in a hug of gratitude. "You're a genius. What would I do without you?"

She laughed, hugging him for a second, then embarrassed, gently pushed him back. "Ah, what have we done? Not only have I sneaked out of my father's house in the middle of the night and lied to the Assistant Commissioner of Posts, now I'm embracing a foreigner. The Wang ancestors must be in despair!"

Tolt flushed. He couldn't tell from her expression how she had experienced the embrace, but the blush in her cheek made him think the thrill might not belong to him alone.

"We can only torment the ancestors so much." Tolt grinned, then asked, "But what do you mean you lied? Everything you said was true. The letter does describe smuggling that the Japanese would see as an action against them."

Diana lifted her eyebrows, then answered, "I told him that I typed the letter," as she held up her perfectly manicured hands with their long, polished fingernails. "If he had been thinking, he would have known that had to be a lie!"

Tolt laughed again. "Let's get you home."

By mid-morning, Tolt was showered, freshly dressed and seated in his office. The adrenaline from the evening's activities was still upon him. As he reviewed that morning's reports laid out on the desk before him, he was smiling at the thought of Diana's triumph. What a gem, that girl.

Lost in thought, he sensed rather than heard the approach of bustling energy. Ronnie filled the doorway, waving his retrieved letter and a note in Tolt's handwriting, bellowing, "Just what is this?"

Tolt looked up, "What's what?"

"Cut the act, Gross. Stealing my letters? Even you must know mail theft is a crime!"

"Hold on," Tolt raised his hand, trying to calm Ronnie down.

Ronnie's face was deep red, anger emanating such that it contorted the muscles of his mouth, making it difficult to open his lips to speak. Realizing their chat was not likely to be a quiet one, Tolt went to close the door. Retaking his seat, he gestured to the chair in front of the desk. Ronnie snarled, "No, I don't want a damned chair. This isn't a tea and crumpets visit. By God, what is this letter doing on my desk when it should be on its way to Hong Kong?"

"You saw my note, saying I needed to explain that to you, right?"

Ronnie waved the notepaper on which Tolt had scrawled his message, "Yes, I saw it. What sorry excuse this time? I'll wager you have a competing offer you want to pass off to my dad."

"Ronnie, that letter was meant to go via Hong Kong to get it to your father as soon as possible, to make a decision on the Fufeng project?"

Ronnie nodded, his expression wary. "

"In Hong Kong, the Brits have censors reading the international post."

The import of this statement didn't immediately register. "So?"

"Re-read the letter, man."

Ronnie glared, trying to assess where this line of discussion was heading.

"Heck, I'll read it." Tolt picked up the copy from his desk, "Let's see ...Here:"

Hong Kong is where the transactions will occur. From there, we'll smuggle the flour out, past the Japanese embargo on the Chinese ports, and onward to the government in Chungking. Returning, a shipment of iron ore will be shipped through the same route, and brought by backdoor into Hong Kong, where we can easily dispose of it. With the military actions under way, ore is in strong demand and will fetch a pretty price. The transportation costs for this project will be high, but the profits (untaxed by customs duties) will offset these costs.

Tolt raised his head and looked at Ronnie, "Very clear for your father to decide, but also to the Hong Kong censors, who are working with the customs." He laid the letter down on the desk. Ronnie's face had gone pale.

"If you still want to send it, avoid Hong Kong."

"You son of a bitch," Ronnie snarled, "Mother was right. All you deserved was to be my valet; she should have stuck to her guns." He slammed the door behind him.

Tolt leaned back in his chair, and shook his head, letting out a bemused chuckle. His ingenuity and contacts had Ronnie's saved Snow Drift from scandal, but all Ronnie cared about was that his deal was dead. At least now he knew who had insisted he depart Seattle as Ronnie's valet. Swell folks, Ronnie and Veronica Planter.

Surveying the river traffic below, Tolt considered his history with Ronnie. It was a rocky one. An incident from the summer before they started college probably constituted the nadir. Or so far, Tolt thought with a grimace. That summer, Tolt was waiting tables and doing odd jobs at Our House, as well as socializing with Jimmy Johnson and Sara Mason. Sara had grown from being a kid he found insufferable for her know-it-all attitude, to being, well, a young woman for whom he nursed tender thoughts.

The Masons always threw a big fourth of July cookout at their house. Mrs. Mason had tasked Sara and Tolt with collecting the little kids playing hopscotch out on the sidewalk beyond the backyard fence to wash hands for supper. As Sara and Tolt attempted corralling the youngsters, who should tootle by in a white convertible Packard but Ronnie. His folks had given him the car as a graduation present; and alongside him was one of his numbskull buddies, a big hulking linebacker type called Roberts.

Ronnie parked the car, jumped out and, obviously inebriated, started cajoling Sara about joining the Mason family barbecue. When that didn't lead anywhere, he insisted on taking a group photograph of Tolt, Sara, himself and the small children. In the hope of appeasing Ronnie so that he would leave, Tolt and Sara agreed. Ronnie handed his camera to Roberts, instructing him to act as photographer, then came to stand on one side of Sara, with Tolt on the other and the kids arrayed in front.

Just as Roberts pressed the shutter, Ronnie bent down and pulled up Sara's skirt, exposing her lower half. Sara screamed and tried to pull down her garments. Tolt failed to wrest the camera away from Roberts, who together with Ronnie fled in the Packard, laughing evilly as they went.

Tolt recalled his sense of rage and powerlessness, as well as shame at seeing his good friend humiliated. When Jimmy eventually arrived, outside of Sara's earshot, Tolt shared the story. Jimmy shook his head, observing only, "He be thinking he know how to make things happen? Huh." Sara rejoined them and Jimmy returned to his usual joking manner, distracting his friends from their misery.

A few days later, Ronald Sr. made his regular Saturday morning stop at Our Place for coffee and *bonhomie*. Bill Gross listened with sympathy, as Ronald Sr. confided how the previous night his son had been arrested for dealing in a large quantity of spirits out of the back of his new car. Ronnie's mother was in a state and Mr. Planter intended to take away the car for the remainder of the summer.

"Craziest thing of all? All four tires were flat. Not that Ronnie should have made a run for it. I'm not suggesting that. But even if he had wanted to, there would have been no chance. Maybe it was the cobblestones they still have down there at the end of Madison Street..." Mr. Planter grimaced. Tolt's grandfather listened with a sympathetic ear.

Tolt and Jimmy sat across from one another at a table near where Mr. Planter relayed his family's woes. They ate their pancakes slower and slower, trying to catch what was being said. Hearing that Ronnie had been arrested, Jimmy looked up from his plate and winked at Tolt. Tolt gave a start. That the police should show up when illegal substances were being doled out, and that *all* four tires on Ronnie's pristine car should go flat was indeed improbable.

Comprehension dawned, soon replaced by a strong conviction that the mastermind behind Ronnie's misfortune was sitting across from him. Jimmy's eyes twinkled as he continued to fork in mouthfuls of egg, pancakes and sausage. Savoring revenge, Tolt consumed his last bites of pancake with gusto.

After finishing their meal, the boys prepared to depart for the tennis courts. They heard Mr. Planter say, "The other odd thing is that Ronnie swears the new camera we gave him for graduation was in the car with him that night, but it can't be found anywhere. On that roll of film, he had all the pictures from our Independence Day celebration, including the pictures of his great-grandmother's birthday party. She celebrated her 100th that day. Even got a telegram from Mr. Hoover, and Ronnie photographed her holding it. Have half a mind to wonder if one of those police fellows made off with it, but with Ronnie in the mess he is, can't exactly run down there making accusations." Ronald Sr. sighed, then took a long swallow of coffee.

Tolt looked at his friend with even greater wonderment, but Jimmy was focusing on matters at hand.

"Mr. Gross, we're done," he asked politely. "Need us to do

any chores 'afore we head out?"

Bill gave an encouraging nod, and he and Ronald Sr. wished them a good contest, as the boys grabbed their racquets to leave. Tolt felt a pang of guilt at Mr. Planter's distress. Then he remembered Ronnie's maniacal laughter at seeing Sara in her panties, and it abated.

Despite heavy questioning from Tolt, Jimmy refused to admit having had anything to do with the matter. The next week, Sara was mystified, but also relieved, when she opened an envelope addressed to her in crooked printing. It enclosed no letter, but a shower of torn strips of unprocessed film fell out from the envelope when she shook it. Jimmy deflected her queries as well.

Ronnie's misfortunes eased their sense of humiliation, and life resumed its usual rhythm. Later, much later, Sara turned down Tolt's pleas that she make a life with him. She assured him of her continuing friendship, but not love. Unable to find a job in Seattle, she left for Chicago. As promised, however, she maintained contact. Every two weeks, Tolt could look forward to an insightful and entertaining update on life in Chicago's 'Brown Belt.'

All during the misery of law school and then his fruitless quest for a job in Seattle, Sara's letters had continued to flow, making him laugh and buoying him up. Until, that is, he told her he was going to work for Ronnie in Shanghai. His decision to work under Ronnie's leadership couldn't be countenanced and correspondence ceased. Despite the excoriation contained in Sara's last letter, it remained tucked into the small sliding compartment at the back of Tolt's portable chess set, a keepsake of what he had had, and what was lost. All these many months later, his heart still ached a bit when reflecting on what his choice of working for Ronnie had cost him.

Tolt looked at his watch. It was time for tiffin. Maybe he'd pop by Tak's office to see if he was free. As he collected his hat and coat from the rack in the corner of the room, he wished Jimmy were in Shanghai. He'd know how to handle Ronnie, or at least, how to make Tolt laugh.

6

FEBRUARY 1941

FEBRUARY WAS almost over, yet the weather was as gloomy and gray as it had been before the Chinese New Year holiday. The day before, Tak had phoned Tolt inviting him to join Diana and Quentin at his and Sumiko's apartment for lunch on Saturday. Given the dreary weather, spending the afternoon in a cozy home with the radio on, enjoying a meal and company, sounded like a pleasant way to while away a Saturday.

When Tolt arrived, Diana and Quentin were already ensconced in armchairs. Tak was standing in front of the heater, chatting with them. After removing his shoes and donning slippers, Tolt joined them, joking as he sat on the sofa, "Tak-san, come away so I can get a shot at some of that!"

Tak laughed and moved aside, waving his hands as if fanning the warmth in Tolt's direction. "Here you go!"

Sumiko entered the room, bearing a tray on which were arranged a pot and tea cups. As she set them down on the low table in front of the sofa, the friends laughed and chattered about the movies they had seen, bands that were coming to town and charity galas that were on the calendar.

Sumiko reached for a brown paper package on a side table, smiling as she announced, "Look what I have!"

She placed the package on the coffee table and unwrapped

it, revealing five picture frames. Diana picked up the top one. "Oh, it turned out so well! Thank you, Sumiko-san, for having it framed."

Quentin picked up the next, holding it for Tak and Tolt to admire. "Not bad at all! We three gents make handsome Blind Mice!" And indeed, the picture showed the three friends in matching gray mohair suits, attached to the back of which were tails stiffened with wire. Their costumes were completed with matching dark sunglasses and dark gray hats.

Shortly before the Lunar New Year, the friends had attended a charity ball with the theme "Fairy Tales of Old." Sumiko and Diana chose to go as two of the four tree fairy elves of the Chinese fable, 'The Flower Elves." Diana as the Pomegranate who was saucy and outspoken, wore a deep ruby red traditional Tang-style dress onto which pomegranate seeds had been embroidered with crystals forming the nub of the red seeds. Sumiko chose to be the Peach tree and wore a matching dress in varying shades of peachy pink, and onto hers were embroidered silk peach blossoms. They wore matching shawls of soft green fine mohair, the color of spring leaves. Their hair was set in similar low buns, held back at the nape of their necks, each with a silken sprig of her respective flower tucked in as a grace note.

Both girls had looked enchanting, but Tolt recalled that he was especially taken by the charms of the Pomegranate Flower Elf. At the Ball, a photographic area had been arranged, with a background depicting various elements from Western and Chinese fairy tales. The scrim was painted with a colorful melange of dragons, pearls, moon maidens, Mother Hubbard, black sheep, and so on. The five friends had arranged themselves with the girls at the center and the Blind Mice surrounding them.

Looking first at the framed photo, then with an appraising gaze at his sister and Diana, Tak observed, "You two really could pass for twins."

Looking at the picture and recalling the fun of the evening, the two leaned together, posing in an attitude of sweet smiles.

"The only difference is that my sister has a gap between her front teeth and yours doesn't," remarked Quentin.

"Brother! What sort of thing is that to say?" exclaimed Diana.

Tolt laughing along, but nevertheless tried to smooth Diana's ruffled feelings. "Not to worry fair Pomegranate Maiden! You and Peach Maiden are equally lovely."

"Coming from a blind mouse, I'm not sure how comforting that is," Diana retorted.

"Well, it sure was a fun time. Thanks, Sumiko-san, for the memento!" Tolt replied.

Sumiko smiled as she knelt down to pour out the tea. Then, standing to hand around the cups she said to the group, "That was a fun evening. And you know what I'd like to do another evening soon?"

"What?" asked Diana. "Is there a new nightclub?"

"Well, new to me. I'd like to go to one of the casinos out on Jessfield Road."

"Oh yes, I've never been there. The clubs there sound like something out of a gangster film. Let's go!"

Tak, Quentin and Tolt looked at each other, then Quentin spoke up. "I don't know, girls. The Badlands area *does* have its fair share of gangsters."

"And opium joints," added Tolt.

"And bad characters," Tak noted.

"Oh come on — the Badlands must have at least one club that is acceptable," Diana said.

The houseboy entered, announcing that lunch was served. As the friends stood to move to the dining room, Quentin said, "How about we look into it? We'll see if there's someplace decent we can take you two."

"But not too decent!" Diana laughed, wagging her finger at her brother. Sumiko smiled in agreement.

Soon they were seated around the table, plying their chopsticks and exclaiming over how delicious their lunches were. Tak had found a new restaurant he admired and ordered bento lunches for everyone. Each guest had a dark lacquered rectangular box set before his place, whose interior was divided into little squares and rectangles. Various delicacies reposed inside: a portion of grilled fish, topped with bonito flakes, steaming white rice, pickled vegetables, and a swirl of neon green strands of seaweed, dressed as a salad.

"Before you came to Shanghai, had you ever seen bento boxes?" Sumiko asked Tolt.

"Oh yes! Many times." Tolt took a swallow from the cup of tea placed next to his box, then laughed, "In fact, it was through a bento box that I became friends with my best buddy growing up."

"How was that?" asked Tak. "I don't recall them being especially common in Seattle when I was there."

"Well, see, the elementary school I attended wasn't far up the street from Japantown and Chinatown. Nearby were kids with families from Japan, China, the Philippines, plus us Negroes and some White kids. Most of us brought sandwiches for lunch, but one day, in first grade, there was a kid, Jimmy, who looked like me," ... at this Tolt pointed to his hair ... "but he had a bento-style lunchbox."

Sumiko frowned slightly in puzzlement, but didn't interrupt. Tolt continued, "So, he sits down at the table where all the first graders from Miss Walsh's class were, and opened up his box. It's filled with slices of egg omelette, some broccoli, a rice ball wrapped in seaweed. And this other kid says to Jimmy, 'Hey, what you doing with some Japanese kid's lunch?'"

"Jimmy pays him no attention, just answers, 'It's my lunch.' Well, that doesn't clear things up for the other kid. I think his name was Willie. Anyway, he says, 'Your lunch? You Colored; what you doing with a Jap kid's lunch?'"

Tolt was enjoying the transfixed expressions on his friends' faces, as they listened to his tale. "So Jimmy says, 'My mama made it for me.' Well, that just set off more questions. 'Your mama?! Who she?' Then Willie took another look at Jimmy and noticed that the shape of his eyes was more similar to our classmates from Japanese or Chinese families. So being a clever kid, Willie asks, 'Hey, your mama be Jap or something?'"

"By this time, Jimmy was getting tired of all the questions. He was hungry and wanted to eat his lunch, so he just answered Willie, 'Yeah, she's from Japan.' But before he could dig into his meal, Willie started laughing."

"Why?" asked Sumiko.

"Well, I guess he thought it was strange that a kid who looked Colored had a mother from Japan. So, he starts pointing at Jimmy saying, 'Ha-ha, you a mixed paddy!' Then the other kids joined in."

"'Mixed paddy?' Diana raised her eyebrows.

"It wasn't an expression I had heard before, but from the other kids' faces, I could tell it was intended as an insult. Jimmy was up in a flash. Before I knew what was happening, he had pulled Willie off the bench, shoved him down on the ground and was kneeling over him, punching him for all he was worth!"

His friends' astonishment made Tolt wonder if lunchroom brawls didn't happen in Chinese or Japanese schools. He continued, "So, Jimmy and Willie get sent to the principal's office. After school, I went home and asked Sato, our handyman, if he had a bento lunchbox and could make me my lunch for the next day."

"You did?" exclaimed Sumiko.

"Sure did. Nutty kid, right?" said Tolt with a smile. "Next day, lunchtime rolls around.This time, Jimmy's got a peanut butter sandwich and I'm the one with the bento. Of course, Willie and his buddy George started in on me, 'Hey, Tolt. You got your lunch mixed up with that Yellow Paddy's there?' I ignored them, started eating my lunch. And it was tasty, too."

Tolt grinned. "They didn't like that. So they kept needling, 'Hey Tolt, you mixed, too? Got some of that yellow blood in you?' I got tired of it, and said, 'Why don't you eat your lunch? Who cares what I eat?' That just stirred them up. One of the kids started teasing Willie then, 'Ooh, I think he's saying it none of your business, now! Whatchya gonna say to that, Willie?'"

Tolt's friends sitting around the dining room table were engrossed by Tolt's vivid telling of his tale. He grinned at the contrast between the refinement of being served by the Takematsus' houseboy, while reminiscing about a Seattle public school lunchroom years earlier.

"Well, George decided it was time to back up his buddy, Willie, so he got up from his place and came up all close to me and said, 'Who you talking to like that? You messin'?' Before I could say anything, who should chime in but Jimmy!"

"What did he say?" asked Diana.

"He was real calm. He just said, 'Shut it. Leave him alone.' 'Course, George, he didn't like that any too much. So his eyes get all narrow" — Tolt demonstrated with his own eyes, adopting an outraged expression on his face — 'Who you talking to?' George says. Jimmy, he's had about enough of this mess, so he takes things up a notch, says, 'You. Fool. I be talking to you.' Next thing you know, another fight breaks out."

"Oh my, you must have gotten into such trouble with your grandfather!" Diana said.

"Well, I'm ashamed to say I was so surprised that I hadn't even joined in to help Jimmy before Miss Walsh swooped in. She broke things up and sent Jimmy, Willie and George to the principal's office again. Poor Jimmy, another day with no lunch spent in the principal's office."

"Then what happened?" asked Quentin.

"Well, when the end of school bell finally rang, I waited outside the principal's office and started walking Jimmy home. I felt bad, but didn't know what to say. Before I could figure it out, he asked, 'What'd you do that for anyway?' I didn't know what he meant. Not fight? Not help him?"

"What Jimmy wanted to know was 'Why'd you bring one of them lunches. You ain't Japanese.' I told him it just looked better than my regular lunch. Jimmy thought that made sense, so then I asked him to come home with me. Ping fed us cookies, which made up for our missed lunches." He gestured to the bento box before him on the white tablecloth, Tolt concluded, "And that, my friends, is the story of how a bento box created a lasting friendship."

Diana, Quentin, Tak and Sumiko laughed at this. Tak raised his cup of tea, toasting, 'To bentos and friendship!'

"I don't think we ever met Jimmy when we were in Seattle," Diana said. "Did we?"

"No, and it's too bad, because you'd like him. He's in Hawaii now. Packed up from Seattle to go be with his mom's folks, working in the cane fields or some such. Hard to imagine."

Taking a sip of tea, Tolt gestured to the table and asked Tak and Sumiko, "So this must have been what you had for lunch at school, too, right?'

"Not really," answered Tak. "Remember, my parents brought us here to Shanghai and sent us to international schools. I went to the American School and Sumiko to the Catholic girls school run by the French nuns."

"Why didn't your parents have you grow up in Japan? Even if your dad was here for the business, don't most businessmen leave the wife with the kids in Japan to be educated there?"

Sumiko gave an almost imperceptible nod, and Tak replied, "Well, when we were in primary school was when big changes started."

"How's that?"

"The militarism. My father says really since the Sino-Russian War. When was that? In '05? Since then, war and patriotism have been in the elementary school curriculum. Mathematics classes did calculations about military matters. Japanese language classes studied the imperial edicts on war and letters from soldiers at the front. PE included war games, and Music classes used war songs." Tak shook his head, "My parents didn't like it."

Sumiko's expression was sober as Tak continued. "Then, in '25 all middle and senior schools in the country had active duty military officers assigned to them and military training became part of the standard curriculum. Girls schools were exempted, but by then, my parents were so concerned, that when the opportunity came for my father to work here, they decided to move the entire family."

"We'd go home to Japan for the summer holidays, of course," Sumiko added. "And when we saw our friends and relatives, it was clear that they were being told exactly what to think. Part of what our friends were learning was to despise anyone who wasn't Japanese. After the Manchurian Incident in '31, we heard so many people we had known as small children saying vile things about the Chinese, about the Americans. How the League of Nations was stupid and should just do what Japan wanted."

"Our parents were saddened to see their country changing," Tak said. "They wanted us to appreciate the good things in

Japanese culture and escape the worst."

"And in the years leading up to the overthrow of the Manchus, your countrymen did so much," exclaimed Quentin. "Dr. Sun Yat Sen and his revolutionaries depended on being able to live in Japan when the Imperial Government sought their heads!"

"And, just like our father, many of the Chinese scholars who went to study in Japan fell in love with Japanese women and married them," added Diana.

"Today those ties are unimaginable," Tak observed with sadness.

"So would you say that you and Sumiko are friends with so many non-Japanese because of how you were raised? I mean, you two are so different from the society you've described," Tolt observed.

"Maybe," Tak said. "I hadn't considered."

"Actually," Sumiko observed, "all five of us are different from the standard in our home countries."

"How's that?" asked Tolt.

"Well, Quentin and Diana had a mother from Japan and were raised in an international way. Your grandfather raised you to learn foreign languages and be exposed to people from different places. Our parents took us away from Japanese militarism."

Tolt grinned. "Now you mention it, we are sort of a special bunch, aren't we?"

"We're like the Mongolian ponies." Diana laughed. "Remember what Ronnie said last fall after he rode one? He called them 'screwy little animals that couldn't hold a candle to real American horses...'"

Tolt interrupted, "Yeah, right before the cunning beast took a leap over a creek that a 12-hand horse would have thought twice about before attempting."

"Exactly! On the exterior we may appear like shaggy little

animals, but in fact we possess all sorts of qualities that you can't tell from the outside: grit, stubbornness, toughness." Diana laughed.

Quentin laughed too. "Shaggy? Stubborn? Speak for yourself, sister!" Diana began poking him in the side to tickle him and the serious mood was broken.

Soon after finishing the meal, Diana looked at her watch. "Brother, we should get going. Remember Papa wanted us to be at home for tea with some visitors from Ningbo?"

The friends rose from the table to see off Quentin and Diana.

"Promise us, next weekend we'll go to the Badlands together. A big night of excitement!" Diana admonished.

Tak, Tolt and Quentin assured her they would make a plan for a group adventure.

Once the Wangs had departed, Tolt said, "You probably have things to do this afternoon, too. I should be on my way."

"No, no," Tak answered. "Please stay and sit for a bit. We can have some more tea."

He, Tak and Sumiko settled in the cozy living room, shutting out the chill of the foyer and enjoying a fresh pot of tea that the houseboy had brought in. As Sumiko was pouring it, the doorbell sounded. When the houseboy went to answer the door, Tolt joked, "What do you want to bet Quentin forgot something!"

The living room door opened. The three friends looked up from their seats, ready to tease Quentin for his absentmindedness, but it was not Quentin.

The visitor greeted them, and gave a brisk bow. Sumiko and Tak scrambled to their feet, their expressions surprised and their bodies awkward as they tried to offer a suitably deep welcoming bow. Tolt was two, no, three beats behind them.

It was Takeda.

What was he doing in Shanghai?

7

MARCH 1941

"SOMEONE should tell him to march himself right back to Tokyo," Diana exclaimed, throwing herself back in the armchair.

Tolt offered a wry grin, "When Tak asked me to fill you two in on what transpired after you left, he figured you wouldn't be too pleased."

Quentin pronounced, "And this is why it's best if you do not meet him," Quentin pronounced.

Bristling, Diana answered, "Little brother, I've no need of your guidance. Don't worry about me embarrassing you."

Quentin's face betrayed mortification at having his sister chastise him in front of Tolt.

Seeking to shift the discussion, Quentin asked Tolt, "So what did Tak have to say?"

"When I dropped by today he was pretty gloomy. He says Takeda is here until the weekend, wanting to spend as much time with Tak and Sumiko as possible. But he does have some meetings. Maybe they'll take up time, and his visit won't be as bad as Tak fears."

Diana wrinkled her nose in distaste, but simply asked, "Would you like to stay for dinner?"

"Would like nothing better, but told our pal I would go to dinner with him and Takeda tonight."

"Tolt to the rescue?" she said, raising her eyebrow.

"Something like that."

Takeda spooned more of the sukiyaki broth into his bowl, "... and that's the second Japanese businessman stabbed and robbed this month. Cousin, you either need to get a bodyguard or even better, a gun. Who's to say the next time at the docks whether it's going to be you that gets attacked?"

Tak put down his chopsticks, exclaiming, "The docks! I just remembered...there's a shipment leaving tomorrow and I was supposed to sign the paperwork." Rising from the low table set in the middle of the private room where he, Tolt and Takeda had been enjoying their meal, he bowed, "Thank you for your concern, Cousin. I will consider your recommendations about the gun. I'm sorry to step away, but will return as soon as I can."

"No worries. I'll keep Takeda-san company," Tolt offered.

After Tak's departure Tolt resumed consuming morsels of tender beef. Takeda picked up his tea cup, looking at Tolt in an assessing way and n Japanese said, "Tolt-san, tell me about yourself."

Tolt chewed his mouthful and swallowed. "My parents... they died of the Spanish flu, so I was raised by my father's father. I call him "Papa." Papa has a small hotel he started during the Alaska gold rush. Seattle was a small, Wild West town then."

Takeda appeared intrigued, so Tolt continued. "The hotel's cook is Ping, a Chinese fellow, and there is a handyman, a Japanese named Sato. I've always liked to eat, so from the time I was little, I was under Ping's feet and he taught me Chinese. At first, it was mostly by yelling at me to get out of his way! Later, he started tutoring me, teaching me to read and write. Papa thinks all knowledge is useful, so throughout my childhood, he insisted that I carry on studying Chinese, and then Japanese. At university I took Chinese, but not Japanese classes."

Takeda smiled and took a sip of his tea, nodding at Tolt to continue.

"You'll enjoy this; when Ping first approached Papa for a job, he announced he was an excellent cook. But he neglected to tell Papa that as the pampered son of a scholarly family, he had spent all his waking hours studying for the imperial civil service exams, and had never before been closer to a kitchen than Papa had been to the Great Wall! The early days were rocky, but Ping...he had a gourmand's palate. With his love of good food, combined with his intelligence and effort, he ended up becoming an excellent cook."

Takeda laughed outright.

"Ping and Sato... they are best friends and best enemies. To them, nothing could be better than arguing over whether Chinese or Japanese culture is superior. With two such teachers, how could I fail to learn to speak Chinese and Japanese?"

Takeda smiled at the tale. "And, in addition to learning the languages, did you also learn about the history and societies of Japan and China?"

"China's history, and Japan's, too? They're so long and complex, in all honesty I can't claim to be knowledgeable," Tolt replied. This seemed to satisfy Takeda, as Tolt suspected it would.

"And what are your views about more recent events?" he probed.

"Oddly enough, it was a German — a former soldier — who lived for a time at my grandfather's hotel, who exposed me to more recent history. He, Ping and Sato loved to analyze the events of the past fifty years: Japan's rise, Germany's withdrawal from Asia after the Great War, China's decline during the end of the imperial age."

Tolt gave a rueful smile. "Well, I should say, China's decline wasn't something Ping liked discussing, but he enjoyed explaining what he saw as the causes."

"And the surging tide of international communism, led by the Russians. Don't forget that." Takeda tapped his forefinger on the table. "This is an issue you Americans will maybe one day finally pay attention to. At present, it is we Japanese who have taken on the task of blocking an expanding Soviet Union. With a weak and ineffectual state buffering us, in the past twenty years the spread of communism has been a key concern for us."

Tolt smiled, and asked in what he hoped was a respectful-sounding tone, "But is communism truly the source of Japan's concerns with Russia? After all, in 1904, wasn't it the Russian *Imperial* Navy that Japan attacked, not the Soviet Navy?"

Takeda had the good grace to smile. "There is truth in that, Tolt-san."

Tolt picked at the food on his plate, looking downward and wondering what sensitive political issue he would next have to tackle. He hoped Tak would soon return. This tête-à-tête was turning out to be more challenging than anticipated; even so, Takeda's next question surprised him.

"I have the feeling that my cousin spends quite a bit of time with you. With you and that Chinese fellow. Does my cousin's sister also socialize with you?"

"Ah… yes, Tak, Quentin and I are like strawberry and soda; we belong together. Often, Quentin's and Tak's sisters join our outings."

"I see. And does Sumiko-san seem to like the Western way of socializing?"

"If you mean does she like to dance and laugh, well, yes. But don't folks in Japan like that, too?"

"Yes, of course. But with the current situation, people in our country are mindful of not being frivolous, so entertainments these days are more restrained."

The chief waitress scurried into the room bearing a fresh flask of hot water to refill the tea pot on their table. Takeda paused while she performed her task, then waved her away, himself picking up the pot to refill their cups.

"I'm curious," Takeda said in an idle tone. "What is a typical evening's arrangement here in Shanghai?"

Tolt was relieved that this question too avoided the minefield of Chinese-Japanese military hostilities. "Well, that's simple enough."

In an animated voice, he explained, "If you're talking a full evening out, from sundown until sun up... first it starts with dinner. The Chinese like to dine early and the Europeans have adjusted their habits to fit the local scene. Six-thirty start time, finished by eight-thirty or nine. Then it's on to a dance club. Or, two. Three if you're ambitious. Depends on where the best bands are that night. Once your feet are finished, if you're still keen to keep going, perhaps finish the evening with a nightcap at a smaller club, listening to a jazz trio and nursing your bunions."

"Interesting." Takeda sipped his tea.

Tolt took a deep draught of his beer. While still mid-swallow, he heard Takeda's next question: "Do you think it might be possible to arrange such an evening while I am here?"

How had he made such an elementary mistake? Ping and Sato, who taught him the encircling chess game popular in their countries, would have chastised his failure to perceive his opponent's move. Chagrined by his failure to hedge his response, Tolt answered, "Er...sure. Why not?"

Why not? Even such a dolt as he could think of any number of reasons why arranging a light-hearted evening of leisure for a Japanese Imperial Navy officer amidst the stormy waters of

Japanese-occupied Shanghai would be a challenge.

The leather of Tolt's shoes squeezed tight against feet swollen from a night of dancing. The leather's pressure struck Tolt as apropos given the sense of constraint permeating the arrangements he and Tak had devised for Takeda's amusement. Knowing the Takematsus as well as he did, Tolt could tell they found the experience of entertaining their cousin draining and were not sorry to see the evening end. The friends' usual carefree enjoyment of being together was replaced by stiff formality. Nevertheless, the food, music and dancing were as outstanding as ever. As Tolt and Takeda repaired to a dingy little bar after bidding Tak, Sumiko and one of her Japanese girlfriends good night, Tolt felt that overall, he managed pretty well. Most importantly, he felt certain that his friends appreciated his efforts on their behalf.

The hour was late, yet Takeda was abuzz, eager to share his observations. It occurred to Tolt that given the frequency of assassination attempts on Japanese military personnel and representatives of the Chinese puppet government, Takeda's presence in Shanghai was not without risk. Leading the way into the still open, but now quiet establishment, he tried to recall whether the assassination attempts usually involved injury to bystanders. Compared to the glossy candle-bedecked birthday cake that was the Paramount Ballroom, where they had spent much of the evening, this bar was closer to an over-cooked English steamed pudding. Nevertheless, it would do.

The establishment's only guests, he and Takeda placed their orders, then swung gently back and forth on their respective bar stools. They watched while the bartender poured their drinks.

Although Takeda generally abstained, this evening he announced that he wanted the full night-on-the-town experience, so had consumed a not inconsiderable amount of alcohol. His cheeks were flushed and his eyes were bright. He swayed a bit on his stool.

"What does your commanding officer make of your visiting Shanghai given all the assassination attempts on Japanese military?" Tolt asked.

Takeda shrugged, "Mostly army. Occupying forces. We Navy have a lower profile here." It occurred to Tolt that Takeda hadn't answered his question, although the fact he was using English suggested an awareness of the risks of standing out. Swinging his bar stool back and forth as he gripped the side of the bar, Takeda shook his head and declared, "Western nightclub culture."

The bartender set the two drinks down in front of them and returned to restocking the bar.

Swirling the cognac in his glass, Tolt chuckled. "Well, if you call listening to a Filipino band play for an audience of Chinese and some Europeans and Americans swirling around the floor of a nightclub in China, Western... then sure!"

"Whether really Western or not, isn't the point. The people tonight are trying to be Western. Modern. International. What's that word people use?" Takeda paused for a moment. "Aping. They're aping the lifestyle of the West."

Tolt wrinkled his nose. "How's that?"

Looking around the darkened, empty room as if to remind himself of what he had experienced earlier in the evening, Takeda didn't answer Tolt's question. "And frivolous," he added.

"Yes, gaiety can involve some frivolity," Told answered in a grave tone, but with a smile dancing in his eyes.

"Yes, well... and all that dancing. With different people!" Takeda shook his head. "Dancing with one person you know, that can be quite enjoyable. But this constant switching of partners. Even men and women who don't know each other taking turns dancing together!"

They took a sip of their drinks.

The door opened and a couple peered in. Tolt and Takeda swung their stools around in unison to see who it was. Perceiving the absence of a crowd and the sleepy feel of the place, the would-be guests withdrew.

Tolt swung back to face the bar. "You were keen for a chance to see how Tak and Sumiko spend their time living here in Shanghai. Did this evening give you the glimpse you were hoping for?"

Takeda's face turned stony. "Yes, I see how things stand, but no, it is not what I had hoped." He glared. The bartender, who had been approaching to see if their drinks were satisfactory, turned and scuttled back to the other end of the bar. "In fact, it is appalling."

"Come again?"

"In Japan, wives don't socialize with their husbands. And certainly, they wouldn't dance or flirt with other men, much less men that they haven't been introduced to."

Tolt nodded but was unsure how to respond. No matter. Takeda continued to rail. "You saw how that Westerner tapped me on the shoulder. What is it called? Cut in – he cut in when I was dancing with my cousin. None of you knew him. Yet I had to give way. Some man none of us knows was holding her in his arms." Takeda's face reddened as his speech quickened. "This entire evening was in contradiction to how a proper Japanese lady should behave!"

Tolt countered, "But, Takeda-san, Sumiko isn't a wife. And, I hate to break it to you, my friend, but this isn't Japan."

"Exactly," Takeda hit the top of the bar with his palm. "This Western way of living… she is too caught up in it. Too comfortable in it. Failing to see what is proper; how she, a young woman from a good Japanese family, ought to be living."

"I'm not following you."

"Out several evenings a week. With a group of friends, not at home with family. Wearing expensive and revealing Western clothes. Dancing, drinking cocktails, not getting home until very late. It's frivolous. Not a proper way to live."

By now, Takeda was almost steaming in his outrage. "And all this socializing isn't limited to men in her family's circle of friends. It can even include total strangers!"

Befuddled and tired after a long evening of politeness, as well as a fair amount of alcohol, Tolt tried to rebut Takeda's characterization. "For the kind of evening we had tonight, light-hearted fun is the name of the game. But, Sumiko...she's not doing anything wrong. No shady joints. And believe me, if that's what one's looking for, Shanghai has them in spades."

Tolt felt a twinge of guilt, recalling that just a few days earlier, Sumiko and Diana had been eager to visit the risqué clubs of the Badlands. He tried to assess if his words were having any impact. He couldn't tell and forged on. "Plus, Tak is always with her. He's family. She may not be sitting at home knitting socks, but she doesn't go out with people who haven't been properly introduced. Don't get the wrong idea."

Takeda remained silent, staring at Tolt.

Still unsure of whether he had succeeded in correcting the impression that Sumiko's conduct was improper, Tolt continued. "In fact, by our lights, Sumiko is quite reserved. Even formal. She doesn't play the tipsy filly at some ring-a-ding. She doesn't flirt. That fellow — he just likes to dance. I see him at clubs all the time. He's harmless."

Waving his arm to encompass the bar, Tolt added, "Look at this place...it's fine, right? Nothing shady going on here, but even so, it's not top-notch. Sumiko wouldn't come to a place like this."

From the safety of the far end of the bar, the bartender looked over to them, curious about the animated discussion.

"Yes, by Western standards I can see why you say it is not improper. But Sumiko isn't Western. The problem is she's like too many of our young people: intoxicated by the West. Too drunk on Western champagne and music to see reality."

Takeda took a hefty swallow of his drink, then said with sullen distaste as if he were spitting out something foul. "The West." It occurred to Tolt that Takeda's usual teetotaling demeanor was preferable to that currently on view.

"The West's time, it's past," Takeda said looked ahead, as if not really seeing the bottles arrayed on the shelves of the wall behind the bar. "Caucasian domination: that age is over. Now the era of the East is starting."

Picking up steam, he went on with more energy. "A Japanese way. A Japanese style of living is what we in Asia should be following, not a mongrel version of so-called Western culture."

He waved his hand for emphasis. "The example of modern Japan is what everyone ought to admire! Japan — a society that holds to tradition, honor and respect — while also succeeding in the industrial age."

"You won't get any argument from this fellow on the downsides to Caucasian domination," Tolt replied, attempting to ease the mood. "Hasn't worked too well for my people, either."

Takeda's expression remained stony.

Ignoring the temptation to needle Takeda by observing the Japanese way of life wasn't necessarily appreciated in all of Asia, Tolt focused on the question at hand. "Forgive me for being so direct. It's not the Japanese way, but I feel like we need to be frank."

Takeda's head continued to face the bar, but he shifted his eyes sideways to gaze at Tolt, and gave a wry smile. "Last year when I was posted to London, I learned that when Westerners say they must be frank, it means they want to say something the other person won't like to hear."

"Well, there's some truth in that," admitted Tolt. He looked down at his hands clasping his glass and thought for a moment. "Word is that you're interested in marrying Sumiko." Tolt paused. Takeda raised his eyebrows but said nothing.

The light in the fixture above the bar sputtered and the bartender stepped to the side door to check the fuse box. Tolt looked up at the flickering bulb, then at Takeda. "Obviously this isn't something that I have discussed with her. But as a general rule... that is, if a fellow wants a girl to be sweet on him, he's got to play detective a bit. He's got to figure out what she likes."

Takeda regarded him with an unconvinced expression, but Tolt plowed ahead. "Show her that life with him offers a chance for enjoyment. If she likes music, to dance, travel, meeting different people, being exposed to new ideas; well, insisting she give all that up for the go-back-to-tradition route, it just doesn't seem like such a good deal."

"Yes, with Western girls, that is probably the case. But you forget Sumiko isn't a Westerner."

The overhead light stopped sputtering and the bartender stepped back into the room, a proud look on his face at having resolved the problem.

Takeda turned on his bar stool to face Tolt. "Sumiko is Japanese. In our society, tradition is important. Duty is important. Family is important. Frivolous ideas — of what an individual likes or wants — these are not important. When you look at a hybrid society such as Shanghai's, well, it's clear that they have lost the foundation of core principles. And when that happens… well, look at the state of China today!"

Now it was Tolt's turn to become agitated. "But that's where you're wrong!" He tried to moderate his tone a bit to fulfill Japanese norms of *politesse*. "Takeda-san, someone like Sumiko, she's a hundred percent Japanese. But she's a modern Japanese girl. She can like the things we did tonight, and still consider herself Japanese. Her family has no objection to her conduct. There's no violation of duty towards them."

Takeda's expression remained neutral. Notwithstanding Tolt's intention to be circumspect, his words sped up and the tone of his voice intensified. "If the story you're peddling is 'come back to Japan, marry me and wear drab kimono while sitting around at home all day waiting for me to return from work and serve my supper,' that isn't going to sell."

Takeda's eyes narrowed but he did not reply.

"You say the age of Western domination is over," Tolt said with irritation. "Could that be wishful thinking? Look around Shanghai." Tolt spread his arm wide.

Takeda gave a cursory look around the bar. The bartender thought he was being called over, started again to make his way to them, but then realizing his error, stopped and took up wiping a different, and already very clean, glass.

"It's been years since Japan came to China," Tolt said, picking up steam. "The army, the navy, they're all here. But Shanghai continues as it ever has. The French run their settlement. The Brits, Americans and others running the International Settlement. Not even the European war has made much difference. The biggest difference is the Germans and Italians no longer get invited to the British consul's receptions. Fact is, things aren't changing much. The West controls much of the world. Politically, economically, socially, you name it. Japan to dominate? I don't see it happening."

"The White race has everyone cowed," Takeda said with contempt. "Even the most oppressed. Even Colored people, such as you." He snorted and took another swallow. "In America, I saw how the Whites despise you. Yet you cannot see what's happening here."

Tolt wondered if during his sojourn, Takeda had also noticed that White Americans weren't too keen on Asians either, but refrained from posing the question.

"It's this combination of Westerners' superiority and their frivolity that makes it so that they — you — cannot perceive that power is shifting. The days of Western control over the international system, of Western cultural values being at the top, these are passing."

Tolt gave a dry laugh. "Ah, the 'Greater East Asia Co-Prosperity Sphere.' But is Japan simply mimicking England's approach from a hundred years ago? A new version of empire for a new age?" He swirled the amber liquid in his glass and continued. "The difference is that a century ago, England's competitors didn't have her same level of industrial capacity. They couldn't block her expansion. But today it's changed. Japan has to take into account the power of America, as well as Russia, England and its empire. Much trickier seas for an island nation to navigate."

Takeda countered, "Like I said earlier, you Westerners are blind to what is really going on around you. Whether we are talking about women or how Japan fits into the international system, you think you have all the answers and that things will continue as they have for the last fifty, a hundred years."

He paused, placed his hand on the bar as if to steady himself. "What if I told you a transformation is coming? That my country was going to seize the initiative? Maybe even attack yours?"

Feeling the effects of the cognac on top of the earlier cocktails, Tolt laughed. "I would say that would be idiocy." He gave a little bow as far as his perch on the barstool allowed. "With all due respect, of course."

"Ah, and this validates my point. But try to put aside your Western superiority; consider it from the perspective of the chess board…"

Here Tolt interrupted, pulling out the board he always carried in his inside jacket pocket. "By all means, let's."

Takeda looked surprised, then smiled. Taking the board from Tolt, he opened it on the bar, then arranged the pieces as if a game were well underway. He gestured to the white side of the board, which faced him. 'You see where things stand. Many options for a win are possible, but none is without risk. One must assess how best to weave through the obstacles. A combination of daring offense and strategic defense can get one to victory."

Pointing to the black pieces, Tolt asked in a joking tone, "Assuming the chessboard is the international political situation, if black represents the vast continental mass of the United States, how does a small island nation, say an England or a Japan, prevail against so much larger a foe? How does White seize the Queen?"

"Too literal," replied Takeda. "Pretend you are playing this game." He pointed at the board. "One doesn't necessarily attack the Queen. Perhaps first one secures a rook, a less important, but still strategic, piece."

He picked up the rook, and said, "In the case of America, that would be Hawaii. Not the United States proper, but an important piece of the game."

"Hawaii?" Tolt asked a bit befuddled. "How did we go from debating how to woo Japanese girls to attacking Hawaii?"

Takeda laughed, but without warmth. "Both campaigns involve strategy. Tolt-san, you may be a chess player, but you're not a military man."

Takeda replaced the rook on the board. "Hawaii. That is where the Pacific Fleet is based. Where the battleships the United States can deploy to the Orient are located. If they are destroyed while sitting at anchor, America doesn't have its knights. Mounting a successful offensive attack would then be impossible for America. It would be left on the defense."

Takeda swept several black pieces from the board.

"I see." Tolt answered in a dry voice. The conversation had lost the tone of a casual chat after a few drinks. Now more like a smoldering, angry fire. Tolt attempted to dampen the flames.

"If what you're talking about are war games... practice for how hostilities could play out, then yes, your point makes sense."

He took a sip of his drink, then continued in what he hoped was a dispassionate tone. "Both Japan's and America's navies play out various battle scenarios all the time. At least, that's what people tell me." Looking at Takeda, he asked, "I suppose this is one that Japan considers from time to time?"

Appearing ruffled at perceived condescension on Tolt's part, Takeda replied, "Yes, each side conducts war games. But what I just described now... this is not such a scenario."

"Ah, I see," Tolt allowed. "Some strategizing going on. Thinking out loud."

"That's not what this is."

Takeda's face was still red, but his gaze was unflinching, steely.

"What is it then? From where I'm perched on this little barstool, I see a fellow I took out for a night on the town with the girl he's sweet on, we listened to some tunes, swung around the floor, had a good time. But now, well, the girl's on the road to ruin and the decadent West will be overthrown."

He looked directly at Takeda. "Why are you telling me these things?"

"For tonight... I must thank you. I expected merely an

evening of relaxation with my cousins. But it has turned out to be much more enlightening. I didn't just get a chance to see how my cousins live here in Shanghai. No, this evening made clear to me how cut off from reality the West is." Takeda took another swallow of his cognac, then continued. "You're right: everyone is dancing as if nothing has altered. This is our chance. The opportunity my country needs to change the tune, to break out of the constraints the West has erected."

"Do you mean that Japan is planning to attack America?"

"No."

Tolt's shoulders dropped, prompting him to realize how tense the discussion was making him.

"Japan isn't planning such a move." Takeda placed his glass back on the bar. "But I am."

Tolt shook his head. Takeda was planning an attack on Hawaii? But Japan wasn't? He tried to think of what made sense to ask next. "You? On your own?" he asked, befuddled.

"I am tasked with planning such an attack. But it is not simply a dream I came up with on my own. No, Admiral Yamamoto himself has assigned me this responsibility."

Tolt looked at Takeda, feeling his mind trying to process what he was hearing.

Takeda continued as if discussing a mundane question. "Is attacking the U.S. fleet while its ships are at berth without a battle, is that feasible? That is what I have been asked to determine. And, if such an attack is feasible, how to accomplish it?"

"And is it? Feasible, I mean."

Seeing that the level of cognac in the two guests' glasses had dropped, the bartender took courage and approached with an open bottle. Both Takeda and Tolt waved him away. He resumed wiping the already gleaming bar top.

Rotating the stem of his glass back and forth, Takeda said, "For the past two months, that is the question I've been considering. Night and day, I have pondered this puzzle."

He glanced at Tolt. "Last November, did you see the news that England used aerial torpedoes to attack the Italian fleet in the harbor at Taranto?"

Tolt nodded.

"That attack was audacious. The British fleet was offshore in the Mediterranean. But the Mediterranean is a mere pond compared to the mighty Pacific. The outdated planes had to fly only a short distance. Could a fleet cross the Pacific, and so far from land and without back-up support, launch a major air attack from open water against an enemy's battleships? And the attacking force then retreat in safety to be deployed elsewhere? These are the questions I have pondered."

"And?" Tolt asked, his throat dry.

Takeda paused, but the rhythmic rotation of the glass continued. "I have concluded it is."

He removed his hands from the glass and placed them flat on the top of the bar, on either side of the glass. "Next week when I return to Tokyo, I will submit my report to Admiral Yamamoto."

A combination of anger and bewilderment suffused Tolt. "Takeda-san, forgive my bluntness, but what gives? Are you irritated that tonight didn't go as you hoped?" Tolt could feel his cheeks getting hot. "If I didn't know better, I'd say a man who goes from an evening of fun to talking about the overthrow of the West is a bit… well, a bit off his rocker."

Takeda was unperturbed. "Yes, that fits with what I said earlier about how resistant Westerners are to reality. You see, these things as unconnected and hence, illogical. But I realize these pieces all are part of a bigger picture."

"Takeda-san, Did the cognac go to your head? Is this some joke you're pulling on a gullible American?"

Takeda looked at Tolt, his cheeks red, but his eyes focused with lucid clarity. "About both my cousin and Pearl Harbor, what I have said is true."

"Fine. What's to keep me from telling people in the U.S. government about it? Remember that retired German officer I mentioned the other day who boarded with us? He spent time in Japan. He said surprise is always a key part of Japanese military strategy. What if I spread the word? No surprise."

Takeda continued to regard Tolt, saying not a word.

Tolt tapped the bar top with his forefinger. "Let's say the Japanese Navy adopts your plan to ambush the U.S. Pacific fleet. What is to keep me from telling them? A prepared defense would thwart the attack." Tolt then gave an emphatic thump of his hand on the bar. "And that's why it seems like you must be pulling my leg."

"It's late, even for Shanghai. We should be going."

Tolt laid his hand on Takeda's arm. "Takeda-san, please, answer my question. Is this just the booze and fatigue, or are you serious about the coming of a war between our countries?"

"This question I have already answered."

"But, to talk about such a plan with me — a civilian, a foreigner — a citizen of the country you contemplate attacking. This seems reckless to the point of illogic!"

"You keep using that word. It's not my thinking that is irrational." He removed Tolt's hand from his arm.

"From the time I have spent in your country, I know how Negroes are treated. You are worse than second-class citizens. You are almost non-persons. What did people say to me when I was in Washington? Infantile, unreliable, unintelligent. This is how your countrymen view you."

Takeda's smile was chilling. "You question the logic of my views towards Sumiko, of my views towards Western culture generally. Your pride blinds you." His tone intensified. "You see the world through the blinders Americans wear. But I know. I know that to your countrymen, you are not a real American. You are barely even human."

Takeda's words both fascinated and repelled Tolt. The statements themselves were undeniably true. After all, he came to Shanghai because no matter his education and abilities, in America he was never going to be able to find employment at a level even close to that of a less-competent, less-educated White man. But the way the Japanese officer marshaled these awful truths to turn Tolt into a safe receptacle of his secrets was sinister.

"Only three people in the entire Japanese Navy currently know of my plan's existence. And now you. This I can tell you without any recklessness on my part as to the operation's being defeated."

Now it was Takeda's turn to tap the top of the bar with his forefinger to emphasize each word. "No one in your country would believe the word of a Negro on a matter such as this. Even if you were inclined to try, my colleagues here in Shanghai would make sure you and your friends had nothing further to say." Takeda's smile was mirthless.

Cold drops of sweat formed between Tolt's shoulder blades. The West was blind. American Negroes were blind. Yes, he too was blind. Realization soaked in like the icy November rains that deluge the Puget Sound, biting one's skin and chilling through to the bone. Takeda was serious. And, worse yet, he might even be right.

8

May 1941, part 1

Tolt's exchange with Takeda troubled him for some weeks, but given that life continued as it had when he had arrived in Shanghai the previous year, he eventually ascribed Takeda's claims to liquor-fueled boasting.

He, Quentin and Tak were often together. As the warmer weather arrived, the three enjoyed pre-work morning horseback rides, and together with Sumiko and Diana, they started planning summer houseboat outings on the canals surrounding the city. On the weekends, they played laughter-filled tennis matches. Tak made no further mention of Takeda and his aims towards Sumiko.

Work continued to be filled with interest. Ronnie's anger over being thwarted in his Chungking-Hong Kong smuggling scheme finally abated. The prestige of being Snow Drift's public face he now found sufficiently delightful. Meanwhile Tolt controlled day-to-day operations, finally confident Ronnie would not attempt to shoehorn him into a flunky role as feared when accepting the job. For all stakeholders — the local employees, Tolt and Ronnie — the status quo represented a pleasing state of affairs: Ronnie could play, Tolt could prove his mettle, and local employees reported to someone respectful of their views. Tolt used their insights to shape the decisions taken by him and by Ronnie and his father; face was maintained and the business flourished as never before. Ronnie Jr. was convinced it was all his doing. When Ronnie preened, Mr. Li and Tolt would exchange smiles.

One bright May morning, Mr. Li tapped on Tolt's door, hesitantly inquiring in pidgin if Tolt might have a few minutes. Monday afternoons the two had a standing meeting, and this was a Wednesday. Tolt's curiosity was piqued.

"Sure, Mr. Li. Come on in." He gestured to a chair in front of his desk. Li took it, perching on its edge.

"How are things?" Tolt asked.

"Fine. Tomorrow shipment go Tientsin, like schedule."

"Good." Tolt paused, hoping this would create an opportunity for Mr. Li to share the reason for his visit.

Mr. Li looked downward, appearing in no hurry to speak. Finally, in Mandarin he said, "I regret I have not performed to your satisfaction. The operational challenges you identified, I thought I had handled, but I see now that my efforts have not been sufficient."

Tolt frowned, trying to recall anything they discussed at Monday's meeting that would have prompted this comment. "Mr. Li, everything's fine," he said, baffled. "Monday did I say something to make you think otherwise?"

Mr. Li glanced at Tolt's face, then in the direction of Tolt's shoulder. "In terms of increasing production levels, you have set targets. We have been trying to meet them. On a weekly basis we may not reach the target, but on a monthly average, the targets are met."

Tolt tapped his desk with his pen, even more perplexed. "Yes, I have been following your progress. Things are going as hoped."

"But perhaps you doubt whether this is sustainable?"

"Well, there are always variables beyond our control, but I

have no reason to doubt your ability to continue to produce so long as sufficient grain timely arrives in port."

"Yes, we agree."

Tolt stopped tapping the pen, and asked, "I'm still at a loss, Mr. Li. Please, just tell me: what's up?"

Equally bewildered, Li gave Tolt a quizzical look. "Well, Japan. Snow Drift is making a joint venture next year to double production." "Joint venture? Japan?" Tolt frowned in a baffled way. "This time I'm afraid the bamboo telegraph's inaccurate, Mr. Li."

"This isn't rumor. It came from top management."

"Well, you didn't hear it from me. Are you saying that Mr. Planter contacted you from Seattle about this?"

"Yes, Mr. Planter. But not Seattle. Ronnie Planter."

"Ronnie? Japan?" Perplexed, but not wanting to create loss of face for either Li or himself, Tolt said, "Well, perhaps Ronnie heard something from his father that got turned around." He stood, hoping to bring this odd exchange to a conclusion. "Given tensions between Japan and China, as well as between Japan and American, it would be risky to depend on a Japan-based operation to meet expansion goals."

With a relieved expression, Mr. Li also stood. "Yes, exactly."

"Not to worry, Mr. Li. Just keep working as you have."

Mr. Li excused himself and departed. Tolt sank down into his chair, swiveling it around to face the window overlooking the busy Huangpu. Putting his feet up on the windowsill, he tilted his chair back.

The window panes rattled as a passing ship blew its whistle, the waters of the river, greeny-gray, pushed against the edge of the Bund. The passing boats moved at varying speeds, and as Tolt stared out on the scene, it assumed a Saturday matinee movie-reel quality.

What was Ronnie playing at? After being thwarted from smuggling to the wartime capital of Chungking, Tolt had assumed Ronnie was content to leave aside such ambitious schemes. But if he was now up to something else, direct questions weren't likely to be productive.

More information was needed. How to get it when the local staff didn't have the facts? Tolt recalled overhearing Ronnie mention a visit to Japan the following week: a tour to Tokyo with some American Chamber members, and a work visit to Snow Drift's Yokohama office.

Tolt sat up. His next step was clear.

Monday morning at nine, Tolt opened the door to the Snow Drift Yokohama office. His entrance elicited surprise, but no displeasure. The office manager escorted him to the usual office. He met with staff to ascertain the state of the business, whether any big orders were on the horizon, if shipping and customs clearance processes were operating smoothly.

As the hour approached 11:30, the mood in the office shifted. Tolt noticed an increasing flutter of people hurrying along the corridor, apparently involved in some arrangements at the office's meeting room. He heard the front door open, and a clinking and clanking reached him that sounded like a restaurateur may be delivering and arranging a catered meal.

After using the washroom, Tolt slipped into the meeting room and made his way to the sideboard-height cupboard that ran along the rear wall. He slid open its door and retrieved one of the finely-sharpened pencils kept there. As he stood up, Mr. Abe, the office manager came in to supervise the caterer. "Ah, Gross-san, may I help you with anything?"

"Got just what I needed, thanks. That brand of pencil you get here keeps the sharpest point. I always need to restock when I visit!" He smiled, holding up the pencil. Mr. Abe and the caterer both smiled in return, and Tolt returned to his office.

Not long after, he heard the front door opening. Bang. It hit the wall as it swung open. Bang again, as the door swung closed. Tolt knew who created such a trail of havoc in his wake.

His office was far enough down the corridor from the reception area that he couldn't hear distinct words, but he could discern the tone. He smiled even wider as he detected the mumbles of a conversation, first low and then more emphatic, which he imagined involved an exchange along the lines of:

"Welcome Mr. Planter!"

Grunt.

"Mr. Gross is in his usual office and we have put you in your regular office."

"Gross? What the hell's he doing here? When did he arrive?"

"This morning, sir."

"Where is he now?"

"In his office, sir."

Heavy footsteps made their way down the hall at a rapid pace. Tolt bent over the ledger in front of him. The door swung open and Ronnie swept in, stopping in front of Tolt's desk with his coat and hat still on and his face flushed.

"What the hell are you doing here?"

Tolt looked up from his work. "Good morning to you, too!"

Ronnie's didn't answer. Gesturing to the ledger in front of him, Tolt added, "Me, I'm checking figures. What brings you here this fine spring day?"

"You didn't know I was coming? Why are *you* here?"

"I come quarterly, remember? I asked Mr. Ma to remind you I was heading over."

"He didn't." Ronnie looked at Tolt with an assessing gaze. Tolt endeavored to maintain a neutral expression on his own face.

"This afternoon I've got some meetings," Ronnie added in a somewhat mollified voice. "Perhaps afterwards we can catch up."

"Sure, sounds good."

Departing Tolt's office, Ronnie must have run into Mr. Abe, as Tolt overheard snippets of conversation that included Ronnie replying with the words, "... no need for him to join. If he wants lunch, you can order him one."

A minute later, Mr. Abe popped in to inquire whether Tolt would like to have lunch ordered for him. Tolt declined, and Mr. Abe withdrew.

Just before noon, he heard noises indicating Ronnie's guests had arrived. After a few minutes, Tolt walked with a purposeful stride towards the meeting room. The receptionist stood up, endeavoring to signal it was occupied. "Yes, I know, won't be a moment," he reassured. Opening the door, Tolt entered the room. Three guests and Ronnie all looked at him, the guests in curiosity, Ronnie with an expression of irritation and apprehension.

Tolt gave a bow and in his most polite Japanese, said, "My apologies for disturbing you. I left something earlier, and I'm afraid I must retrieve it."

Almost before finishing his explanation, he headed across the room to the cupboard. The Japanese guests were surprised and delighted to hear a foreigner speaking fluent Japanese. They stood to bow in turn. Ronnie, remained seated.

"Sorry, man," Tolt said. "Left my notebook and need it before my lunch meeting."

The guests, occupying the side of the table closer to him, bowed again and held out their business cards. Tolt bowed in return and exchanged his with them. They made polite remarks, noting that he was based in Shanghai. By this time, Ronnie has risen, his hands placed on the table in front of him, looking as if he was exerting efforts to refrain from barking at Tolt.

Tolt noted the eldest man's resemblance to a Chinese 'happy' Buddha statue: the remaining hair on his bald head was close-shaven, his face was round and his earlobes exceptionally pendulous. It took all of Tolt's restraint not to gape at the man's unusual appearance. He apologized again, and with a wave to Ronnie, made his exit. On his way to lunch with Tak, who was also in Yokohama that week, Tolt examined the business cards.

Tak was already at the restaurant. As Tolt slipped into his seat, the waitress filled their teacups, and Tolt dealt the three name cards out on the table. He took a sip of the tea and waited for Tak to digest the information.

Tak looked up, smiled, then said, "Did you just meet?"

"Yes, indeed."

"Well, this is a coincidence. Actually, it's two."

"How's that?"

Before Tak could answer, the waitress returned. "Okay if I order for us?" he asked.

That important matter handled, Tak pointed to the card the Buddha-faced man had given Tolt. "Last Friday, my father told me that Mr. Yoshida recently came to see him about investing in an international project."

"Yoshida's card says he's in charge of a logistics company."

"Yes, he is, but the way he got started was as a grain miller. His first company milled grains for growers and farmers, then eventually he got into transportation and logistics, first for grains and now for other products."

"So, what project did he want to do with your father?"

"Well, that's just it. My father has no use for Yoshida. He's never explained details, but it sounds like Yoshida may have cheated my dad on a deal years ago, and ever since, he's refused to do business with him."

"In that case, why would Yoshida come to your dad for a new project?"

"Oh, you know how things are with us Japanese. My father can't stand him, but they know so many people in common that it was easiest to avoid an outright break, so Yoshida has no idea of my father's true views."

Tak slurped his tea, then continued. "Yoshida's known to run his businesses in an aggressive way, always trying to expand and go into new lines. In order to get capital, he often has to borrow funds or take on partners. My father runs our family's businesses more conservatively, so he tends to have plenty of cash on hand. Yoshida was keen for funds, but my father hinted at recent losses in China. That headed off a discussion on the details of Yoshida's plans."

"I had no idea your family's interests had taken a bad turn," said Tolt, suddenly anxious.

Tak laughed and threw back the rest of his tea in a big swallow. "They haven't! You should know us well enough to know that Father did that just to avoid a discussion of a project with someone he wouldn't want to be partners with."

Tolt grinned, as the waitress arrived with their deep-fried pork chops on rice. The friends dug in with gusto and after a few mouthfuls, Tolt recalled Tak's original statement. "So, what's the second coincidence?"

"Last night when I was at the Hotel New Grand waiting for you, I sat in the bar for a while and who should be there? Yoshida, along with a couple of other fellows."

Gesturing to the cards on the table, he added, "Perhaps these two. In any case, Yoshida was boasting. Just won a concession to the Imperial Army to supply wheat flour at a nice price."

Using his chopsticks with dexterity to corral the last grains of rice in his bowl, Tak said, "A big deal. But the key to success in the project is securing a steady supply to meet the contract demands. Yoshida was bragging about how he had lined up a foreign partner... American with deep pockets, *and* guaranteed access to a steady supply of grain."

"Sounds logical enough."

"Sure. But then, one of the other fellows asks, 'so what happens if there's a war with the U.S.? How's the American partner going to fare?'" Tak placed his chopsticks across the top of his now-empty bowl.

"Yoshida seemed to think that was the funniest thing he'd ever heard. Want to know his reply?"

Tolt's grin was perplexed. "I'm all ears."

"He said that would be the best result of all; the Army would need more flour than ever, their conquered territories would supply the grain and the American partner... well, they'd be left in the cold, their share of the joint venture forfeited and Yoshida holding all the cards."

Tak watched Tolt digest this information. "Yoshida's companions seemed to think this was hilarious." He continued, "They left before you came down. It didn't occur to me that the boastings of a low-life my father detests could have anything to do with Snow Drift. But, here you come from the Snow Drift offices, bringing me these cards. Between last night and today, how many other American suppliers of grain with offices in Japan could Yoshida have met?"

Tolt frowned slightly . "True enough. But I'm curious. Last night when you were waiting for me, listening in to this whole discussion, how did you know it was Yoshida anyway?"

"Yoshida's got a pretty distinctive mug, wouldn't you say?"

Tolt nodded in agreement.

"So I recognized him right off. But I was still in university when

we met; that was years ago, and my face isn't so memorable."
Tak grinned.

Tolt laughed. "Be thankful!"

"Between when I left you last evening and lunch today, how
did *you* meet Yoshida?"

Tolt relayed the events of the prior week: his discussion with
Li, the decision to come to Japan without telling Ronnie, and then
his subterfuge to learn with whom Ronnie was meeting today.

"So, Snow Drift *is* the potential partner," concluded Tak.

"You mean patsy!" replied Tolt with a grimace.

"What are you going to do?"

"Talk to Ronnie. He's not going to like me putting my two
cents in, but not sure I have much choice."

"Well, good luck with that." Tak finished the last of his tea.
"Got plans for tonight?"

"To catch onto your coattails and find some fun. That's the
extent of my planning."

"Well, I better get to work then and make some arrangements!"
replied Tak, smiling as he waved to the waitress to bring the
check.

When Tolt returned to the office, Ronnie's luncheon with
Yoshida had concluded. There was no sign of any of them. Tolt
felt relieved, preferring to delay confrontation. At the end of the
workday, Tolt headed out to meet Tak.

The next morning, Tolt was back at the Snow Drift office,
going through the overnight cables. To his surprise, Ronnie
popped his head in, inquiring, "Got a minute?"

Tolt stood up, gesturing Ronnie to enter, "Come on in."

Ronnie wasted no time. Settling into a chair, in a cool, steady
tone he said, "The meeting I took yesterday, it involves an
opportunity; I want to give you the lowdown."

Tolt nodded. He could feel the vibration of his desk against which Ronnie was tapping his shoe. "The project this Yoshida proposes is looking real. Based on the last go-round you and I had, well, it strikes me that it's best to air things out early. Might as well hear all the negatives now, because eventually, they'll be there waiting to bite me on the backside."

Tolt started to reply, but Ronnie raised his hand. "Just as oil opposes water. It's like a scientific law or something. Better lay all the cards on the table, before you put a bug in the old man's ear."

Tolt sat back and gave a rueful grin at Ronnie's assessment of their communications.

"Fair enough. Shoot."

Ronnie started. As his explanation gained ground, the toe-tapping ceased and his enthusiasm for the project became ever-more apparent. "Well, the old man wants to expand milling capacity here in the Orient. You've been working on improving operations in China and those efforts are bearing fruit."

Tolt noted Ronnie's recognition of his accomplishment, which was a first. "But China being China," Ronnie continued, "and especially now with the disruption from the military operations among the Japanese, the Nationalists and the Communists, it's just too unsettled a situation to give us confidence that it's going to improve in the short term. Increasing investment in China may be too risky."

Tolt considered asking why six months earlier Ronnie had been agitating to do just that, but he refrained. Ronnie barreled on. "So, we need a locale with direct and regular shipping routes with the Pacific Northwest, a ready workforce and a stable political and economic situation."

He fiddled with the watch chain in his waistcoat. "We could do it on our own, but building up our distribution capacity at the same time as expanding production capacity has some downsides. It occurred to me that Japan is the most stable of the locations that fits the bill. There are frequent shipping routes between here and Snow Drift's home base, and Japan's the most developed economy in Asia."

Tolt nodded.

"Then I thought, what if we did the project as a joint venture? Yoshida's operation we've worked with from time to time on the distribution side, so he seemed like a natural candidate. Yesterday's meeting validated these points. Not only is Yoshida enthusiastic, but he's just signed a major supply contract with the Imperial Army. His biggest concern was how to guarantee meeting the supply requirements."

Dropping his watch chain, Ronnie clapped his palms together, the sound reinforcing his conclusion. "With Snow Drift as a partner, Yoshida's chief worry is gone. He says the terms of the Army deal allow him to assign the contract to the JV. It could be the foundation stone. Profit margin wouldn't be high, but volumes would be good. Having the Imperial Army as a customer would help build the JV's reputation."

Ronnie stopped and looked at Tolt in a fashion that was direct, but not antagonistic. It occurred to Tolt that Ronnie's attitude indicated a truce of sorts: this project was important to him, and Tolt's support was needed to make it work. Wasn't this what Tolt had been hoping for, a chance to be recognized? Not dismissed as ignorant on account of his race or respected only due to his being Bill Gross's grandson? For a fleeting moment, it occurred to Tolt that he and Ronnie shared more in common than surface appearances suggested: both faced the possibility of being deemed dilettantes advancing solely because of their relative's status. Not a comfortable sensation.

Turning from the discomforting prospect of kinship to

Ronnie, Tolt considered the pitch. His analysis made sense, but the problem was the possibility of Japan and America going to war. Observing Tolt's silence, Ronnie couldn't resist needling. "My presentation has left you speechless? Can't say as I've managed that before."

"Sorry, man. Just taking it all in." Tolt considered how to convey the respect Ronnie's sharing of confidences deserved, while reflecting his own concerns.

He looked down at the desk, then after a moment, looked up. "The plan seems like it'd be hitting on all eight. The sole hang-up could be Jap's military aims. Right now the bullseye is only China, but I keep hearing they are planning on a move south."

"Well, last year what happened in French Indochina answered that question. No one loves the Tri-Partite arrangement, maybe not even the countries in it... but now that Japan has some troops based in Vietnam, it really has nothing to do with the Yanks."

"Sure, but Japan might have its eyes on more than just Vietnam. The Philippines, British Malaya. Maybe even Java for the oil fields there."

"It's just speculation. That or Chinese rumor-mongering against the Japanese. China was — is — a basket case, a fragile basket waiting to break, and it's the only thing separating Japan from the communist hordes in Russia."

Ronnie resumed turning the links in his watch chain, "Vichy France's allowing Jap troops into northern Indochina helps contain opposition in China's southwest. Between the Japanese forces inside China, and now in Indochina, it's like a crab claw pinching from either end. They can crush the Chinese. The situation all seems pretty measured. It's not like they're itching to crawl over the entire map of the Orient, wallpapering it with the Rising Sun."

"Could be," Tolt fiddled with a pencil, then looked up. "I get your line. Honest, I'm not trying to push the brake. I just need to think through the angles." He put down the pencil. "Give you my thoughts in a day or two?"

"Sure. As long as no wires are going out to the old man in the meanwhile," Ronnie replied with a genial expression on his face, but an edge in his voice.

"He won't get the lowdown until after you tell him," Tolt assured him.

After Ronnie departed, Tolt resumed twirling his pencil. Ronnie willing to join forces? Who would have predicted that? But what if he put the kibosh on Ronnie's plans with Yoshida? Ronnie would be telling his pop to get Tolt to take it on the heel and toe, that was for sure. But maybe this time Ronnie was right. Even if Yoshida turned out not to be the partner Snow Drift needed, maybe the idea of expanding in Japan had merit. After all, Asia was in turmoil. Had been for years. Was Snow Drift supposed to stand still in the meanwhile? It occurred to him that there was a way to kill two birds with one stone: figure out whether expanding in Japan was worth pursuing, and whether Takeda was merely blowing smoke.

Meet with Takeda. If he is in town. If he is available.

Big ifs.

9

MAY 1941, PART 2

IN THE CENTER of the dojo, Tolt and Takeda both stood encased in kendo armor, and bowed toward each other. Takeda had been surprised, but not unwilling when Tolt proposed getting together for some kendo practice.

"I did not know you were a *kendoka*!" he exclaimed as he and Tolt donned their gear the day after Tolt's discussion with Ronnie. Tolt demurred. Unsure of Tolt's level, Takeda replied, "Shall we do *gokaku-geiko*?", meaning that they would engage on an equal level of skill.

"Ah, I'm sure *hikitate-geiko* would be more appropriate for a poor kendoka like myself!" laughed Tolt.

Takeda grinned, unsure of whether Tolt was merely being polite, but nevertheless appreciative of good form.

Each spread their feet apart, and bent their knees with torsos upright, then extended their *shinai*, so the points of both touched. Straightening their legs to stand erect, they backed away, holding the *shinai* extended.

Their movements looked like a dance, but instead of partners moving in unison, their mirrored movements unfolded as if under a repelling force. After reaching the required distance, they stopped. Takeda approached. With a sharp exclamation and a stamp of his front foot, he raised his *shinai*, striking the side of

Tolt's body armor. They took turns striking and defending, using the various approved zones: the wrists, head or body.

The day was warm, and vigorous sparring soon had them both panting. Pausing to take some water, Takeda remarked, "Your sensei must have been quite good."

Tolt smiled, thinking of how proud Sato would be to have his teaching praised by an Imperial Japanese Naval officer. "He lacked a talented student, but his determination compensated for the student's deficiencies!"

They retook their positions, Takeda and Tolt facing each other with knees bent. Tolt was a few inches taller than Takeda, but both men were of similarly agile, slim builds. Tolt parried Takeda's *shinai* while advancing and simultaneously thrusting against the side of Takeda's *bogu* and Takeda exclaimed, "Ah, very nice *harai-waza!*" describing the defensive-offensive move Tolt had deployed.

On the next round, Takeda retreated several times as Tolt sought to make a strike, then suddenly, he lifted the *shinai* over his shoulder, gave a shout and stamped his foot as he struck Tolt on the top of his helmet. Through the helmet, Tolt's muffled voice praised Takeda's use of surprise. "My sensei was right. You Japanese are good at *katsugi-waza*. Well done!"

Takeda bowed. "We Japanese like the element of surprise in our sparring."

After an hour had passed, Takeda looked at Tolt. "Do you enjoy the Japanese bath? Shall we go to the *sento?*"

"Do I!" exclaimed Tolt as he removed his helmet and pulled off the towel encasing the top of his head to wipe his dripping face.

After scrubbing themselves with tremendous thoroughness and repeated rinsings at the small spigots lining the tiled room, they finally settled in the large tub of water whose heat to Tolt felt almost scalding, but to Takeda apparently offered no discomfort.

"You are good at finding *suki*," he complimented Tolt, referring to opportunities to strike one's opponent. Tolt nodded but was too focused on enduring the torrid temperature to say anything.

"I expected that you would use more direct techniques, but your style relies a great deal on feints and moves in anticipation of your opponent. It is rather subtle."

Takeda's compliment seemed to embody an assumption that as a foreigner, or as a Negro — precisely which was unclear — Tolt would be a straightforward opponent relying on brute strength.

Takeda lifted his hand from inside the bath, and watched water droplets fall into the tub. "In planning strategy, assumptions are necessary, but they can also be one's undoing. I must bear that in mind."

Unsure of how to respond to this second observation, Tolt chose to focus on the first.

"Takeda-san, in all truth, you are too polite. I am a poor *kendoka*. Despite my sensei's instructions invoking the saying 'try, try and try a thousand times,' I am not skilled."

Takeda grinned. "Your instructor was indeed wise. His advice on persistence is one I use not only in kendo, but in my work."

"My sensei used to say that persistence is necessary for any accomplishment."

Takeda nodded.

Tolt dribbled water over his head. "Any technique I have comes from the lessons of my two sensei. One, Sato-sensei, was strong in focusing on cultivating the third eye. The other teacher, Rupp-sensei, taught me European fencing and inspired me with tales of the man who is my hero, the Chevalier de Saint-Georges."

"Fencing." Takeda's expression and the tone of his voice were as if describing a vulgarity not suitable for discussion in polite company. "Westerners often confuse the techniques of European fencing with kendo, but of course the discipline of kendo is meditative. A spiritual practice as much as a martial art. Your reference to your sensei's comments about the need to cultivate the third eye shows you are aware of this."

In a less astringent tone, he added, "I have not heard of this Saint-Georges. What technique did he espouse?"

"He referred to the need to develop a 'cat's eye' in fencing, to envision where your opponent will move and get there first."

Takeda nodded, "Ah, yes, that does sound rather similar. From your use of the *debana-waza*, this is a lesson you have followed."

They sat in silence, enjoying the water's heat. The evening rush had not yet started and the room was otherwise empty.

Tolt then ventured onto the subject that had prompted him to contact Takeda. "So, if in kendo sparring you expect an American to use the technique of wearing down and overwhelming, what style of attack would the Imperial Japanese Navy use to engage with America?" he asked, in what he hoped was a neutral tone, although his heart was pounding and droplets of sweat beaded his hairline.

Takeda appeared as cool and unconcerned as if he were soaking in a pool of tepid water on a crisp autumn day. "Ah, that is an easy question: *Katsugi-waza*. A surprise attack, such as I used at the end of our session."

"Just like in 1894 and 1904, eh?" Tolt replied in a light voice that to his ears sounded faint.

Takeda sat up with a splash, "I didn't realize Americans knew so much about Japanese history!"

Tolt tried to chuckle in an off-handed fashion. "I'm not sure

Americans generally do."

Takeda nodded, and sank back into the bath.

"How is that project coming, the one we discussed when last you were in Shanghai?" Tolt asked, trying to seem casual.

"It is consuming all my time. Talk about assumptions. So many to sort through and then alternative scenarios to consider. It's like a giant puzzle." Takeda said.

This was it. Tolt tried to process the significance of what he had just heard without revealing the wheels spinning in his head. He cupped his hand and swirled it through the water. "Have the pieces all come together now?" he asked.

"More or less. Of course, with such projects, after developing the plan, one has to practice and assess weaknesses, but such adjustments come down to fine-tuning."

"Fine-tuning and timing, too?"

"Timing is always a consideration in using *katsugi-waza*," Takeda replied with a wry smile. "But as you know from kendo, one must prepare all sorts of techniques for both attack and defense. Whether and which you use depends on the situation. All your planning and practicing might never be used."

Pondering how to apply the kendo metaphor to the possibility of Japan's attacking America, Tolt ventured, "I suppose a would-be opponent could also concede that you are superior, and then you prevail without ever having to do battle."

Takeda scoffed. "That is not man's nature. Look at your country's leaders! Can you imagine such men conceding the reasonability of Japan? Of our need for stability in our region, our need for raw materials to power our industry?" He snorted. "You Americans have your Monroe Doctrine. How are the efforts of Japan any different?"

Takeda wrung out a cloth, draping it round his neck. "Imagine if America required oil imported from Venezuela to operate its economy. If Japan or Germany blockaded you, what would happen? America would strike that country."

America wasn't occupying Venezuela, killing hundreds of thousands of civilians, raping its women and torturing its combatants, but Tolt refrained from dispute.

"Noted," he said. "So if the status quo persists — either because America comes to accept Japan's position, or we refrain from provocation — then Snow Drift can continue operating in Asia, with you and I sparring, visiting the *sento*, and finishing with a good meal."

Takeda smiled. "Well put. As long as the objective conditions don't box my country in, there will be no reason for hostilities."

Removing the cloth from his neck, Takeda gestured. "Shall we?"

Towards the end of dinner, a mellowed Takeda confided, "Before today, I had never gone to a *sento* with a foreigner, much less a Negro. It occurred to me that you might not know what to do. What if you jumped into the bath without cleaning yourself first? Most awkward!"

Grinning at the thought of possible humiliation, Takeda chuckled, "But it turned out that you did know how to bathe! All very proper. It is most interesting. And a Negro, no less!" He shook his head in wonderment.

Afterwards, Tolt returned to his hotel and lay in bed pondering the events of the day. How to interpret his discussions with Takeda? Propped up against the bed's headboard, his legs stretched out before him, he tossed the room key in the air while considering the curiosity value their interactions afforded Takeda. It was hard to avoid a sideshow freak feeling. Not pleasant, but if his status as an 'oddity' yielded an information-gathering advantage a White American wouldn't enjoy, he would use it.

Tolt dropped the key onto the bedside table. Considering the implications of what Takeda had said, Tolt concluded that it was not a certainty that Japan and America *would* go to war. Takeda had agreed that America might not take a step precipitating a Japanese attack. If he assigned a mathematical value to the situation, he concluded the percentage of war currently stood at 25%. Was that high enough to stymy Ronnie's plans? He suspected that in the next several months, the direction of events would become clearer. Perhaps the best thing for Snow Drift and his relationship with Ronnie was to accede. Pursue the project, but slowly, allowing developments to reveal which way the wind blew. Having reached that conclusion, Tolt felt the tension in him ease. He sank into sleep.

The next day, when Tolt told Ronnie his joint venture idea had merit, Ronnie raised an eyebrow in suspicion. "The other shoe's going to drop. What is it?"

"There is no other shoe. I just told you, I've considered all the factors. Your analysis makes sense. I'm still worried about the possibility of wider hostilities, but it's speculation. You've sound reasons why a joint venture is worth pursuing. If you want to propose it to your father, I'm not going to oppose the idea."

"Won't oppose it. But will you support it? We both know the old man's first question will be whether both of us think the idea is worth pursuing."

Tolt paused. "Yes, I will. It's your brainstorm, so you should take the lead. We both know that with partnerships, the devil is in the details, so we'll have to see what Yoshida wants, what he's willing to concede. But I'll do everything I can to support, including managing the Shanghai employees' expectations."

Ronnie gave Tolt an appraising look. "What gives?"

"What do you mean?"

"Is this some new offensive-defensive move you've learned from your slant-eyed buddies?"

"I just said I support your idea. Where's the offense? Where's the defense?"

"Don't softsoap me, Gross. We both know that pretty much every time I've ever said up, you say down. All of a sudden you're throwing your chips in with mine. Why?"

"Maybe because this time you're right."

Ronnie continued to eye Tolt, assessing whether to take his response at face value.

"Man, you've known me long enough to know when I don't agree with you, I'll say my piece. That hasn't changed. It's just that in this case, I don't disagree with you. End of story."

Ronnie seized on this statement. "So, you don't *disagree* with my proposal, but you don't necessarily agree. That's the sort of lukewarm dishwater my old man will use as a reason not to proceed. I knew this was too good to be true."

Tolt shrugged. "It's been almost four years since hostilities broke out between Japan and China. Unless the U.S. moves to block Japan's access to oil, my worries are just nerves. Even though our name is 'Snow Drift,' the company can't stay frozen forever. We have to keep moving ahead. And, if we want to grow in East Asia, the reality is that Japan *is* the most stable country here."

They parted with the decision that Ronnie would prepare a memo to his father, copying Tolt. The next afternoon, Tolt was due to sail back to Shanghai. Before heading to the dock, he met Tak for breakfast.

Stirring his coffee, Tolt said, "Thinking about whether Ronnie's joint venture makes sense or not has got me in a tangle. Is Japan a modernizing, stabilizing force? Or, is it the big bully on the block, wrecking all the other kids' marble games?"

Tak looked around to confirm no one was nearby. "My country complains of being bullied. We say our actions are self-defense, but in China or Korea, *we* are seen as the oppressor. I'm proud of my country's heritage, but I worry about where we are today."

"What if you knew of something about to happen that would truly be an act of aggression by Japan with potentially devastating consequences?"

"I'm a mere businessman. Who would listen to me, even if I did know of such a thing, or spoke out about it?"

"True. But what if the government or the military were planning something big, something shocking that would destabilize the situation across Asia, and maybe beyond?"

"How would I come across anything like that?"

"Who knows? But just say you did. Go back to what you overheard Yoshida and his men discussing the other night; say you overheard them talking with a military man, discussing a plan to attack another country, say Britain."

Tak laughed at this vision.

"Man, why you laughing? I'm talking war here!"

"It's not the idea of war that makes me laugh." Tak managed to stifle his amusement. "It's the idea of here, where everything is secretive and people fear being overheard in public discussing sensitive topics, that Japanese would be discussing such a matter in public. Even now, you and I must be careful to lower our voices!"

"Fair enough, but humor me. Assume that on Sunday night, Yoshida wasn't chuckling over the prospect of planning how much money he would make if Japan and the United States went to war. What if he was talking about what was being planned to *start* the war. A war with a foe that could eventually destroy Japan as we know it.What would you do?"

"I'm trying not to laugh at the idea of Buddha-eared Yoshida being a threat to U.S.-Japan relations. So, for the purposes of your discussion, I'm to assume that I've overheard him talking about this with someone in uniform, someone credible. Someone like my cousin Takeda, correct?"

Tolt flinched. "Yeah, that's right. Takeda or some Army fellow… an officer type."

"Well, then the possibility could be more real. But, two points: first, some objective change would have to take place. Something to show the general level of hostile speech is changing towards outright military aggression. I haven't seen anything like that. And second, if you're asking me, what I as a Japanese could do, it's hard to think of any effective action."

Tak looked around to confirm there was still no one within earshot before continuing. "You know what has happened to Japanese society in the last fifteen years, the assassinations, the military's domination of all branches of our government…"

He lowered his voice even further, making Tolt strain to hear him. "If it were you, an American or some other Westerner, facing such a scenario, maybe you could go to your government and get someone to take steps to defend or prepare to counter-attack. But in Japan? No one would help. Indeed, it would be suicidal to try."

Tak sipped his tea and gazed at Tolt, his voice resuming its normal timbre. "It's only nine o'clock; this is a serious topic for breakfast. You overhear something while you've been here, maybe some Japanese who figured a foreigner wouldn't know the language and talked about sensitive matters next to you at a restaurant?"

"Like *The 39 Steps* or something?" Tolt smiled.

"Yeah, something like that. Do we need to plan to go on the run?"

"Not yet. I'm just wondering out loud. Thinking 'what-ifs.'"

Tak grinned and shook his head at his friend. "What did your grandfather used to say? You're a piece of work."

Tolt grinned back. "I know."

10

July 1941

As July progressed, Shanghai's heat and humidity rose. Peak daytime temperatures were almost unbearable. In the evenings, sidewalks filled with people hoping to catch a breeze. They set up low tables and stools where they ate dinner, and later played cards. Lucky ones stretched out on reclining chairs covered by quilts, trying to sleep. Tolt loved to stroll the neighborhood observing the nocturnal turn of local life. Diana and Quentin had gone with their family to their villa in the cool hills of Moganshan. They invited Tolt to join them, but he was reluctant to head off when Ronnie wasn't taking holiday himself.

One Sunday morning in late July, he found himself reading the weekend papers while enjoying a cup of coffee and feeling relieved that there was nothing he had to do that day, when a headline in the Saturday edition of the *Shanghai Evening Post and Mercury* caught his eye:

JAPANESE TRADE WITH U.S. TO END;
Experts See a Complete Cessation
Following Order 'Freezing' Tokyo Funds

Tolt eagerly scanned the article. The paper reported that with the agreement of France's Vichy Government, on the 24th,

Japanese forces had occupied Southern Indochina. The U.S. didn't see Petain's Vichy regime as legitimate representatives of France, and objected to the occupation as a further threat by Japan towards China, as well as the rubber reserves of Malaya and oil wells in Java. Roosevelt had signed an executive order freezing trade with Japan.

Accompanying the report, was a reprint of an editorial from the *Los Angeles Times* observing that as of June, Japanese companies reportedly had obtained licenses to export from the United States over 7 million barrels of gasoline and more than 20 million barrels of crude oil, supposedly enough to supply the country with crude oil through to the end of 1943. The President's order had not referenced an oil embargo, but the *Los Angeles Times* hoped U.S. regulators would so interpret it, and cancel the export licenses.

Tolt recalled a visit to the Snow Drift office by one of Ronnie's Marine buddies over the winter when the topic of US-Japan relations had come up, the Marine joked that the prospect of an American war with Japan was as likely as Germany opening a second front against its Russian allies. Yet in June, Germany did just that. Implausible things sometimes happen.

In May, Takeda had stated that as long as conditions didn't constrain Japan, there would be no reason to attack America. Drumming his fingers on the table, Tolt pondered: was this the change that would turn improbability into likelihood? America might be facing a risk greater than it could imagine. Closer to home, the president's order probably also meant Ronnie's treasured joint venture was up in smoke. Takeda's assessment that America's government wouldn't heed the warning of a Negro was probably correct. Tolt smiled ruefully at his disinclination to test the proposition.

With his thoughts pinging inside his brain like a pinball

machine, Tolt took another swallow of coffee, then grimaced: more caffeine was hardly likely to support calm reasoning. After a few minutes of gazing at the newspaper without seeing the text, he decided there was no sense in courting trouble. Soon enough events would show which way the wind was heading. The houseboy brought the morning's mail on a tray. His grandfather's strong hand stood out on one envelope. Anticipating one of his newsy letters, Tolt grinned. Inside he found not only a letter, but also a postcard, bearing a picture of a smiling brown-skinned woman wearing a grass skirt and her chest covered in multiple necklaces of flowers. Tolt flipped over the card. It was from Jimmy!

Dear Mr. Gross,
How you been? Things here are good. Miss you and Tolt tho. How's Ping's cooking these days? Me, I'm gonna be doing some cooking myself! Enlisted in the Navy, and I'm assigned to mess duty. No more fieldwork for this fella — gonna be at the Navy base at Pearl Harbor!
Thanks again for all you did for me. I can never really thank you enough, but I'm trying!
Yours respectfully,
Jimmy Johnson

Tolt dropped the postcard, leaning back in his chair with a thud. Jimmy was at Pearl Harbor? He rushed to unfold his grandfather's letter. Halfway down, it read,

This card just arrived from Jimmy. Thought you'd enjoy seeing it. It's been a spell now that he's been over there in Hawaii. Think it was one of them smaller islands where his mama's kin was at — Kauai or some such. Expect working on the sugar cane got old. Probably figured the Navy was a step up.

Tolt paced between the living room and dining room. The houseboy came out from the kitchen, inquiring if Tolt needed anything, but Tolt just shook his head and continuing to pace.

Saying to hell with America might be one thing. Let Takeda and his buddies scare the pants off of Uncle Sam. But Jimmy? That was something else. If Takeda was for real, then Tolt's best friend was sitting smack-dab in the center of a target. Noticing the day's other newspapers stacked on the breakfast table, he began rifling through them, comparing coverage of the U.S. embargo story. One contained a report quoting Japan's foreign ministry as scoffing that the U.S. action would not have an adverse impact on Japan because the country had oil reserves to last for 24 months, so there was plenty of time to arrange for alternative sources of supply. Another reported on the Chinese government's reaction from Chungking, stating that the embargo didn't go far enough.

Tolt thought back to the session with Takeda at the *sento*: Takeda said if America was ever blocked from getting oil, it would attack, and surely he meant that the same was true for Japan. Tolt picked up the telephone.

As the sun set and the day's heat started to dissipate from cauldron-like to merely sweltering, Tolt made his way from the French Concession to the Embankment Building. The complex was vast, supposedly the largest in Asia, with all the modern amenities, including an in-house swimming pool. The Takematsus' was one of the many units on the south side of the complex with balconies overlooking Suzhou Creek. The houseboy welcomed Tolt inside. The door to the balcony from the living room was open, and a somewhat cooler breeze wafted in from the water. Tolt gazed longingly at the balcony's rattan chairs arranged invitingly, but the houseboy was resolute in showing him into the kitchen where Tak was furiously fanning a large vat of rice.

"Cooking for an army?" Tolt enquired.

"Ha! No, I'm experimenting."

"To see how much rice it takes to feed an army?"

"To see which vinegar makes the better sushi rice. Come on, get an apron and help me before the rice gets cold."

"Hard to imagine cold rice in this weather, but hold your horses, a refreshing beer is required before I can get to work."

"Of course!" Tak laughed and asked the houseboy to serve, while Tolt donned an apron. The houseboy went to hang up Tolt's hat, leaving the two friends at their work.

Tak separated the rice into two bowls, dosing each with a different type of rice vinegar into which he had already added salt and sugar. He handed Tolt a paddle to mix up one, while he tackled the other. Once the vinegar was incorporated, Tak directed his friend to take a seat and keep him company while he finished preparations for their meal. Tolt marveled as Tak deftly shaped the rice into compact oblongs, sliced fish, and arranged glistening morsels of sushi. He made sure to keep the pieces from the two bowls using different vinegars arranged on two separate platters, all the while keeping up a steady stream of chatter with Tolt. "Sister is visiting Diana and will be back from Moganshan by the end of the week. Her postcard hinted they'll have lots of stories for us!"

Tolt grinned in reply, trying to match his friend's liveliness. "Hey, how'd you learn to make sushi anyway?"

Tak reminisced with zest about how his grandparents' cook had trained with a sushi master, and loved to show Tak his tricks. Tolt laughed along. When it was time to eat, Tolt consumed copious quantities of the delicious sushi. Tak ate his in an appraising manner, pausing between bites as he meditated on the differing qualities the two vinegars added. "On balance," he concluded, "The Mizzen vinegar's flavor is more delicate. Going forward, that's going to be my vinegar of choice."

Tolt grinned.

"What?"

"You, man. This is all delicious. And here you are, analyzing away. Like we were back in law school briefing a case, you making out the strong and weak points of each side's position."

"Hadn't thought of that," Tak broke into a grin, "but perhaps that's why I was always the best at doing the case notes!"

Tolt wadded up his napkin and tossed it to Tak, who caught it and then started batting it back and forth between his two hands, as if preparing to juggle.

"What say we leave this to Hsiao Fan and sit on the balcony for a bit?"

To ward off mosquitoes, Tak lit an incense stick in a small dish on the balcony ledge, and they each sat in rattan armchairs facing the creek. A few boats were still moving, but most had tied up for the night.

Tak sipped his beer, closed his eyes and leaned back.

"Been reading the news?" Tolt asked.

"Not today," Tak replied with his eyes still closed. "At dawn I was heading to the market."

"Remember those 'what-if' scenarios I mentioned over breakfast in Yokohama?"

"The Japanese version of *The 39 Steps*?" Opening his eyes, Tak smiled.

"Yeah, that's it. If you recall, the story needed a catalyst to be credible. A real threat to Japan."

"Yes, something that would turn Buddha-eared Yoshida's speculation about hostilities between Japan and America into an actual crisis." Tak sipped his beer, then looked idly at Tolt. "So, what does that have to do with today's news? Yoshida's on the front page?"

"President Roosevelt has issued an order freezing Japanese assets in the U.S. People are interpreting it as meaning the government will move to block exports of oil from the U.S. to Japan."

Tak's expression became serious, but he didn't say anything. Tolt looked out into the night and swatted a mosquito. "The news reports say Japan's navy has two years' worth of oil reserves. But over 80% of its supply comes from the U.S."

He glanced through the screen door to confirm the houseboy wasn't in the living room, then continued. "I remember your cousin's saying that Japan's total oil reserves are only enough to last six months. So, if the U.S. is thinking about implementing an embargo on oil exports...." Tolt paused. "Well, it would be like jabbing a hornets' nest with a stick."

"True. I mean, that's logical," Tak responded in a slow tone. "But, there's no way of knowing whether America is going to adopt such an interpretation. Surely your government will recognize that doing so makes a war more, not less, likely."

Tolt nodded. He considered what to say next, wanting to enlist his friend's help in analyzing this conundrum, but recognizing the risks to him. Concluding there was no help for it, he said, "Here's a hypothetical for you...."

Tak grinned, "Law school days really are back: first briefing cases, now hypotheticals! Shall we invite Quentin for a moot court session?"

Tolt gave a wry smile. "Assume a respected Imperial Japanese Navy officer who was senior enough to have access to sensitive information about Navy strategy, and engaged in first-hand, front-line planning, confided in a foreigner top-secret details of a plan to attack a potential enemy."

"An Imperial Navy officer telling a civilian, much less a foreigner, internal planning details? This really is an imaginary scenario!" Tak interjected.

"Hear me out. Let's assume that the officer himself recognized the absurdity of such a breach of security, but argued that by virtue of the foreigner's identity, it was almost as if he wasn't disclosing the matter at all. Given this foreigner's identity, no one would ever believe him."

"How's that?"

"Say the foreigner were an outsider in his own society."

"You mean like a criminal? Or a mentally ill person?"

"Worse." Tolt grimaced. "Imagine he's a Negro."

The expression in Tak's eyes changed from joking to seriousness. He listened with careful attention. "It's just a hypothetical, remember, but imagine this: the Japanese officer is tasked with developing a blueprint to attack the Navy's chief rival for control in the Pacific, an audacious plan forestalling a major open sea battle. Imagine an entirely unexpected ambush that critically weakens the enemy, enabling Japan to commence a wider offensive."

Tak pursed his lips. "Fine. What's the catalyst? Is there a set date? "

"Who knows, but maybe this Executive Order has started a clock ticking."

Tak's response was measured. "So, we're speculating."

"True. But let's take the information that's not supposition, that's from a reliable source: your cousin. He says Japan has enough oil for only six months. It's the end of July. Come January, the reserves will be getting pretty darned low. By February, they'd be out. Unless..."

Tak pondered that, looking out over the balcony.

Tolt took a swallow of his beer. "When we spoke in Yokohama, you said an objective event would have to occur to cause Japan to conclude it had no option but to attack America. Bottom line, I need to go see Takeda. Then I will know if this is for real and if it is... well, if it is, I'll have to think about what to do next."

In a wry tone, Tak replied, "I thought we were talking in hypotheticals."

Tolt looked at him. "So far as it concerns you, we are. None of this is actually real."

"Hmmm. Sounds like hypothetically, we need to get to Japan."

"*I* need to. But I'm not so sure you do. In fact, I'm pretty sure it's best if you stay right here."

Tak gave Tolt a baleful look. "I'm not going to sit back while one of my best friends takes on the risk you're talking about. I'm going with you."

"What risk? All I'm going to do is talk with your cousin about recent developments."

"And the mysterious Naval officer who confided in you the existence of a plan possibly to launch a surprise attack on America?" Tak said with raised eyebrows. "I know we're talking about conjecture and suppositions. You've not breached any confidences, but..."

Tolt looked at Tak with a level gaze.

Tak continued, "We both know who is behind this. You are not going alone."

Tolt tried to argue, but as he prepared to head home, Tak assured him, "First thing tomorrow, I'll check the sailing schedule. Who knows, maybe on Tuesday we'll be able to catch a boat."

Fortune was with them: Tuesday morning they were indeed embarking for Japan. Tolt has spent Monday sorting out various work responsibilities. Unsure whether from Japan he would be going on to Seattle, or returning to Shanghai, he tried to think of everything that Mr. Li would need to know to keep projects on course if he was gone six weeks or more.

That afternoon as he rushed from Mr. Li's desk to his own, he and Ronnie collided in the hallway, each preoccupied with reading some papers, which all cascaded in a jumble. Both bent down to collect them, Tolt saying, "Hey man, sorry about that. Just going over the schedule for some of the big milling projects that Mr. Li is tackling in the next few weeks, and..."

"Not a problem," Ronnie interrupted, standing to shuffle his retrieved pages.

"We need to talk about that executive order — the ban on trade with Japan. How are we going to fill pending purchase orders when we won't be able to export there?"

"Not a problem. I've got Smythe on it. We can still bring wheat into China, mill it here, then sell it to a middleman. Where they sell it, well, that's up to them..."

Tolt frowned. Maybe that would work, but he suspected it wouldn't necessarily be as clear cut as Ronnie suggested. No time to argue about it now, in any case. "Well, glad you're already on it. Fact is, I've got too much on my plate as is. Tomorrow I'm heading to Japan, and I wanted to let you..."

Ronnie interrupted in a sharp tone. "How's that?"

"Oh —it's..." How to reply? Say it's work? No. That will make him anxious. Tell him...

"It's Tak."

"Tak?"

"Well, the other night he and I got to talking, and drinking. Next thing you know, we had a wager going. Rock, paper, scissors. If Tak won, I had to go with him to Tokyo to try his favorite sushi restaurant."

"And if you won?"

Tolt could almost feel his brain sending out signals, reaching for a lifeline to devise some sort of plausible response.

"Uh, Hong Kong. We'd take next week's boat to Hong Kong and find the best Cantonese place." Tolt could feel his face grinning with what felt like forced hilarity. "Certifiable, isn't it?" he added.

"I take it Tak won," Ronnie answered in a dry tone.

"Yes, siree. So, tomorrow we're off. Tokyo, here we come. Anything you need me to look into while I'm there?" Tolt felt ridiculous, acting a manic zest he wasn't feeling.

Ronnie's suspicious tone evaporated, replaced with indifference. "No, not at the moment. Yoshida is pulling together some figures for me, and once I have them, we can discuss."

Tolt bit his tongue. Presumably Ronnie was also planning to use some sort of middleman to sidestep the embargo's application to his cherished joint venture. How could he be so indifferent to the risk such a scheme faced? Tolt thought about raising the topic, but decided it would simply set off another round of acrimony. Waiting for events to develop might be the smoothest course. Attempting a confident smile, Tolt merely replied, "Fine. Well, the rest of the week you won't see me, but Mr. Li is on top of things, so I don't expect there will be any snafus."

Ronnie nodded and held up his stack of papers. "Good. Well, must be getting on."

"Sure. Don't let me hold you up."

What an idiot I sound, Tolt thought, shaking his head as he headed back to his own office.

By Thursday night, he and Tak were in Japan, and had sent a message round to Takeda's quarters. Friday morning, Tak dropped by Tolt's hotel to update him.

"No luck. Takeda's adjutant says he's away. Expected back tomorrow, but he was doubtful that Takeda would return as scheduled." Tak's expression was glum. "Worse, when I dropped my things off at the house, my parents mentioned how his work seems to be requiring him to spend more and more time away from Tokyo."

Tolt nodded.

"The next passenger ship departs Yokohama for Seattle on Monday," Tak continued, his voice anxious. "Just three days. There's not another until early September. If he doesn't get back in the next two days, we're not going to be able to talk to him about what is going on."

"Maybe," Tolt said as he swallowed the last of the beer in his glass.

"Maybe what?" queried Tak with a raised eyebrow. "The sailing schedules are fixed. Without Takeda's return, what information can we gather?"

"The mere fact that he's gone more now than before tells us something. There's no evidence that the war in China is changing shape. Pretty much all the action is inland, so the Navy's role is limited."

Tak nodded, but then asked, "So?"

"So if your family and Takeda's aide are telling you he's now noticeably busier, doesn't that suggest planning on the Pacific project continues? And maybe that it's intensifying?"

"Maybe."

"What do you mean, maybe, man?"

"This is all hypothetical, remember? I need more data before I can draw conclusions," Tak responded tartly.

Tolt looked around the darkened bar. Except for two businessmen in the far corner whose reddened faces suggested they had imbibed enough to put them past the point of overhearing strangers' conversations, it was empty.

"Fine. Here's data for you: when I saw Takeda in Japan in

March, he was for real." Tolt leaned his forearms on the table, his hands clasping the base of his beer mug. In an intense, but quiet voice, he continued. "That night...it was the night he insisted on an evening out with Sumiko. After we wrapped up and you took the girls home, Takeda was keen to rehash the evening."

For emphasis, Tolt struck the table with his palm. "Two topics. One was this question of a plan to attack the U.S. The other: how to woo your sister."

Tak flushed. Tolt recognized that in mentioning the two confidences in conjunction with one another, the possible attack had assumed a new level of credibility. They were now beyond the realm of claiming theoretical possibilities.

"Takeda mentioned some admiral dude who had tasked him to figure out if an attack was possible... I think his name was Yamamoto."

"Isoroku Yamamoto? That's who Takeda said assigned him the job of planning an attack on America?"

"He didn't say the first name, just Yamamoto. But, yeah, I guess so."

"That seems odd. Yamamoto is known to be favorable to the United States. Studied at Harvard. And, the militarists hate him. It's well-known that he opposed the expansion into Manchuria. And the Tri-Partite Pact. In fact, the reason he holds his current position as leader of the Joint Fleet, was to get him offshore, away from land where the Army could assassinate him. Are you sure Takeda wasn't pulling your leg?"

"He didn't say anything about Yamamoto's views. All Takeda said was that Yamamoto assigned him the mission of determining whether an attack was feasible, and if so, how to execute. You know how Takeda can be high and mighty when he wants to, but that wasn't what this was. Sure, he liked rubbing my nose in the fact that because I'm Colored, he could reveal this scheme and no one would believe me. But as to details, the substance? The man was all business."

"Did he really come right out and say he was telling you because you are Negro?"

Tolt nodded.

Tak looked even more disturbed. "Say Japan really does have enough oil reserves for only six months, and Takeda really is working on a plan to attack the U.S. fleet at Pearl Harbor. And, because my cousin is who he is, I guess the plan is a good one?"

Tolt nodded again.

"Who's to say that Japan doesn't have other plans, maybe involving coordination with Japan's allies Germany and Italy, to deal with this situation? We don't even know if the U.S. is going to impose an embargo on oil exports. People have been calling for one for years. But it hasn't happened."

"History. Look back, Tak," Tolt answered in a low, but urgent tone. "What's that thing Ping and Sato were always saying about the past foretelling the future? I remember them talking with that fencing teacher who boarded at Our House, the German war vet, Rupp. I told you about him… he had been posted in Japan and also in Tsingtao?"

Tak nodded.

"Rupp talked about how Japan's M.O., the key samurai battle strategy, was using surprise attack to overwhelm opponents. And Sato agreed with him. 'Strike first, declare war later.' That's what he said was the *bushido* tradition."

"Tolt, you're talking about *bushido*; that's like talking about the rules for European jousting in the Sixteenth Century. Sure, Japan's military still treasures our country's traditions, but they are also pragmatic. Attacking a country with industrial and national resources capabilities like the U.S. is a different proposition than invading a backward, weak country like China.

You know this better than most Westerners."

"All true. But countries, nations, people... they don't change. Or if they change on the surface, they don't change all the way through. Look at America. Eighty years ago, people like me were enslaved. In many states it was a crime to teach us to read. To read!" Tolt shook his head. "But eighty years on, here I am, a university graduate. A trained lawyer. That's change. As big a change as that is, it doesn't mean many folks in America don't still see me — someone with dark skin and kinked hair — as an ignorant fool."

Tolt frowned. "Japan may now be an industrialized, modern nation, but I see how much of traditional thinking still remains in how people treat each other. The *bushido* ways are obviously influencing today's military men."

Tak took another swallow of his beer and pursued a different angle. "All right. But how do we know Japan is going to activate a plan to attack the U.S. Navy thousands of kilometers away?"

"Because Japan has done it before; maybe not as far afield, but still it's previously used this approach. There was the sinking of the *Kowshing* by the Japanese navy in 1894, a week before war — I guess it's now the *first* Sino-Japanese war — was formally declared; then, how in 1904, Japan torpedoed Russian ships at Port Arthur two days before the Russian-Japanese war was declared."

Tolt tried not to let his voice rise, "In both wars, Japan started with a surprise naval attack. And in both, Japan won. That's what Sato and Rupp meant when they said surprise is a key part of the Japanese military tradition. If it worked thirty some years ago, wouldn't it make sense to try that same approach again? Some of the people running things today may have even been junior officers then. Heck, that Yamamoto admiral fella, for all we know he was a junior seaman in the Sino-Russian war."

Tak gazed down at his beer mug, his expression troubled. "In fact he was. Lost two fingers when the cruiser he was on was hit in the Battle of Tsushima." He sighed. "I want to argue with you. I want it to be like when we were in constitutional law class and we could argue just to argue. But..."

Tak paused and looked down again. "Your reasoning makes sense. And my cousin with his pride in Japan's military might, a pride strong in my country... well, I fear you may be right."

Hesitating a moment, Tak then asked, "But even if these theories are true, what does it mean? We're not supposed to know. Even if we were willing to say something, would people believe it?"

Tolt nodded grimly. They waved the waiter over and ordered another round of beers.

The next day brought word that Takeda was returning to Tokyo on Saturday but had an evening engagement with fellow officers. That left Sunday as the last day to meet and still be able to catch the last August sailing to Seattle. Saturday afternoon, Tolt was relieved to receive a message from Tak reporting the location and time for Sunday's dinner. He booked a berth for Monday's departure, hoping he would be traveling with up-to-date information on Takeda's mission. If it turned out the operation had been scratched, he could enjoy a home leave visit during Seattle's gorgeous summer, a welcome relief from the oppressive humidity of Tokyo and Shanghai. He would telegraph Ronnie, but he didn't think Ronnie would object to his absence.

Sunday's dinner unfolded much like previous evenings spent by the three. Once seated on the tatami around the table, Takeda was as he had previously been: serious, focused and with polished manners that bespoke a person of substance. Tak's face bore a preoccupied expression, leading his cousin to comment that business must be wearing him down. Casting about for an innocuous topic that would keep Takeda talking, and relieve Tak from his attention, Tolt started to quiz Takeda about aviation developments in general. Not surprisingly, Takeda had strong views on which manufacturers' products were worthy of admiration.

"Boeing." He grunted dismissively.

"I don't know, Takeda-san. Pan Am has been using Boeing planes for their Clipper service around the world for a while now, and the folks my grandpa knows in Seattle say other long-range aircraft are in development."

"Maybe. But in military aviation, nimbleness and flexibility are what matters. Boeing designs don't have finesse, they lack the elegance to provide agility." Takeda selected a morsel of fish and swallowed it almost without chewing, as he warmed to his theme. "Consider who Boeing's first engineer was."

Tolt and Tak looked at each other.

"Bill Boeing?" Tolt ventured.

Takeda swallowed another mouthful of tuna. "No. Not Boeing himself. It was a Chinese. One of those who were sent abroad at the end of the last dynasty. That fellow, Wang Tsu, was one of the key people trying to develop Chinese aviation. That is, before '37. We saw how that turned out!" Takeda gave another dismissive snort.

The dinner continued until Tak looked at his watch, as he and Tolt had pre-arranged. "Cousin, I'm sorry, Father asked me to take visiting customers for some entertainment. Will you excuse me?"

Takeda laughed. "You businessmen; always focusing on making money. Run along. Who knows, maybe we'll meet up with you later in the evening? Send a runner once you settle on a place."

After Tak departed, Tolt picked at the remaining food on the table, and then asked in what he hoped was a casual tone, "Last year when you were in London and saw the German-British air battle, what did you think of the British planes?"

"England's Hurricane and Spitfire both did well, as did Germany's Messerschmitt. But the Mitsubishi Zero could easily out-maneuver any of those European aircraft."

"Do you think Japan would be superior to the U.S. in the air?"

Takeda gave Tolt a sharp look.

Shrugging his shoulders, Tolt added, "I remember your telling me about some scheme that an Admiral had asked you to work on." Tolt tried to look as if he was puzzling to recall a hazy remembrance, then he broke into a smile. "Did your boss have a bet with some of his fellow admirals that the Japanese Navy could attack the U.S. somewhere? Where was it? Somewhere in the Pacific. All that good cognac we drank clouds my memory!"

"Pearl Harbor."

Tolt nodded as he swallowed the last of the sake. The waitress stepped into the room to refill the cup, then withdrew.

"I have since refined the model considerably," Takeda said, his voice taking on a quiet intensity. "It represents the realization of ideas I have been working on since early in my career."

"Naval battles are all about big battleships blazing their guns at each other, right? So the goal is to… lure the American battleships out to open water?" Tolt asked.

"For hundreds of years, yes, that has been the way naval battles have been fought; ships blazing cannon at each other. Like a larger version of a kendo duel. But now, with the advent of aviation, there's a new way to fight." He paused, then added, "And to win."

Takeda's eyes shone with excitement. "What if instead of having battleships fighting each other on the high seas, the ships were used as mobile airfields to deploy bombers and attack planes in raids? You could fight ships at sea *and* attack targets on land. It would be a much more flexible way to fight; the kind of nimble engagement that Japan has always excelled at."

"The British did something like that last year in Italy, right?"

"Britain's deployment was much more limited." Takeda shook his head in a dismissive fashion. "To destroy the U.S. fleet at anchor, using planes instead of battleships, you must attack with low-flying torpedo bombers. But unlike the British, this attack must be launched from a great distance to avoid detection. It is ambitious. Such a thing has never been done on a large scale."

Takeda's normally pale face had become flushed.

"Many traditional officers think it cannot be done: that a navy is defined by its ships, not through the use of planes. But I am going to show them they are wrong."

Takeda sipped his lukewarm tea, as Tolt digested this information and the fact that Takeda had shifted from discussion of an imaginary case study to a concrete exposition.

"So, what would happen then? If your theory is correct, and you successfully ambush and destroy the U.S. forces?" He gestured with his chopsticks to a pile of raw fish slices sitting on a dish. "If that sashimi is Hawaii and the table is the Pacific, then what would you do? You'd be stranded in the middle of the Pacific!"

Takeda considered for a moment. "It depends on how successful the first attack is. If not all the ships are disabled, I would order repeated attacks by air."

Takeda sipped his tea and continued. "The fleet includes troop carriers. Once the initial air attacks succeed, the troops can be deployed to occupy the Hawaiian Islands, and then use them as a forward base to attack the U.S. West Coast. Whether or not to attack the West Coast depends on various factors, but the threat of such attacks would put the U.S. on the defensive, freeing up the Pacific for Japan's navy and army to move south, all the way to Indonesia and Australia. The European powers are focused on the war in Europe. In Asia and the Pacific, Japanese forces could sweep aside all defenses. At that point, any U.S. effort to attack Japan by blocking access to fuel and other raw materials would be stymied."

Tolt nodded. "Sounds risky. But what do I know? A mere civilian." He tried to sound jovial. "You have given this scenario a lot of consideration, my friend. Does your admiral think you're brilliant or deluded?"

Takeda lowered his voice. "Admiral Yamamoto has great confidence in me. But Japan's navy is conservative. The Admiral has lived in the United States. He is doubtful about the wisdom of attacking America, but says that if Japan does strike, it must be done unreservedly. I agree. Of course, whether these ideas will be adopted or not remains to be seen."

Tolt felt a wave of distaste wash over him, but he strove to sound casual. "So if this operation is greenlighted, will you and I still be able to enjoy dinner together? Should I be getting my affairs in order?"

Takeda's expression was earnest. "War is coming one way or another. Americans are like the British. They are convinced the Caucasians will continue to rule the world. They presume the peoples of the Orient, of India and Africa don't have the power to run their own affairs. That will change. Japan offers a new model, a vast Oriental empire. Once it is established, we will show the world the power of Asiatics."

His gaze bored into Tolt. "I tell you these things because I know that no one from your country would believe a Negro bearing such tales. But these are highly secret topics. Within the Imperial Navy itself, even as of today, only a handful of men know of these plans. Do not discuss with my cousin. You will put his life at risk."

Tolt nodded. He wondered about the risk to Takeda's own life if it should become known that he had shared such top-secret plans with a civilian, much less an American.

"As to your question, while in the end a Japanese empire will be much better than European colonialism, in the short term, the war will be brutal."

The window of their private room seemed to frame a living picture of great serenity: a tiny stream trickling beneath a pine lit by the waxing moon. Takeda gazed on the scene, and Tolt felt an inward shiver at the contrast between the garden's tranquility and the foreboding in Takeda's words.

"Sweeping the Caucasian from the Orient will require a heavy hand. You would be wise to wrap up your affairs in Shanghai before year's end. Although Seattle may be a bit too far West for total comfort, you would at least have room to retreat inland, if needed."

A tap came at the door, which slid open to admit the runner bearing a message with the location where Tak awaited them. Tolt stood up and donned his straw hat.

"Let us set aside these serious subjects and go see what games your cousin has afoot."

The following day, as the ship steamed out of the harbor, Tolt stood at the rail. A year away, when he left Seattle, he couldn't even get a job. Now he was successfully managing a major business in a competitive market. Could he also come through in persuading the U.S. that it faced an ambush? And do so without the news reaching back to the Japanese, thereby putting the Takematsus and himself at risk?

11

August 1941

As the days aboard the Admiral Oriental Line steamer passed, Tolt devoured the bulletin of major news circulated by the captain. It reported that the anticipated freeze of Japanese assets and disruption of exports from America had occurred. News that an NYK line vessel en route to Seattle had spent two days sitting 150 miles off Cape Flattery while its captain negotiated a guarantee that the ship would not be seized upon entering American waters left the crew on Tolt's ship abuzz.

They were on the fast northern route. Ten days from Yokohama to Seattle, with only one stop in Victoria. Before departing, he had sent a telegram to Ronald Planter Sr., asking him to request a meeting for Tolt with Senator Smith. The brief telegram format eliminated the need to explain the request, but Tolt realized an explanation would eventually be required.

It would be mid-August before he arrived. Senator Smith should be spending the summer recess in the Pacific Northwest. But would he consent to meet? Tolt hoped Smith's ties to Planter from his days as a lawyer to the Port of Tacoma, of which Snow Drift was a major customer, would aid Tolt's cause.

Sending the telegram to Mr. Planter reminded Tolt that Papa would not be expecting him. Another telegram was dispatched: "Arriving 8/14. Tell Ping. Pie."

"So, how is it?"

"As good as ever!" Tolt enthused as he shoveled in another mouthful of tender blueberry encased in flaky pastry.

Bill Gross crossed his hands across his ample belly and chuckled. "Good to see some things don't change!" Next to him was his best friend, John Gayton, who lifted his coffee cup, "To Ping's pie-making talents!"

Tolt made a noise that sounded like, "yes, indeed," but the fullness of his mouth made it hard to be sure. They were seated in the cozy family living room, to which they had retreated after Tolt's arrival and respects being paid to Ping and Sato. The room was cool despite the piercing sunny August day beyond.

"How long you staying?" Bill asked.

Tolt swallowed, then drank some milk to clear his throat. "Hard to say, Papa. Depends on a meeting I'm hoping for. Then there's the sailing schedules back to the Orient. What with the freeze of Japanese assets, the Japanese ships aren't going to be sailing anymore and getting to and fro is going to be tougher."

"Ah, that reminds me," said his grandfather. "Got a letter for you here. Mr. Planter sent it round the other day. Just 'afore he and the Mrs. went off to their place on Hood Canal. End of the week they'll be back."

Bill stood up in a manner that suggested lifting his bulk took effort. He walked over to the Queen Anne secretary, opening the drop-front desk and extracting an envelope from inside.

"Here you are," he said.

Tolt scanned the note, then dropped it on the coffee table, next to his plate of pie. "What is it? You look like your cat's done drowned?"

"Mr. Planter's news. I asked him to set a meeting for me. With Senator Smith. He says he has, but Smith's not free until the end of the month, the 29th."

"He mentioned that. Day they were heading to their beach place. Stopped off for some coffee and pie. Said you wanted a meeting with the Senator. Didn't say why though."

"He doesn't know why. In a telegram I couldn't say."

"Well, no need for telegrams now. You're here in the flesh. Go on ahead."

Tolt paused, then replied, "I can't tell you."

Mr. Gayton set his coffee cup down on the table and started to rise.

Tolt put out his hand, "No, no, Mr. Gayton, it's not you."

"Well, what is it then?" asked Bill.

"It's just… it's probably best if I speak with Senator Smith."

Bill dropped his chin and looked at Tolt over the tops of his spectacles.

"Papa, I know what you're thinking and no, I am not getting too big for my britches. Really, this shouldn't be discussed more than it needs to be. If you knew, you'd agree."

"Well, why don't you try me, and we'll see?"

"Good try, Papa." Tolt shook his head. "How's about bringing me up to date on what's what around here. I liked that postcard you forwarded from Jimmy."

"Humph." Bill's dim view of Tolt's reticence was apparent.

"So why did Jimmy go away in such a rush anyhow? It's been what — three plus years now? What's the story?"

Bill again looked over his spectacles at his grandson, but this time with a twinkle in his eyes. "Well, that *is* quite a story. Perhaps after I hear about your meeting with Senator Smith, I'll feel comfortable sharing that secret of mine."

Mr. Gayton chuckled, while Tolt shook his head and grinned at his grandfather.

U.S. Senator Preston Smith held up his hand, "Now, young

man, just a moment. I've got a Navy friend who was in ONI waiting outside for lunch. He should hear this."

Tolt frowned, "ONI?"

"Office of Naval Intelligence. Was posted to Hawaii, as a matter of fact. Now he's on the operational side of things. Now a Lieutenant Commander, stationed at Bremerton. Fulton's his name. I'm going to call him in."

Tolt hesitated; he wanted the news he brought to reach those in the Navy who could take action, but mindful of the risk that his warning could circle back to Asia, he wondered whether this was the officer to whom he should confide his tale. Too late. Senator Smith had already opened the door to go collect Fulton.

Smith re-entered the room accompanied by a man of medium height who appeared to be about forty, and who moved with a confidence suggesting he was accustomed to being heeded.

Smith performed the introductions, explaining, "To bring you up to speed, Fulton, young Gross here works for my longtime friend Ronald Planter. The Planters have a flour milling business with operations in the Pacific Northwest, and also the Orient, both China and Japan. Very successful." Fulton nodded.

"Mr. Planter has known Mr. Gross since he was a child, and last year sent him to work in Shanghai, helping with the company's Asia operations. He asked to meet with me."

Fulton slipped into his seat, taking Tolt's measure as he did so. His expression didn't betray hostility or even doubt, but rather curiosity. "Hello, there. Happy to hear what you have to say," he said.

"Good to meet you, sir. Long story… no time to get into it here, but I speak Japanese and Chinese, so Mr. Planter thought I might be a good fit to help with their Asia operations."

"I see," nodded Fulton.

Smith resumed. "Mr. Gross tells me he's learned that Japan is planning an attack on the U.S."

An expression in incredulity flashed across Fulton's face. "Really?"

Amid the beauty of a Seattle summer day, with the serene majesty of Mt. Rainier in the distance, Tolt was conscious this statement sounded jarring, if not melodramatic. Frustration welled inside him. Thinking of his kendo training, he tried to stay calm and focused.

Trying not to sound defensive, Tolt explained, "To give a little background, when I studied law here at the U, I got to know a couple of fellows from the Orient, both from big tycoon-type families, the kind that have ties stretching all over the place. One was from China and one from Japan. After we graduated, they went home to work for their family businesses."

Fulton nodded.

"So, the Japanese fellow, Saburo Takematsu, has a cousin who's a big deal in the Japanese navy. An aviator, and considered a pioneer in naval innovation. He was also a hero in Japan's invasion of China. A few months back in Shanghai, I had a conversation with this navy fellow, his name is Takeda — Hajime Takeda. We got into a debate about politics and such. He's no fan of the West. He argued that Western domination of the Orient is coming to an end, and Japan will be the controlling force."

Smith and Fulton frowned.

"When I pushed back, he told me about a plan he was developing for Japan's naval forces to attack the U.S. Navy at Pearl Harbor."

"If true, why would he possibly take the risk of telling you about such a thing?" asked Fulton.

Tolt took a deep breath. "I asked him that. His response was that he had previously been posted to the Japanese Embassy in Washington and observed how most White Americans look down on Negroes, so he figured that even if I tried to tell anyone, no one would believe me."

The faces of Smith and Fulton both reddened.

"So," Tolt said, "here I am."

"May I ask you some questions?" Fulton said. Tolt nodded. What did this Takeda fellow say specifically? How did he seem? What month was it when they had this discussion? Was Takeda trustworthy? If he was senior enough to be entrusted with such a mission, why would he have time to leave Japan and visit Shanghai? Had Tolt seen him again? Discussed this further? It's now August: why had Tolt waited so long to raise this concern? Did he talk with anyone in the U.S. Consulate about this? Why not? And on and on.

Tolt had a ready answer to each of these questions. But, from their tone, he could tell Fulton and Smith were dubious.

Finally, Smith said, "Young man, I know you've come here in good faith. Mr. Planter tells me you're a fine fellow, a credit to your people. But you yourself must concede, you've not had a lot of experience in the world. And what experience you've had, it's been in business, not the military, not government."

Smith's condescension seeped into Tolt the way the icy rains of a November Seattle downpour permeated the thickest raincoat. It was a familiar sensation, but this time unacceptable. By God, he was risking his position, risking harm or even death to his closest friends, and these fools couldn't be bothered to take him seriously? Anger mixed with defiance, and Tolt struggled to maintain a neutral face.

Fulton chimed in. "The mere fact that Japan has sketched out some scenarios for possible attacks, including an attack on one of our bases, is nothing unusual or particularly sinister. That's what we in the military *do*: develop theories for possible wars, then use exercises — 'war games' — to test them and practice our skills. We do it to the Japs. They do it to us. It's the way the thing works."

"Yes, sir. For some time I assumed that's what this was. But the usual Japanese war games involve *battleships;* ships fighting out at sea. This is different. As I mentioned, this is ships at anchor, with no chance to defend themselves against the attacking forces."

Tolt laid out Japan's past use of surprise attacks to launch military hostilities, the fact that Takeda had conceded a precipitating incident would be needed to bring the plan into play, that such an event had now occurred and Japan's oil reserves were actually lower than reported, that Japan viewed denial of access to necessary raw materials as akin to a declaration of war by the U.S. Would the weight of the evidence not sway them?

Tolt finished answering the men's questions. They stood, and Tolt followed suit. "Well, let us make some inquiries," Smith said. "See if any of this can be substantiated,"

"With respect, sir, it's quite likely not to be verifiable by U.S. sources. According to Takeda, only a handful of people in Japan's own navy are privy to the plan. It's more a matter of letting the U.S. forces in Hawaii know to be on the lookout, so as to be able to defend against ambush."

Fulton spoke up. "Well, it's not like we don't have professionals on the case. ONI has folks looking at the Japs both in Hawaii and on the Mainland. Hell, in June we just broke up a major spy ring involving them. Don't suppose news of the Tachibana case reached you over in China? Major haul of documents, codes, plans — the whole shebang. Jap navy was in it up to their eyeballs. If execution of an actual attack were underway, that motherlode would have had word of it. And there was nada. Trust me, I would know."

Tolt started to respond, but Smith headed him off. "Still, as young Gross mentions, it may not hurt to pass along a warning. I need to start first with the State Department. Don't want to step on any toes. It's already Friday, and next week many people may still be returning from their summer vacations, so no promises. But I will check."

Tolt picked up his hat from the chair next to him and bade them farewell. It was done. He had taken the plunge. Relief washed over him. His stomach gurgled and he chuckled at himself. It had been quite the morning. No wonder he was hungry. Boarding the elevator to the lobby, he considered going to his and Jimmy's favorite fish shack. Would their fish and chips still taste as delicious as when they were kids?

The following week, the chief of Smith's Seattle office sent for Tolt. Tolt set out, filled with nervous anticipation. The fact that it was the chief-of-staff calling the meeting, not Bone, didn't seem favorable. With all the resources at the State Department's and military's disposal, however, some other piece of corroborating information might have been uncovered. He hoped for the best.

The chief-of-staff welcomed Tolt to a cramped conference room. "The Senator is visiting constituents in Eastern Washington, so asked me to see you."

As he spoke, Tolt noted that the aide's tone was jolly, suggesting a combination of condescension leavened by affected friendliness. It did not bode well. His next words confirmed Tolt's impression. Reading from a note, he said, "The Senator has shared your news with the State Department. Indeed, there had been a similar rumor received via a U.S. national employed as household help by the Peruvian embassy. Considering the status of the informants, well…"

The man had the decency to appear chagrined, but continued, "The State Department was inclined against further action. There would be no recommendation that the U.S. military take action to prepare for the rumored attack. In all likelihood, this was either mere gossip or at the most, attempted disinformation."

Tolt sat stunned, unable to marshal a response.

"So you see, no need to worry. Good to have brought the report to our attention of course. The Senator asked me to extend his appreciation. But matters of statecraft are complex; many swirling currents, you know. For civilians, it's difficult to see where the action is. In any case, you can rest assured, comfortable you've done your duty. No need to worry."

Tolt heard the babble of the man's voice, and although he had half-expected this sort of response, marveled at how deflated it left him. As Tolt walked back from the Federal Building to Our House, his sense of dejection started to smolder and transform into anger.

"How'd it go?" asked Bill, looking up from the sofa where he was reading the newspaper.

Tolt tossed his hat onto the table. "Fine."

Bill lowered his newspaper. "By the looks of it, you don't seem any too fine. Are you finally going to fill your granddad in?"

Tolt threw himself into a chair. Might as well tell him the whole sorry tale. Bill sat, listening and scratching his sideburns, not saying a word. When Tolt was done, silence lingered between them.

"I see." Bill pulled on his sideburns. "Did I ever tell you…"

"No! No, Papa." Tolt bolted upright, standing over his grandfather on the sofa.

"Son…"

"No, not another story. Another fable. This can't be mended by a parable. The Life of William Gross, a Negro legend, where all manner of tribulations are overcome by dint of hard work and decency."

"Tolt..."

The door slammed.

Sara Mason was in town to visit her family, and Tolt pondered whether she would see him. Given how angry she had been a year ago at his taking the job working for Ronnie, it wasn't a sure thing. After his argument with his grandfather, it occurred to him there was nothing to lose. If Sara refused to see him, he'd be at loggerheads with two important people in his life, instead of just one. In for a penny...besides, now he could tell her just where that nutty requirement of going to Shanghai as Ronnie's valet had originated.

When Sara answered the knock at the Mason family door, surprise was evident on her face, but no unfriendliness. She urged Tolt to come in. Soon they were sitting on the porch, drinking lemonade and gabbing as freely as they used to.

"You still haven't told me what it's like to be *you* though!" Sara exclaimed.

"Ah. Well, to be me." Tolt grinned. "Now *that* really is a racket. I be getting on some stiff time!"

Sara laughed, "How so?"

"Obviously all the social things I told you about are swell. In Seattle, you might do one of them in a weekend, but in Shanghai, you'll do five in one day: a morning ride, followed by tennis, a tea dance, then a rest to refresh for dinner, and after a dinner at a swell joint, a visit to the nightclubs. It's solid. But really, it's the feeling that you can reinvent yourself — you're all thrown into this mix, that gives you a sense of freedom."

Tolt tried to think of how to explain the feeling. "It's...it's intoxicating. People are focused on making money. It's the reason Shanghai exists, so if you're good at that, then your hair could be green and your skin purple, for all they care."

"And are you?"

Tolt held his hands up in front of him and gave them a look, then grinned at Sara. "Not purple yet, at any rate."

"Fool! You know what I mean. Are you good at business?"

"Well, now," Tolt gave a slow smile. "Turns out I am."

Sara laughed. "Well, go on... tell me. Brag on yourself a bit. Just this once, I'll let you!"

"Let's see. Well, since I've joined, Snow Drift's revenues are up by about 10% and profits are up by 18%. Mr. Planter is pretty pleased."

"And did you have something to do with that?"

"Yep, sure did. The Planters had been looking at the Shanghai operations as serving the China market. They hadn't really explored the possibility of a regional play, using China operations as a base to serve other parts of Asia. My buddy Quentin Wang, he's from one of those Chinese families with branches spread all over the Orient, each tending to one kind or another of the family's businesses. We looked into whether there might be a demand in Southeast Asia for high-quality flour milled from U.S. wheat, but fresher than if shipped all the way from the States."

Sara listened with interest, a small smile playing at the edges of her mouth.

"Turns out there was demand, so now the Wang family companies are distributing Snow Drift Flour in Burma, Malaya, and Thailand. And because they can access the markets directly, we've been able to cut out a couple of links of middlemen. That's part of what's making the additional revenue streams much more profitable."

"Well, look at you! Who knew you would turn out to be a John D. Rockefeller?"

"And to think, I passed up an offer to serve as maitre d' at old so-and-so's law firm dining room in order to take on this gig!"

With a smile in her eyes, Sara observed, "I'd say you made the right choice. Even if it does mean working with that devil." She broke out into a grin. "Does Ronnie Jr. really let you run things as you want?"

"Yeah, the other good thing about Shanghai's active social scene is that young Ronnie has taken to it like a duck to water. He's content to leave the heavy lifting to yours truly. Occasionally he gets some bee in his bonnet about a project. But I've been able to sideline them or buy time, like with a joint venture that the Japan trade embargo will put the kibosh on. So our financial performance has been good."

Resolving that information shared with Sara wasn't likely to reach Takeda, Tolt decided to confide the purpose of his trip. As Tolt concluded, Sara took a sip of lemonade, but didn't immediately respond. "You think I'm blowing smoke?" he asked.

Slowly, she spoke. "No. You tell me that the Japanese are planning an attack, I believe you. Japan? I know nothing from nothing. Military things are a mystery. But you, I know, and you're no gumbeater."

Hearing Sara's assessment, Tolt's shoulders dropped an inch, the tension he had borne since hearing from Smith's chief-of-staff abating. "But I can't say I'm surprised these folks in the U.S. government don't believe you. On that, Takeda spoke truth "

"So, what do you think I ought to have done?" Tolt asked, his sense of mollification evaporated. "Not say anything to anybody? If you heard a storm was on its way, wouldn't you tell your neighbors with open windows and the laundry hanging outdoors, to close things up? Plus Jimmy's in Hawaii."

"You're not getting it. I'm not saying you shouldn't have tried to warn that a dark cloud is approaching. I'm just saying that you shouldn't be surprised when they react like you're some crazy zigaboo talking mess."

Tolt scowled.

"Even if you were white as snow — Ronnie Planter, Jr. himself — you gotta admit, this story would sound implausible. Coming from some Colored fellow, it's fantasy"

Tolt remained silent, absorbing Sara's words. She mused, "Maybe this is the downside to how you were raised."

"How's that?"

"Maybe Our House should have been called 'Our World.' That's what your grandpa created for you... and maybe a bit of what my folks created for me, too. Growing up here with so few Colored people, Whites in Seattle maybe felt like they could give us a bit more room to experiment. Your grandpa and my family, they ran with that, and created all sorts of opportunities. Both for themselves and for us. But leaving Seattle, now I see how things really work for us as Negroes. Our folks were naive — well-intentioned, but naive, blowing a glossy bubble to shield us from the dirt of racism."

Sara took another sip of her lemonade. "So instead of worrying about the entire United States, I'd focus on what concrete things you can do to protect the people you care about."

"Yeah, well, if you were listening, that's what I *was* doing. Jimmy, I care about."

"No need to go snarling at me. You know how I feel about Jimmy, but that's not who I meant."

"Who then?"

Here Sara paused and raised her eyebrows. "How about that Diana Wang whose name you keep dropping?"

Tolt smiled. "Ah, I see."

"See what?"

"You're jealous."

"Men! Always thinking that we women are concerned about

getting your affections."

Tolt laughed, "Fair enough. I withdraw that comment. Anyhow, that's enough about me. Tell me what's going on for you in Chicago."

Sara started to fill him in, and the two old friends whiled away the afternoon, chatting and bickering in a friendly fashion. Before Tolt left, he pulled his chessboard from his jacket pocket. Sara watched, perplexed. Sliding open the little compartment at the back, he extricated her letter. He handed it to her, now crumpled and worn, but her boldly written "Hello my friend!" still visible at the top. Fingering it, she marveled, "Why you holding on to this relic?"

"Well that's just it, Miss Mason. It's a *treasured* relic. Back when you still wrote to me."

Sara looked up at him with a wry smile. "Fair point. Guess the grudge has been nursed long enough. Write down your Shanghai address, and I'll put you back on pen-pal status." Tolt enveloped her in a hug, jotted down his address, then made his way home for supper.

On the way, he pondered Sara's advice that he ought to focus on aiding those he cared about. Smith and Fulton didn't believe him, but he had proven his credibility to Sara who was no pushover, and Mr. Planter had been pleased at the good results he was achieving for Snow Drift. Maybe he needed to take more risks. What would be his next gamble? The germ of an idea began to sprout.

12

September 1941

"You're back!"

"Just like a bad penny, I always turn up!" Tolt laughed. Despite Bill Gross's appeals, buttressed by John Gayton's reasoned arguments, he had insisted on returning to Shanghai.

Diana had creased her brow, frowning. "Why do Americans say that? What does it mean to be a 'bad penny'?"

"Heck if I know." He took her by the hand and spun her around as if they were on the dance floor instead of the spacious entrance hall to the Wang family home. Diana laughed.

"What's this?"

"Practice! Tomorrow I'm taking you to the Park Hotel. Lord knows that with my being gone so long, you've probably forgotten how to even foxtrot!"

"Ha! Why just last weekend, I was doing the jitterbug."

"Oh really? Be ready to be tested on your moves, Miss Wang. I've got my eye on you!"

The most oppressive of Shanghai's summer heat was past and a hint of autumn delights was in the air. Restaurants with outdoor verandahs or patio seating found themselves in heavy demand.

Resuming the Shanghai life that he missed while in the States, he now inveighed upon Diana to accompany him in all pursuits. On the weekends, they rode ponies in the villages and fields adjacent to the city, finding a local family to prepare them a lunch they could enjoy at a table set up outside. On these outings, Tolt sought to turn the conversation or mood to one of tenderness, but Diana always seemed to anticipate these inclinations, forestalling with banter that would make romantic approaches appear out of sync. Tolt found this perplexing, but so enjoyed their high-spirited exchanges that he was hard-pressed to complain. Nevertheless, beneath the repartee, he was nursing a plan. All he needed was the right opportunity to present it.

Dancing turned into Tolt's and Diana's favorite pastime. The Metropole Gardens, the Paramount, the MGM, Vienna Gardens (which offered not only an open air dance pavilion, but also a miniature golf course), the Park Hotel; they visited them all, plus many others, sometimes two or three in an evening.

Before the summer, late-night dancing had been restricted to the weekends, but Tolt now went during the week as well. When Diana marveled that he could work after staying up so late, he dismissed her concerns, saying that they were young and needed to enjoy life. He didn't tell her that he was caching away memories in the way he had hoarded Sara's last letter. Soon, there would be no carefree dancing in Shanghai, nor maybe elsewhere. Occasionally the entire group went out, but Quentin and Tak were both busy with work. Sometimes they could persuade Sumiko to join them, but often it was just Tolt and Diana. By this point, he was so much a part of the Wang family's circle, Diana no longer had to find a way for her father to allow her to be seen alone unchaperoned.

For each dancing excursion Diana wore a different evening gown of tissue-like shimmering silk. Some were in the ch'i-p'ao style, form-fitting with long slits up the sides and made of colors or patterned fabric that looked anything but traditional. Others were Western style and to Tolt, looked like the gowns pictured on the covers of fashion magazines. Whether Diana adopted Chinese or Western-style attire, she walked with a fluid gait that conveyed both elegance and zestful energy.

This particular evening they were at the Park Hotel, enjoying dinner before heading into the ballroom to kick up their heels. Tolt had asked Diana to wear her 'fish dress,' to which she responded with puzzlement. Tolt reminded her, "You know, the shimmery silver dress I said looked like a sockeye."

Diana laughed, promising she would indeed wear her 'fish dress.' In the light, the silver paillettes shimmered, and so did the glossy sheen of her fashionable pompadour-styled hair. Tolt found it hard to concentrate on the words emanating from her plumply red lips.

"Why are you staring so?" she finally asked in a mock exasperated tone. "If you were Chinese, it wouldn't be a problem, as we stare all we want."

"Along with telling people they've become fat and asking how much someone earns or spends... all of course, without being rude."

Diana, laughed. "True, it's fine for us Chinese to do those things. But I know from experience that you Americans don't think it's polite to stare. So, tell me, Mr. Gross, have you now abandoned American good manners?"

"Hmmm, Miss Wang. According to good Chinese manners, isn't it the case that a well-bred young lady isn't supposed to ask direct questions or contradict others? Based on what I've observed in my sojourn in this fine country of yours, those are things you do all the time, so who's to talk about consistency?"

"Ah, so this is like when you are fencing and strike with a 'touché'." She laughed.

They were awaiting dessert. Diana's hands with their long

slim fingers tipped with scarlet polished nails rested lightly on the table. Tolt looked Diana in the eye, holding her gaze steady while he reached across the table to cover her hands in his. As he did so, he marveled at how slight and delicate they felt. Diana appeared surprised for an instant, then she recovered her usual poise.

"I know we usually joke, and no one does it better than you," he said. "But I want to talk about something serious."

"All right," Diana replied, with a look of concern.

Tolt gave her hands a squeeze. "Don't worry, it's not something bad. At least, I don't think it is, and I hope you won't either." He took a deep breath and then withdrew one hand, reaching into his jacket pocket and pulling out a small jewelry box.

"Diana, you may not know this, but my name — Tolt — it's the name of a river. You know from your Seattle days how sweet the drinking water there is. Seattle's water comes from the Tolt River. Salmon thrive in it, and my daddy loved it so much that he insisted on naming me for it. I wanted you to wear your beautiful sockeye dress tonight because I wanted to ask you something."

Diana's expression was puzzled, but she didn't interrupt.

"I want," and here Tolt was forced to swallow as he realized the emotion of the moment was making his voice quaver, "I want you to be like the salmon on the Tolt River and return home with me. To Seattle... as my wife."

With that, Tolt opened the box revealing a platinum ring set with a brilliant emerald-cut pink sapphire, bordered on either side by baguette diamonds.

Tears filled Diana's eyes. "How you manage to make comparing a girl to a fish sound romantic, I'll never know, but any man who can contrive to do that is worth 'hooking'!"

They both laughed at the pun, as Tolt slipped the ring on Diana's finger.

Diana looked at him, her eyes shining and her voice tremulous. "But how? How did you know that this would fit?"

"One of the benefits of dealing with the Wang family is their insistence that there is always the 'right' way to do things, and that includes the right suppliers of certain goods. I knew your family had to have an 'approved' jeweler and it wasn't hard then to get Quentin to tell me which Shanghai jeweler the family deigns to patronize."

Diana laughed.

"With that information in hand, it was pretty simple to find out the sizing that would fit Miss Diana Wang."

Tolt then added in a rush, "I hope you like it? It's not a standard stone for an engagement ring, but with Jeweler Dong's help, I took the risk."

"Of course I love it, you silly! But did you tell Jeweler Dong what it was for?"

"No! I knew I had to do this thing lightly, slightly and politely. I told him it was for a Shanghai girl with sophisticated tastes. By rights, I should have asked your papa first before asking you, but I didn't have the nerve without first knowing if I had a prayer."

He paused and gave her a searching look. "It sounds like I might?"

Diana laughed and stretched out her hand to admire the sparkle of the ring. "I think you just might, indeed."

"To be safe, though, I recommend you put that baby away until I talk to Papa Wang. We don't want to set him off thinking his prospective son-in-law is some sort of stormbuzzard."

"Stormbuzzard? Is that another kind of fish?"

Tolt laughed. "Don't you remember? It was my favorite epithet for some of the worst of the law students your brother, Tak and I were stuck with! A stormbuzzard's someone who's no good. I don't want your daddy to think that of me. Until I can collar him for a chat, you want to hold onto the ring, or shall I?"

"You better," Diana answered, sliding it off her finger with reluctance. "Hsiao Ch'en is so thorough at cleaning my room and organizing my things, that there's not a hope of hiding it from her. And once she knows, the entire household will know."

"That's what you get for training your people to high standards," Tolt joked.

At this she gave a wry smile, but stopped removing the ring. "Let's be like that fairy story... Cinderella, and wait for the end of the evening before we turn into pumpkins. I want to enjoy wearing my ring now while I'm with you."

"Fine by me! I'm just relieved that you like it, and the person who gave it to you, enough to consent to accept it. Now I can finally start enjoying this evening!" Tolt replied. He dabbed his cheek with his handkerchief.

"You poor thing! Let's forget dessert. I'm too worked up to sit still. Let's dance!"

"You don't have to ask me twice, Miss Wang, soon to be Mrs. Gross!" answered Tolt. He stood and reached out his hand to Diana.

As they circled the dance floor, Tolt leaned his head close and spoke into Diana's ear. "I love you, Mrs. Gross-to-be." He could see Diana's neck flush, but she didn't say anything.

The rest of the evening passed in a whirl of happiness, and when the car stopped at the Wang family home, before alighting, Tolt leaned over to kiss Diana. Rather than a demure averting of her face, as he half expected, he was taken aback by the degree of intensity with which she responded. It occurred to Tolt that it was fortunate he had arranged for the Snow Drift driver that evening, rather than the Wang's.

When they broke apart, she took his face in her hands. "You know enough about China and Chinese to know we don't go around saying the words 'I love you' in the casual way you Westerners do, so I'm telling you now, but warning you that you won't hear it often. You have to know and trust that it is true: your heart is in my heart. Your life is my life. I love you and I always will." With that, she slipped the ring from her finger, gave it to Tolt and alighted from the car.

Tolt leaned back against the cushions of the seat as his driver sped him home and savored the happiness that coursed through him. In between being giddy with excitement, he and Diana had managed to discuss the fact that as much as the Wang family was fond of Tolt, the prospect of their daughter's marrying a foreigner, much less a Colored one, was going to come as a shock. Would his race be an implacable barrier to Mr. Wang's approval?

Seated in the small sitting room adjacent to the Wang family drawing room, Diana poured out the tea, asking, "But why November?"

"Then we could take a ship back to the U.S. for Christmas."

"Yes, but that's so soon! We still have to get my father's permission, and then arrange with the fortuneteller to figure out an auspicious date. Around the New Year Festival is probably the earliest we could hold the wedding."

"That's not until February!"

"Remember you'll be stuck with me for the rest of your life. November to February: what's an additional few weeks before your prison term begins?"

Instead of a joking reply, Tolt's answer was a flustered one. "No, no... it's too late. We need to be leaving Shanghai before the end of this year." "Well, what's one Christmas away from home? After all, many Westerners here don't go on home leave for four or even five years!"

"It's not Christmas. It's...it's..."

"What?"

"It's that we need to be away from Shanghai. Before much more time passes. And with the U.S. freeze of Japanese assets, half the ships that used to provide passage between Shanghai and America are out of commission. Travel options are slim."

"Dearest, I'm confused. You love Shanghai. Why are you saying we must leave?"

Tolt fiddled with the buttons on his suit vest, pondering how much to tell Diana.

"You must promise me not to share what I'm going to tell you with anyone. No one. Not Quentin, not Sumiko, no one."

"Not even my father?"

"Before we leave Shanghai, we can tell your father. And Quentin. But not now. Not yet."

Diana picked up her cup and took a sip. "I'm not sure I want to know."

"Well, I'm not sure you do either. But you ask why I'm so insistent on heading to the States before the end of the year. And, there is a reason."

Rat-a-tat tapped Diana's red-tipped nails on the marble-topped table next to the sofa. "Well, what if *you* were to go home, to see your family at the holidays, and then return around Lunar New Year for the wedding?"

"It's not about a family Christmas!"

Diana looked at him, surprised at Tolt's vehemence. She leaned forward and picking up the teapot, she refilled first Tolt's cup, then her own.

Tolt nodded his thanks, picked up his cup and tried to calm his voice. "The key is that before the end of the year, we need to get away from Shanghai, back to the U.S. If we're not married, you can't travel with me. It's that simple."

"But you love Shanghai! If you're telling me that once we get married, we're always going to be living in your country — in America, then that's something you need to say now. Directly."

"No, no. That's not what I want. I want to be near your family. I want our children to grow up with their cousins, uncles and aunties. Hell, living right here in the bosom of the Wang family home, and making daily kowtows to your daddy, that'd make me plenty happy."

Diana smiled at that. "Well, we probably wouldn't force you to kowtow daily, but fine, I get your point. So?"

Tolt finally blurted out, "It's because America and Japan are about to... They're likely soon to be at war. If I stay here, who knows what will happen, and I..."

"Japan and America?"

"Yes, by year's end, war is coming and once it does, will Japan respect the rights of enemy citizens? Shanghai's foreign concessions will become just another hostile territory. My government won't be able to help us."

"But how do you know this? Have the Americans at the consulate told you this?" Diana frowned. "No, that can't be it, because then everyone in Shanghai would know." Her forehead wrinkled deeper as she pondered the possibilities. "Who told you? How sure are you?"

"How I know is what shouldn't be divulged."

"For the last four years the Japanese have occupied most of Shanghai, and as long as there's nothing political, they mostly leave you alone. And even if the war spreads — especially if the war spreads — they'll still need access to goods. Supplies like the flour that Snow Drift mills and distributes. Why can't you stay?"

"A source I trust tells me we will not be safe."

"Who?"

"I'm willing to tell you, but it can't go any further."

Diana fell silent. She looked at him with a steady gaze. Tolt held his teacup between his two hands and let her examine him, saying nothing.

Finally she spoke. "I trust you. If you tell me that war is likely, that's enough for now. But how to tell my father? How do I ask him to be married in just a few weeks, to a foreigner, and then to leave Shanghai for who knows how long?"

She took a long drink of tea. "You think my family is so modern and Western. And we are, but a daughter still doesn't simply announce she is getting married to the man of her choice. Family wishes matter."

She stood up before he could reply, and he started to rise, too. "No, no," she waved. "Sit down. Rest a bit. I'm going to take a stroll in the garden. I'll be back shortly."

Tolt leaned back in his armchair and watched as Diana let herself out the French doors into the garden. Hsiao Ch'en, hearing the sound of the door, popped into the drawing room to see if her mistress needed anything. She was surprised to see Tolt sitting by himself.

"It's fine. Miss went for a walk. She'll be back in a few minutes."

Tolt picked up the day's *North-China Daily News*. As he read the day's editorial, his concerns increased.

Those of us familiar with conditions in the North at the time the Empire of Greater Japan began its expansion into that territory now referred to as "Manchukuo," will recall Mr. Tojo, Japan's newly announced Prime Minister.

To refresh the memories of those more recently arrived in the Flowery Kingdom, Mr. Tojo first served as head of the military police force Japan kept garrisoned at Port Arthur. Shortly before hostilities between Japan and China commenced in 1937, Mr. Tojo was appointed chief of staff for all the Kwantung Army. He is known to have played a key role in the events of the summer of 1937. Following his assignment back to Tokyo in 1938, he rose to the post of Army Vice Minister. In 1940, his ascent continued, as he became the Empire's Army Minister.

During his service leading the Army Ministry, first as a Vice Minister and more recently as Minister, Mr. Tojo has consistently been a strong proponent both for continued military action by Japan in China, and for formation of the Tripartite Alliance with European powers, Germany and Italy.

His ascension to the post of Prime Minister appears to signify that the active — some might even say, bellicose — approach of Japan towards pursuit of its perceived international interests is likely to become only stronger. With its ally Germany approaching the outskirts of Moscow, speculation grows as to what new fronts of activity Japan may open up in 1942.

Will Japan bring its considerable determination to the question of subduing its recalcitrant neighbor, China? Or, like Germany, will it decide that a single front of war is not sufficient to assure its strategic aims, and advantage lies in pursuing dominance in new territory? Only time will tell.

"What has you frowning so, my dear husband-to-be?"

Tolt looked up, startled to see that Diana had returned from her walk and was standing before him, her face bearing its usual expression of good humor. She raised her eyebrows.

Tolt shook the paper and said, "Just reading about the Japs' new Prime Minister. Sounds like a dandy fellow."

"Oh, him. Yes, don't get Papa started about Tojo. His blood pressure starts to rise any time he talks about that man's bad deeds when he was in the North."

"Well, now that he's top dog in Japan, I'm afraid we'll all be hearing a lot more about him. And, according to the *Daily News*, he's likely to be even more aggressive than the last guy. Good luck, China."

Diana sank onto the arm of Tolt's chair and put her hand on his coat sleeve. "Enough of that. I've sorted out what we should do."

"Have you now? All right, enlighten me!"

"My father has a sister who lives in America."

"He does? Did you ever tell me that?"

"Dearest, I have aunties, uncles and cousins scattered all over the world. It would take a week just to teach you who belongs to who, much less where they all live!"

"Fair enough. Carry on."

"So, you will go to Seattle and I will be going to visit my auntie in San Francisco."

"What? Given the current situation, you're not going to be able to get a visitor visa for travel in less than a month!"

"Hear me out. In a Chinese family such as ours, things have to be done a certain way. Out of respect for the family, for our position. Getting married at the drop of a hat to a foreigner would invite gossip." "But Diana, we're not getting married because you're in the family way. How does your idea solve our problem? Dates are dates. Time is time. It's the middle of October and before the end of November, we should be on a boat heading east to the U. S. of A. But if you're not with me, I won't be on that boat!"

"Shhh. Let me explain. In the Chinese way. Not the American, dot-dot-dot, straight line way."

Tolt held his tongue.

"So, as I was saying, everyone knows my father's younger sister lives in America. Her health hasn't been good; she wants to come home and see her relatives."

Observing that Tolt was going to ask about this, Diana

quickly added, "Not really. She's in fine health. But this is China. If the story is that I am needed to help a relative of my father's generation, people will understand."

Tolt nodded and let Diana continue. "So, I am going to America to help my auntie make the trip back in time for the New Year Festival. That makes perfect sense."

Tolt frowned, but managed to refrain from interrupting.

"We explain to my father that we would like his permission to marry. You tell him as much as you can without compromising whoever has told you about the risk of war. We hope the situation blows over. Then we can come back next spring and we can be married in a full Chinese ceremony. But, in the meanwhile, we request his permission to marry in a private ceremony and travel together to America."

Tolt's frown was replaced with a smile, but still he held his tongue as Diana concluded her explanation.

"Publicly, the story will be that we're on the same ship so Tolt can help me make the overseas journey and once Stateside, I will go on to San Francisco to collect Auntie and bring her home."

"Perfect!" Tolt stood up and grasping Diana's hands, he swung her around in a circle. But then a thought occurred to him, and he stopped.

"You do realize, though, that if I'm right... if what I've been told is true, well, it won't be New Year when we'll be back. It might be a long time." Tolt, lowered his and Diana's arms, but didn't release the grip on her hands. "Japan and China have been at war for over four years. Who knows how long before we can return?"

"I know."

"You do?"

"Yes, you numbskull. Aren't I always reminding you and Quentin that I'm the smart one in the family?" Diana laughed.

"But you're willing to go, nonetheless?"

"You mean despite the fact that you're a numbskull?" she teased.

"Ha! You know what I mean."

"Yes, I told you the night you asked me to marry you. Your life is my life. This is what it means for us to be together: we are one."

"You believe in me that much?"

"I do. And because you have asked for my hand, you are telling me that you believe in me that much, too."

Tolt's eyes pricked with tears. Diana laughed. "You silly American! You get this hardhearted Shanghai girl talking all sorts of sentimental stuff! Enough."

Tolt gave her a wry smile. "I figured the years amidst the Pacific Northwest's natural beauty had softened your Shanghai toughness. So, what's next? Find your father, drop a kowtow or twenty, and ask permission?"

"Given that he's in Canton at the moment, that won't work. He's got Quentin with him to inspect some factories or something. From there, they are heading to Hong Kong. In a couple of weeks, they'll be back in Shanghai. We can ask him then."

"Two weeks? It will already be November then!"

"Hush. Leave it to me. This part of the plan, I can work out. Your part is to figure out the ship schedules and my visa."

Tolt nodded, his expression thoughtful.

"Remember, next week I'm in Tokyo with Sumiko, so when I get back, your job will be to have all the logistics sorted, and mine will be to get his permission!"

Tolt stuck out his hand, grinning. "It's a deal!"

Diana laughed and batting aside his hand, she threw her arms around his neck and planted a big kiss on his lips.

13

OCTOBER 1941, PART 1

"Was it as you expected?"

Diana pondered, looking up at the ceiling above her as she lay on her futon. "Physically, yes, but as far as atmosphere? No."

Sumiko laughed. "What do you mean?"

"Well, Japan has been so successful at adapting to the West, to the modern world, I expected Tokyo would be advanced. And it is modern. But, in terms of the feeling, well, somehow it's different from what I expected."

"In what way?"

"Well, internationally Japan is energetic... aggressive. Given what it's doing in the rest of the Orient, I guess I expected the mood on the streets would be confident and strong as well."

Sumiko's cat snuck through the barely cracked open the *shoji* door to the bedroom, where the girls were reviewing the first day of Diana's visit. The cat rubbed against her mistress, seeking to have its ears scratched.

Diana smiled at the cat, then continued, "But Tokyo seems subdued. I mean, look at Shanghai: we've lost. The parts of the city belonging to the Chinese government have been conquered. Even so, wherever you go — on the streets, in cinemas and other public places — there's a buzz, an energy. But Tokyo? It feels drab and tense."

Sumiko sat up and bent her knees, clasping her hands around them.

Rolling on her side, Diana tried to discern her friend's expression. "I'm sorry. Quentin is always warning me about my bluntness. Today with you and Tak was wonderful. I don't mean to seem ungrateful."

"Oh, I didn't take your comments as criticism. I'm just trying to think of when it changed. When it became as you describe."

"You mean it didn't used to be like this?"

"Oh no. Or at least, not as I recall. But the change happened gradually. And part of the time, I wasn't living here, so I may not be the most accurate observer."

"What happened?"

"Well, it used to be that kindness and connection to others, were the values that were emphasized. You saw this in day-to-day interactions. For example, shopkeepers — they were respectful to everyone. But, as attitudes started to change, we began to hear from our foreign friends living in Japan that they were being treated brusquely, even offensively by the shopkeepers they had done business with for years."

Sumiko twisted a strand of her hair. "Then we started noticing pilfering. It used to be you could leave shoes and other household items out on the porch, but they were being stolen. People no longer feel as safe in their neighborhoods, as connected to each other."

The cat's purring could be heard over Sumiko's voice. "And the press! The stories began to have a boastful, challenging tone. Next, people started to think that being aggressive in public was good. Then last year the government started to promote 'restoring the spirit and virtues of the old Japan.'"

Diana reached over and scooped up the kitty, to lie on her futon. "What does that mean?"

"Essentially to ensure support for militarism. The government launched an organization, the 'Imperial Rule Assistance Association,' It includes a network of neighborhood associations. These neighborhood groups conduct surveillance of residents. So now, people are wary of their neighbors."

Sumiko continued. "My father knows an Englishman, a famous Japan specialist who worked in Britain's foreign service for many years. Sir George Sansom is his name. He's devoted his life to studying Japanese history. Before he returned to England, he told my father that he could not stand Japan in the way she is now going. He said it was a feeling of distress like a lover might feel when he saw his mistress losing her mind."

"What did your father say?"

"He agreed. He thinks the old virtues are still here, hidden under the surface, but for many, they are no longer important. Everything you do is right if you can get away with it. Especially if you're powerful. What the powerful do is always right. It makes my parents very sad."

The cat stretched its neck, seeking a share of ear scratching from Diana. She obliged as she looked at her friend's dark shape outlined by the light coming in through the window.

"And your cousin? What do your parents think of his attentions to you?"

Sumiko tensed her shoulders, raising them up to her ears. "*That* is a real mess."

"Why?"

"He's somehow set on me." Sumiko shook her head. "Even though he already has three children with a wife he would have to divorce."

"What? But why? If he's already married, why is he pursuing the idea of marriage with you?"

"You know how it is. For all that Japan seems so modern,

AMY SOMMERS

many old ideas remain. Men still choose to divorce their wives or take concubines as they wish."

"China's the same, but why is he so insistent on having you?"

Sumiko gave a bitter laugh. "What? Aren't I a gem worth pursuing?"

"You know what I mean."

"He's never said. But he knows that for someone of my family's status, being a concubine would be unacceptable. It's marriage he's intent upon. So far, all the discussions have been through other family members. But my father says my cousin's... well, obsession — it's tied to this distortion of old values."

"What do you mean?"

"As a naval officer, my cousin can claim to adhere to ancient values of military courage and loyalty. But, in the current age, the militarists also want the benefits of capitalism. My family has many resources. They have given me the chance to have the international polish that, together with our fortune, would give a man like my cousin high status in this New Order."

"Ugh." Diana was silent for a moment. "Can't you run away? Stay in Shanghai?"

"I wish it were that easy. But I am part of my family. I owe everything to my parents. If I refuse, if I create a rupture in the wider family, especially with a man as powerful as my cousin is becoming, that would be unfortunate for my parents, for my brother."

"Yes, it sounds like Takeda could make life unbearable. What a mess."

Sumiko sighed. "So it is. You can understand then why these last months in Shanghai, the time spent with you, your brother, Tolt and my brother...it's been special. I wanted you to come here, to host you in our home because you and your family have been so kind to me. I hope you don't regret coming."

Diana reached out and put her hand on Sumiko's. Sumiko grasped it, pressing it. "Not a bit. I'm glad to be here with you."

"I should have known better than to wear a new pair of shoes out sightseeing!" Sumiko shook her head, grimacing as she slipped her bare feet under the table.

She and Tak spent the morning showing Diana more of Tokyo's sights. A waitress had just ushered the three into a private room of a well-known restaurant serving traditional Japanese imperial court food. Diana looked sympathetically at her friend.

While they were occupied, Tak picked up the teacups on the table and began juggling them. They heard the waitress at the doorway to the room, and as she entered and kneeled to take their order, Sumiko caught sight of Tak's game. She gave a slight frown and with a sheepish expression on his face, Tak returned the cups to their places. Diana giggled.

The lunch that followed was delicious, and between bites the three friends laughed and joked. Midway through, they caught the approach of measured footfalls distinct from the quiet patter of the servers. Curious, they paused their banter and through the room's doorway, they saw their server making a deep bow. Tak and Sumiko scrambled to stand, bowing as well. A few beats after them, Diana managed to stand and offer a bow.

"I heard you were in town and figured there was a good chance this is where you would be enjoying lunch."

"Won't you join us?" Tak asked in a voice of formal politeness. Diana noticed that his face had taken on a stiller, more closed quality from the relaxed happiness of a few minutes earlier.

"If I'm not interrupting...?"

Tak and Sumiko urged the servers to bring utensils.

Tak turned to Diana, who had been standing to the side watching the interactions. "My sister and I are not being polite!

Our cousin, Captain Hajime Takeda. Cousin, this is our friend from Shanghai, Miss Diana Wang. You two met very briefly once in Shanghai."

Takeda gave a smooth bow towards Diana, who tried to replicate a corresponding level of depth in her returning obeisance. "Such an unusual city, Shanghai. It somehow seems more like a transplant from the West than an Oriental city."

Diana managed a neutral tone. "I imagine it was work that took you to Shanghai last time, but I hope you'll have a chance to visit again in more pleasant circumstances."

Takeda smiled, "Work indeed, but I find my work so fascinating, that to me it's a pleasure. A bit like figuring out a difficult puzzle. When I was stationed there, my job was to plan how to arrange our air bases so they could stretch from the coast inland to support operations most effectively. Really a tricky challenge in a territory so large and varied as China's."

Recalling the thousands of civilians killed during that campaign, Diana found herself at a loss as to how to respond. "Indeed," was all she could muster.

Tak gestured for everyone to sit down. His and Sumiko's expressions appeared strained at the situation's awkwardness. Seeking to redirect the conversation, Sumiko said in a bright tone, "Diana has family from Osaka, but this is her first visit to Tokyo, so we're hoping to show her as much as possible."

"Ah, yes. What are your plans for this afternoon?"

Tak nudged Sumiko under the table, and she turned to him instead of responding herself, asking, "Brother, what are we planning this afternoon?"

Trying to think of an activity that wouldn't appeal to their cousin, Tak replied, "Well, we've already shown Diana-san some of the main areas of downtown Tokyo, so this afternoon I was thinking of taking her to Asakusa — give her a feeling for the more bohemian side of the city."

"Asakusa! A bit seamy, isn't it?" Takeda a doubtful expression on his face. "I suppose the climate of the last few years has calmed things down a bit, but still, there are some bad elements hanging around. It would be advisable to have more than one male escort."

"That's kind of you, cousin," Tak replied. "But I know how busy you are. We don't want to impose, particularly with something so frivolous as sightseeing in Asakusa."

"Busy yes, but what better use of my time than to make a Chinese guest feel welcome in Asia's greatest city?"

Both Tak and Sumiko made polite murmurings, while Diana smiled in a fashion that she hoped appeared sincere.

As the meal ended and they prepared to depart, Diana said in a quiet voice to Sumiko, "Lunch was delicious, but I'm not feeling so well. Would it be all right if I go back home to rest a bit?"

"Of course! Let us take you back."

Tak, who had been walking with Takeda down the hallway to the restaurant's main lobby, turned to ask, "What's going on?"

Once Sumiko explained, Tak urged, "We've been overtiring you! Let me take you home."

Takeda proposed, "I suggest that my cousin take Miss Wang home to rest for a bit. I will escort Sumiko-san to Asakusa, and then you two can rejoin us for late afternoon tea at one of the restaurants at the Subway Tower. How does that sound?"

Diana voiced no objection. Tak was focused on her reaction, and didn't notice his sister's slight frown. Calling a rickshaw, he helped Diana in. After instructing the driver, he settled next to her.

They were quiet as Diana watched the busy street scene through which they were passing. "Do you really feel unwell or was our cousin just too much for you?" Tolt asked.

Diana turned her head and started to respond. "I really am not..." She gave a rueful smile. "I'm sorry. I know he's part of your family, but listening to him describe how figuring out air base bombing fields was like working a puzzle, well..."

Diana adjusted her hat. "Thoughts of those killed or their homes destroyed kept flashing through my mind. I had to restrain myself from shouting at him."

Shaking her head, she added, "Quentin's and Tolt's fears about my causing an international incident would have been realized. Claiming a headache seemed preferable."

With a rueful smile she turned to face Tak, "I'm sorry for ruining your afternoon. Why don't you drop me off at the house, then go meet the others?"

"You haven't ruined my afternoon. My cousin is my cousin, but my own views may be closer to your own."

"Sumiko didn't seem keen about spending the afternoon alone with him. I feel bad about abandoning her. Perhaps we ought to try to find them?"

"You mean Tak and Diana save the day?"

"Yes, something like that."

Tak put out his hand to shake and Diana, a bit puzzled nevertheless, extended hers to grasp it. "Shake, partner?" he asked.

"Shake!" she replied, laughing at this quintessentially American gesture.

Calling to the rickshaw driver to change directions, they headed to Asakusa.

"This is my first day of relaxation and no work in months!" Takeda remarked with a smile.

In the car next to him, Sumiko continued to face forward, but glanced sideways at him as she replied, "The burdens on our country's military are heavy, aren't they?"

"I suppose. But, when this period is over and our aims achieved, then all the efforts and sacrifices will have been worth it."

"Yes, I'm sure," she responded. "Meanwhile, your sacrifices to duty continue by accompanying your cousin around town instead of enjoying time with your family."

"You are family! And, it's my pleasure to see you. Indeed, despite the press of work in recent months, I was hoping we would have time to see each other."

"Oh look, there's the Subway Tower — we're at Asakusa!" she exclaimed. "I loved coming here when I was small. Mother and Father thought it was a scandalous place, so my brother and I would figure out how to come without their knowing. All the cinema houses and restaurants! Such a jumbled mix of food from different countries. We were too young to go to any of the revues or cabarets, but just the liveliness of the streets was amazing."

Takeda smiled. "I had no idea of my cousins' rebellious side."

"Well, to be fair, usually I instigated these outings. And my brother, being loyal, would always take care of me."

The cab slowed for a stop light. Looking ahead, Sumiko called out, "Oh, there's Cafe Paulista. Let's go for a coffee!"

"Really?" Takeda asked in a dubious tone.

"It's not like the old days, filled with philosophers and would-be revolutionaries plotting to change the world," Sumiko answered. "Now that our military has taken on the task for us of rectifying society, an officer can take a coffee there without damage to his reputation," she concluded with a smile.

Takeda examined her face to discern whether she was being ironic, but her bland smile made him dismiss that idea. He told the driver to pull over.

The Western-style cafe had none of the liveliness that had characterized it a decade earlier, but it was still quite full. They found a table and sat down. "So, any idea of my cousin's intentions towards your friend Miss Wang?" Takeda's voice sounded casual, but there was a probing expression in his eyes. Preoccupied by settling her purse on the open chair next to her, Sumiko looked up. "I beg your pardon?"

"I know from my trip to Shanghai earlier this year that you often socialize together. Have things between them progressed beyond simple friendship?"

"No, I don't think so. Diana is – well, she's... Let's just say that she thinks of Tak as a brother or a good friend, but her heart is not inclined towards him." Sumiko fell silent, not wanting to discuss the matter when she knew where Diana's true feelings lay.

Takeda, however, was unwilling to abandon the topic. "It would be complicating for my cousin to marry outside our race. He ought to find a Japanese girl from a good family – not go marrying a foreigner."

The server came to take their orders and after she left, Sumiko found Takeda had taken to looking at her intently. It made her uncomfortable. Takeda continued to assess her.

"Sumiko-san, I understand you have converted to the Roman Catholic religion?"

"Yes, that is so." She tilted her head to look at Takeda, wondering why he mentioned this topic.

"I am puzzled," Takeda said, then paused.

"About?"

"A Japanese becoming Catholic is unusual; you will agree, I'm sure."

The waitress brought their coffees and set them on the table. Takeda picked up a spoon and gave his an absentminded stir.

"Catholicism is known for the strictness of its doctrines, and regulation of its adherents' lives. What puzzles me is in some fashion you are a non-conformist. How do you see yourself in terms of this religion?"

Sumiko added sugar to her coffee, as she considered a response. "Please forgive me. Answering your question, I may offend, and I apologize if I do." She paused again, then in a slow voice said, "You're correct of course. Catholicism's prescriptions for adherents' behavior are strict. At their heart, though, is the concept of honoring the presence of God in each of us — of a higher power or order than the rules of this world... an order that connects all of us as creatures made in God's image."

"As a Japanese, we are also taught that there is a higher demand on us, the demand to honor the emperor and our homeland."

She looked up at him. "In the last several years, ideas of what that entails as a Japanese have evolved. I fear they risk crowding out what it means as a human. To have a sense of connection to others, to those who are not Japanese, in ways that I fear are leading to...."

Sumiko's voice tapered off. She paused and then concluded, "Well, here I am rambling, not making sense." She laughed a low laugh, but the sound wasn't filled with humor. "Perhaps my connection to my religion is simply one of those things a person feels, but cannot really explain. I apologize if I can't give a better answer."

Ignoring the implications of her statements, Takeda zeroed in on the issue closest to his heart. "And do you follow *all* the precepts of your faith? Do you, for example, think marrying a non-Catholic is a sin? Or marrying a divorced person?"

Sumiko gazed at him, flummoxed as to how to respond. Before she could answer, she heard someone call out.

"There you are! I knew Cafe Paulista would be your first stop!"

Tak, together with Diana, had arrived. Sumiko's expression changed from grave to delighted. "You're here!" Then, concerned, she asked, "Diana, I thought you weren't well. Are you sure it's alright to be out?"

"Oh, once we got her out in the fresh air, she was much better and insisted that she had to see Asakusa," Tak answered.

"Please, join us!" Sumiko gathered up her purse from one of the extra chairs. Takeda rose, bowing in Diana's and Tak's direction.

The newcomers took their seats and started chatting with Sumiko about what they should see and explore that afternoon. Takeda observed them closely, sipping every now and then on his coffee, but saying little.

As the afternoon wound down, Takeda insisted that he show Diana around the next day. Unable to devise a polite refusal, the Takematsus agreed. So it was that the next morning, Takeda dismissed the Takematsu chauffeur, and was driving the family car. Tak was seated next to him on the front seat, listening as his cousin disclaimed. They had just dropped the girls off at the cathedral, so that Sumiko could attend Sunday services. Diana planned to sit in a back pew, and maybe go for a stroll if mass ran long. Takeda had announced that he and Tak would drive around, then come pick the girls up after the service.

While smoothly navigating the crowded streets, Takeda offered some pronouncements about the war in China. Seemingly out of the blue, he observed, "At least she's not a Korean, but still....you couldn't expect the family to treat her like one of us. A Chinese married into an old family like ours?"

Tak was baffled. "I beg your pardon?"

"Miss Wang of course. The last few days have given me a

chance to observe you. You are taken with her; perhaps you even believe yourself to be in love. Indeed, she is quite lovely. Attractive in face and figure, well-spoken and well-mannered."

Takeda gave a deft twist of the wheel, neatly avoiding several pedestrians who had stepped in front of the car. "Twenty or thirty years ago, she would be the sort of refined Chinese who a Japanese scholar or businessman posted to China might consider marrying and bringing home. And, of course, she is one-half Japanese. So that might account for her apparent good breeding. But she was raised in China with a Chinese father. She thinks of herself as Chinese."

At a red light, he slowed the car to a smooth stop. "Even if she did think of herself as Japanese, today mixed marriage isn't feasible. It would be ill-conceived. Besides, her tastes tend to more animalistic, more tribal."

Takeda's statements left Tak speechless. So preoccupied had he been with cudgeling over how to discuss Takeda's interest in Sumiko, it had never occurred to him that Takeda might have views regarding *his* life.

The autumn weather was clear and warm. Tokyo looked at its best, people filled the streets. Takeda was a capable driver and managed the crowds with no hesitation. Seizing on the last of his statements, Tak asked, "What do you mean by tending toward 'animalistic' or 'tribal'?"

"Oh, that Negro friend of yours. Quite good Japanese he speaks. But he's an American. And worse, he's Colored; nevertheless, from what I can tell by the way she blushes and her eyes light up when his name is mentioned, Miss Wang is in love with him."

The light at the intersection at which they were waiting turned green. Takeda accelerated the car with a steady pace. "Miss Wang doesn't look that way at you. She's fond of you, of course, like a brother; but no, it's that African bushman who makes her heart beat faster. And, you...well, you're too much of a fool to see how she really feels. You're just not rational."

"*I'm* not rational?" It had never occurred to Tak to fall in love with Diana. To hear Takeda characterize him as having an irrational obsession was outrageous. Faster than he could think, words started to spill from his mouth. "You, the man who's already married, yet has set his eyes on my sister? Who cannot recognize that she despises all you stand for, that marrying you would be a repudiation of her deepest beliefs. And you call *me* irrational? Unbelievable!"

Now it was Takeda's turn to flush. For he had danced around the topic of marriage to Sumiko, never directly raising it with Sumiko's parents nor Tak. He hoped that when he finally did broach the topic, it would be with confidence in a positive outcome. "What do you mean?" he demanded.

"You know very well. For the past two years, you've been working every angle you can, expending the same level of meticulous attention to detail and tenacity you bring to your military exploits to the prospect of marrying my sister," Tak answered. "But she shrinks from the mere thought. She finds your work repugnant. The idea of marrying a divorced man is abhorrent to her. Since she returned from Switzerland, why do you think she's spent so much time in Shanghai?"

In profile, Tak could see Takeda's jaw tighten. He soldiered on: "She hoped that you would relinquish this ridiculous scheme. Indeed, the only reason I was able to persuade her to come to Tokyo with me this time was because she assumed you would be away on maneuvers. She is too kind and well-bred, as well as loyal to family, to brush you off, but if faced with the choice of marrying you versus almost anyone else, she'd take anyone else."

Now that he had embarked on the topic, Tak could feel anger and resentment towards his cousin's arrogance powering through his body. "I have no idea whether Diana Wang is in love with Tolt or he with her, but since you've mentioned him, I'll use that comparison. My sister so detests the idea of marrying you that if presented with the choice of having to marry you or Tolt, I'm willing to wager all I own that she'd choose him: a foreigner, an American and yes, a Negro."

Takeda said nothing, but his eyes tightened in anger.

Disregarding the danger, Tak continued. "If my sister's reluctance to marry you isn't sufficient to make you rethink your ideas, you should know that I will do everything I can to block you."

Takeda gave Tak an assessing look. "By the time the new year arrives, your family will see things very differently." He resumed gazing at the road ahead of him. "Marrying me, someone who will by then, the Emperor willing, be a hero to our nation, will not be distasteful. In fact, it will be the desired aim of your entire family."

"I wouldn't be so sure of your success as a military hero. Many things could go awry before your aims to make military history come to pass," countered Tak.

Takeda's anger was evident, but he kept control over his emotions. "You don't understand how things work today in our country. Too much time spent overseas. The acts and words of an officer of His Majesty's Imperial Navy are presumed honorable and correct. In the coming months, this will become only apparent."

As Takeda spoke, his emotions seemed to cool. "I could say you committed a crime. All the evidence could point to *my* being the perpetrator, yet the police and courts would nevertheless believe you guilty and me innocent. *That* is how things stand today in Japan's New Order. So, don't talk about your power to block the realization of my aims. There is no aim I have which you are capable of thwarting."

As he finished uttering this statement, several things combined at once to provide an opportunity to test the cousins' respective assertions. Takeda had circled the car back by the cathedral. Diana, who had indeed slipped out for a stroll, came into view. She was midway across the street, and saw the car bearing Takeda and Tak draw near enough to recognize them. She smiled and raised her hand to wave.

Rather than slowing, Takeda pressed on the accelerator and Diana's eyes widened in fear as she realized it was going to hit her. Tak realized it, too. He tried to wrest the wheel, but Takeda's grip was steely. The car's path was unerring. Striking Diana with a sickening thud, it carried on without slowing. Diana flew up over the windscreen and then behind the car, landing heavily on the pavement. Tak could hear screams from bystanders on the sidewalk.

Tak reached inside his coat. With the vibration from the impact of Diana's body colliding with the car still being felt, hot rage overrode other considerations. He drew out the gun that Takeda had months earlier urged him to buy as protection from attack in Shanghai.Cocking the gun, Tak aimed it at his cousin. Takeda looked at him in astonishment, slamming the car brakes and sending Tak flying against the dashboard. The impact caused the gun to fall from Tak's hand. Takeda reached down and pocketed the weapon, then exited the car. On the street behind them a crowd had already gathered around Diana's limp form. Police were approaching her, and another group of police was coming towards the car. Takeda stood next to the driver's side, dabbing his forehead with his handkerchief.

A policeman rushed up to him and saluted, in a breathless

voice asking, "Officer, are you all right?"

"Yes," Takeda replied.

From the passenger side of the car, Tak emerged clutching his right arm. He ran to Diana.

Pointing to him, Takeda told the policeman, "That man is a menace. I suspect he was drinking earlier. He was driving and hit the pedestrian back there. I was finally able to get the car stopped."

Disregarding the fact the officer had just seen Tak alight from the passenger side of the vehicle, and that Takeda was standing next to the driver's side, he answered, "*Hai!*" and took off after Tak, who was pushing through the crowd surrounding Diana.

Tak dropped down on his knees on the ground next to her. He tried to turn her face to examine it, and winced, perceiving for the first time that his right hand was injured. Using his left hand in an awkward fashion, he touched her face. Diana's eyes were open. A trickle of blood came from her mouth and he could see blood spreading in a widening pool under her head.

She was so like herself, yet so still.

She was dead.

14

OCTOBER 1941, PART 2

TAK COULD hear roaring in his ears. Around him all seemed black. Just a circle of vision big enough to take in the red, halo surrounding Diana's head. He lowered his own head, the hair of his forelock swinging down, touching his forehead to hers. His body started to shudder with sobs. The policeman finally made his way through the crowd and grabbed Tak, his hold firm, but not cruel.

While Tak was leaning over Diana, Takeda was speaking in a quiet, but insistent tone with one of the police officers. In his shock, Tak paid no mind to the hands on him, hands that were drawing him upright. Then he found himself being escorted away. Realizing he was leaving Diana, he stopped and tried to resist.

"No, I can't leave her!" he screamed. "Who will take care of her? I can't leave! Let me stay!" The police were unrelenting, and his entreaties had no effect.

In response to his cries, they merely said, "You're wanted for questioning."

Tak tried wrenching free and then screamed in pain as they held onto his right wrist. Seeing its odd angle, they realized he must have injured it in the car crash, and unbeknownst to Tak, the officers' intended destination changed from the police station to the hospital.

Mass had now ended. Sumiko descended the cathedral's steps, searching the crowd for Diana. The ambulance and crowd surrounding a fallen form caught her attention. As Takeda's likeness registered with her, she broke into a run. A sheet was being pulled over Diana's body, as the ambulance workers loaded it onto a gurney and placed it in the ambulance.

Grabbing hold of Takeda's arm, she cried out, "What's happened? Who is it?"

Takeda looked at her with a sober expression. "Miss Wang. I'm afraid she was hit crossing the street." He reached out to support her, saying, "The force was too great. There was nothing they could do."

Sumiko cried out, and tears flooded into her eyes. She fumbled for her purse, extracting a handkerchief that she pressed to her eyes. Tears continued to pour down her face. Takeda was quiet and tender. "Here, let us get away from this crowd."

With one arm shielding Sumiko, he turned to one of the officers and slipped him the car key to the Takematsu family vehicle, while telling him where it should be returned. Then turning to another, Takeda asked him to call a cab. His attention focused on calming Sumiko. asked what had happened.

Takeda said only, "There was an accident. A terrible accident. It all happened so quickly." The first couple of times he responded this way, Sumiko didn't challenge him, but suddenly she recalled that Tak had been with Takeda. Turning in the seat to face him, she grabbed both Takeda's arms. "What about my brother? Was he killed, too? Where is he?"

"No, no, he was not hit by the car. He is alive. It was only poor Miss Wang." At that, a fresh bout of weeping came over Sumiko.

Wiping her nose, she asked, "But where is he then? Did he not come with you? Does he even know about this terrible thing?"

"Yes, he knows," Takeda said quickly. "It's just he was hurt a bit. The doctor must examine him."

"Which hospital? We must go to him! It might be serious!"

"No, it was not so serious. Think of your poor parents. The family car is going to arrive home at any moment, driven by a police officer, and your parents will not know what has happened to any of you. We should first go home, and then attend to your brother."

When they arrived at the Takematsu home, others were also arriving. The family car was being driven into the driveway. And, more unexpectedly, another vehicle was also pulling up. Tolt had come as a surprise. Sumiko and Takeda alighted from the taxi, with Takeda comforting Sumiko. Concerned by the sight of Sumiko in tears and a policeman driving the family car, Tolt jumped out.

"What's happened, Sumiko-san?"

Sumiko took one look at Tolt and eyes brimming with tears she choked out, "Tolt-san, I don't know how to tell you this. Diana — she's — she was just hit by a car." Doubled over with the pain she was feeling coupled with awareness of how the news would affect Tolt, she was at risk of falling to the ground. Takeda held onto her.

"What?" Tolt spat out. "What do you mean? What hospital is she at?"

Sumiko's face contracted in agony, tears streaming down her cheeks. She couldn't bear to say what had happened. It fell to Takeda to answer. In a sober voice, he said, "I regret to tell you that Miss Wang is dead."

"Dead?" Bafflement was etched on Tolt's face. He grabbed Sumiko's arm, as if pleading with her to contradict this word. "Sumiko-san, what is going on?"

With an agonized expression, she replied, "I wasn't there. I can't tell you more." "She can't be dead!" he exclaimed. He heard the words, but acknowledging their meaning was so agonizing, it felt as if he was being suffocated. Time slowed.

Seeing the shock registering on his face, Sumiko attempted to regain control over her voice. "I'm so sorry, Tolt. She is dead. That I saw with my own eyes. But at the time it happened, I was in church. I didn't witness what occurred."

Both turned to Takeda, who said in a calm tone, that conveyed compassion, "It was indeed a terrible accident."

Looking at Sumiko, he continued, "Your brother was driving. Someone seemed to be trying to merge from the left and he was distracted. He didn't see Miss Wang in the crossing. Indeed, she, too, was distracted waving at us. Unfortunately, the car struck her. Your brother was injured — not seriously — but they took him to the hospital before taking him to the police station for his statement."

Tears were now forming in Tolt's eyes. He kept mouthing the word 'no,' but not a sound emerged from his lips. The world was cracking around him. He felt like he was dissolving. Shock and pain left Sumiko and Tolt standing frozen at the Takematsu's front gate.

Takeda took charge of the situation. "See here, Gross-san. My cousin is distraught. I will take her into the house and we will have the car take you to the hospital — they were going to take Miss Wang there for...issuance of the death certificate. You will go find out what has happened, next we can learn about Sumiko-chan's brother."

Takeda's use of the endearment 'chan' was unnoticed by Sumiko in her anguish, as she watched Tolt turn in a mechanical fashion and re-enter the car. Takeda instructed the driver where to go. The entire ride to the hospital, Tolt kept shaking his head, clinging to the idea that there was a mistake. It must be an error.

And, yet, once at the emergency room, he found himself talking with a nurse who confirmed that the body of a young woman had just arrived and the ambulance drivers were likely at the hospital morgue completing the paperwork.

When Tolt made his way down the hall to the morgue, he came upon the two ambulance workers, who stood at the front desk, just finishing up the forms. Tolt spotted Diana's handbag casually placed next to the paperwork. The sight of the chic leather bag, which Diana carried with such nonchalance, struck a blow making him realize this was real. He was not going to find a case of mistaken identity behind the door to the morgue. He felt a knife-like sensation cutting him apart. The two men ceased the sort of casual chatter that co-workers engage in, and took in the presence of a foreigner, a Negro at that, who had entered the room.

"Did you just bring in a female accident victim?" Tolt asked. The two men nodded, now even more dumbstruck to be addressed in their native language by the man facing them.

"Is that her handbag?"

Again, they nodded.

"The victim is my friend. May I see the bag?"

They nodded for a third time but made no move to hand him the bag. Tolt stepped closer to the desk and opened the purse. It was indeed Diana's: her change purse, compact and comb all lay in place. From constant jumbling, the items in women's purses often assume a shiny, worn appearance. Yet, each of the items Diana carried was simple and elegant. She was always so tidy. He marveled that such mundane thoughts could flow through his head at that moment.

"Do you know what happened?"

One of the men finally got the nerve to speak. "We weren't there. But I heard some of the bystanders saying that the car was accelerating as it hit her. They said it was strange as the traffic there is usually slow there because of the crowds. The cops were taking one of the fellows from the car away, but we just saw him being admitted here at the hospital, so he must have been injured as well. The other fellow — the one in the uniform — he seemed fine."

"Can I see her?"

"When the doctor's done, they should let you. Tell them you're family." He then looked at Tolt and flushed with embarrassment. "I mean, well, you know…"

Tolt turned to go back to the emergency room. At the reception desk, he asked whether a patient surnamed Takematsu had been admitted. The face of the admitting nurse took on a serious cast, as she told him the exam room number and gestured down the hall. Tolt noticed that a couple of junior-looking police officers were standing in the reception area. One was looking at his notebook and reading to the other, who was making additional notes.

Tolt strode down the hall. No one was there and the police hadn't followed him. As he arrived at the indicated room a nurse approached from the other direction, opened the door and entered. Tolt stepped in after her. To one side, Tak was seated in a chair, cradling his wrist and hunched over. He didn't look up at the sound of the door, but did as soon as he heard Tolt's voice saying 'Excuse me' to the nurse. The nurse nodded, briefly checked the chart and left.

Tak rose, and turned to Tolt, his eyes filled with tears. Tolt's mouth was dry. "What happened?" he said.

Tak reached out his uninjured hand to grasp Tolt's arm. Tolt covered Tak's hand with his own. He couldn't bear to say what he knew, that it was Tak who had been driving the car that struck Diana.

"It was my fault. Not entirely, but maybe if I hadn't done what I did, it wouldn't have happened." Tak's eyes reddened.

Footsteps reverberated in the hallway. Between that and the buzzing in his head, Tolt didn't know how to respond. So much needed to be absorbed: Diana was gone. Diana with whom he had been planning to spend the rest of his life. And Tak was the one who had done this. His dear friend. How in God's name was he going to get his head around this?

The door to the examination room opened and the doctor entered. "Please, sit down. I need to check your hand." Tak sat, continuing to look at Tolt with a tormented expression. Tolt stared back, overwhelmed.

The doctor was silent as he probed and Tak winced. "I need to get some materials and a nurse. Please wait."

The doctor left, and Tolt pulled up the just vacated chair, sinking down as though his legs had no more strength. He felt like he was in danger of disintegrating.

"There's not much time," said Tak urgently. "When the doctor returns, we can't talk. I need to tell you now. We may not have another chance."

"Another chance?" Tolt asked in a stupid tone.

"About what happened," Tak hissed.

"I know. You were driving and struck…struck Diana."

"No!" Tak shook his hand for emphasis, then cringed at the pain. "It was Takeda. He was driving!"

"Takeda?"

"We got into an argument. There's no time now to go over how it started. But I told him Sumiko wouldn't marry him. That she despises everything he stands for. Then he saw Diana. Crossing in front of us. Waving."

Visualizing Diana's characteristic jaunty wave, Tolt's face contorted.

Tak bore on. "Suddenly…he accelerated, saying I didn't understand how things work in Japan. If he wants something, he can do as he wishes. If something bad happens and he says I did it, people will believe him. To prove it, he drove right into her."

Tolt closed his eyes and tried to stay present.

Tak's voice was breaking. "So after, after…." He took a breath, then resumed. "When the car stopped, and the police came, Takeda told them *I* had been driving, that I had hit Diana, and…"

Tak stopped as the doctor returned along with a nurse. Tolt relinquished the chair, then turned around, rubbing his forehead, trying to make sense of the mass of horrible facts: Diana was dead. Takeda had done it. As a demonstration of power. But Tak would pay. He and the others who loved Diana would all pay. And Takeda? Unscathed.

Tolt turned back to observe the doctor and Tak. The doctor was checking Tak's pupils. "The wrist fracture is straightforward enough, but I'm concerned there was a head injury. Please wait while we make the necessary arrangements."

As soon as he and the nurse had left, Tak resumed his urgent tone. "We need to make a plan. Now."

A plan? Tolt gazed at him befuddled.

Tak continued, "I got a gun."

"What?" asked Tolt, astonished out of his torpor. "I thought obtaining a gun was extremely difficult."

"It is. But, as with anything in Japan, if you have connections, the impossible becomes possible. We both know war between Japan and America will be a disaster. You've tried to tell your government that an attack was pending. There's no one in Japan to stop the attack." He brushed back the lock of hair falling over his eyes. "I had been considering whether I could…"

He paused. Torment creased Tolt's face. Tak continued. "Our military believe a successful attack in Hawaii is vital to prevailing in a war against America. Without Takeda's genius, could such a complex maneuver succeed? Could removing him create a delay allowing cooler heads to prevail? If you love your homeland, should you not try to prevent its destruction?"

His face flushed. " I hadn't decided whether I could kill someone, much less my own cousin, but there in the car…well, when I realized what he was doing, trying to hurt Diana, I pulled out the pistol. I tried to, to shoot him, but I…I failed."

Tears pooled in Tak's eyes. He hunched down in the chair, shielding his face with his good arm. Tolt tried to say something, but was speechless. Tak lowered his arm and made an effort to continue. "Between what I told him about Sumiko — that she would never marry him — and trying to use a gun against him, I know that he will be merciless."

"You mean he'll get you prosecuted for Diana's death?" asked Tolt, incredulous.

"Or worse."

Tak rushed on. "Unless, unless…my parents encourage Sumiko to agree to marry Takeda. If she did, he would relent."

"Did he say that to you?"

"No, he didn't need to."

"So what happens now?" Tolt asked in a bleak tone.

"This is what we need to decide. And after what I said to him, we also need to assume he now suspects that you betrayed his confidences. He'll be thinking of you, too. It's not safe for you to stay in Japan, much less to be seen here with me."

Tolt's brain was hardly operating. He looked to his friend for a hint of what he was contemplating. "I'm sorry…I can't make sense of it. Just tell me what I am to do."

Tak took a deep breath and shared his plan. Despite its audacity, Tolt recognized that it made a certain sense. He gripped Tak's shoulder. "I will give it my all."

The nurse returned. "Mr. Takematsu, some officers have come from the central police station to see you, along with a navy officer. They want to speak with you, so we need to finish your examination. Best if your visitor waits outside."

The nurse walked over to place a clipboard on a table by the wall, and Tak leaned towards Tolt, saying in low and urgent English, "Go now, but don't try to leave the hospital. Takeda will see you. He can't find out you've spoken with me. That would ruin everything. Find an empty room and wait until you hear them come in here."

The nurse approached with a bowl of water and a sponge and Tolt span around, opened the door, and went into the corridor. Across from him was another exam room with its door ajar. He heard the clomp of boots approaching from the reception area and darted into the empty room, closing its door. He heard the door to Tak's exam room open and several people filing in. As soon as he heard that door closing, he opened the door to his own room and quickly exited. There was much to be done.

Tolt walked through the gate of the Takematsu residence. His feet seemed as burdened as if dragging anchors behind them. He wanted nothing so much as to collapse on the ground and sob, but he had to keep moving. Tak needed him to carry out his plan. Tolt was not confident of success.

When the Takematsu's servant showed him into the living room where Sumiko was waiting, her first words were solicitous, asking in a gentle voice, "Did you see her?"

Tolt realized with a jolt that he hadn't seen her.

"No," he replied. "I didn't." Oh God. Now he never would. That too, was irrevocably gone.

"Did they refuse to let you? Perhaps my parents can help make a request for you. At the moment, they are on their way to the hospital to see my brother."

"Actually, it was your brother I saw. We were able to talk."

"Don't worry, my cousin has gone to the police. He said he will use every effort to persuade them to go easy on my brother." Tolt shook his head.

Time was tight. There was no choice but to plunge in. Tolt took a breath. "Sumiko, Takeda is lying."

"What? What do you mean?"

"I spoke with Tak. Things didn't happen as Takeda said."

Sumiko frowned. "Sit down, Tolt-san." She looked at him with pity.

Tolt sensed her sympathy but pushed it away. He had to stay focused: Diana was gone. Tak was trapped. Thinking back to Sara's admonition, he needed to focus on protecting those he cared about. Sumiko was who he needed to save.

"Tak told me what really happened. He and Takeda were alone in the car, waiting for you and Diana. They started talking about you."

Startled, Sumiko asked. "About me?"

"Yes. You and I haven't talked about this, and it concerns private matters, so I apologize for jumping in, but based on what your brother has asked of me, there's no avoiding it." Tolt took a deep breath and told her all he knew.

Sumiko's face turned pale, her lips tight, her hands clenched in her lap. "Takeda was driving? He intentionally hit Diana?"

"It's your brother's word against Takeda's. My money is on Tak."

Sumiko nodded.

"Takeda may have told you he is trying to clear Tak, but when I left the hospital, he had just arrived with police. He didn't see me. Tak says Takeda will make him the scapegoat."

Sumiko looked devastated.

"From other things Takeda said, your brother thinks that in the next couple of months, the military situation will change and Takeda will be in a position of even greater power. It may become impossible for your family to deny his request to marry you."

Sumiko turned even paler." And what if I were willing to marry him?" she asked. "Would my brother be freed?"

He shook his head. "Maybe, but your brother refuses to go along with such a scheme. He wants me to discuss another plan with you."

"What plan?"

"This is going to sound crazy, but I swear to you, it's what your brother wanted me to ask you to do." Tolt corrected himself. "To beg you to do."

"Very well."

"He wants you to flee. To leave Japan, go somewhere safe. For reasons I can't go into now, we know that the war in China is going to spread. There's a narrow window for you to get away from Takeda's influence."

"To flee? How would I flee?"

"With me. To America."

"America?" Sumiko gasped. "What can he be thinking? Leave him and our parents at the worst moment of our lives?"

"I know. He knew that would be your response. We'll get to that, but first let's talk about the crazy part of the plan."

"The crazy part?" Sumiko gave a shaky laugh.

"Yes, there's a part of your brother's idea you will like even less. Tak specifically wants you to do this, so know that in raising this I'm honoring his wishes."

"I understand."

"You know how people have commented on your and Diana's close resemblance?"

Expression puzzled, Sumiko nodded.

"With Takeda so relentless, getting out of Japan, then out of China as Sumiko Takematsu will be risky, maybe impossible. Instead, he proposes you pass as Diana, in Shanghai we marry, you go to the U.S. as my wife. It would be a paper marriage, and after arriving in the U.S., we would divorce. At least Tak would know you are safe."

The plan was outrageous. How could he convince Sumiko to take the extreme step of walking away from her family at such a dire time?

Looking even more somber, Sumiko answered, "Tolt-san, please do not see this in any way as personal, but I simply cannot. In the middle of this catastrophe, the worst our family has ever known, I flee? What kind of daughter and sister would I be to be so selfish? It would be shameful. "

Tolt pursed his lips, gazing downward. "Your brother anticipated this reaction," he said, looking up. "He said to tell you that *he* feels deep shame that he lost control at Takeda as he did. He feels it was his blunder that set off this terrible chain of events, that he is responsible for Diana's death."

Sumiko started to speak again, but Tolt put his hand on her arm. "Tak's situation gives Takeda increased power over your family," Tolt said firmly. "If you stay and marry Takeda, he wins. Tak told me such a defeat will be a lasting dishonor for him. He begs you to do what he proposes to redeem something positive from a terrible situation."

Sumiko bit her lip. "But what about my parents? How to explain all this?"

"Your brother anticipated this as well. The best way to protect your parents is *not* to tell them. Simply leave."

Sumiko frowned.

"This he didn't tell me, but I believe his intention is after the uproar dies down, he will tell your parents more about what happened. Meanwhile, they will be as mystified as anyone else. Tak thinks this will protect them from Takeda's rage."

Sumiko sat silently for a few minutes, then rose and left the room. When she returned half an hour later, she had cut off her long hair and changed her make-up. She was wearing a blouse of Diana's and she held Diana's passport. She handed it to Tolt, who opened it to the first page. Looking at the picture and then up at Sumiko, he marveled at the resemblance.

"When do we leave?" she asked.

15

LATE OCTOBER 1941

ONCE SUMIKO departed her parents' home with him, Tolt's first act was to check out of his hotel and check them into to a dive near the Yokohama port. He slipped some yen to the desk clerk not to require his companion's identification details be registered. The clerk smirked at this request, and raised his eyebrows further when Tolt requested a room with two beds, or alternatively two adjoining rooms. Sumiko blushed in mortification. Tolt tipped the desk clerk further, asking him to send a steamship agent round the following morning to book passage to Shanghai.

The waiting was tedious, as they dared not go out and risk being seen by police in case Takeda had them on the lookout. Bellboys brought multiple newspapers to the room, which Sumiko pored over, looking for some reference to Diana's accident or a police search for them, but there was nothing. Two days later, they emerged from the hotel, and took a cab to the port. Until the customs officers finished inspecting their papers and they boarded the ship, they both remained nervous.

Sumiko's returning to her Shanghai apartment was out of the question given the risk Takeda could be having it watched. Instead, Tolt took her to his while he broke the news to Quentin and Mr. Wang.

Under Diana's and Sumiko's original plan, they were

supposed to be in Tokyo another week. When Tolt went to surprise the girls, Quentin was away on business, so Tolt had left a note, telling of the plan. When Tolt showed up at the Wangs' home, they joked, "Welcome home, traveler! Did the girls drive you so mad you had to retreat home?"

Tolt attempted a smile, as they ushered him into the large drawing room. Various members of the extended Wang clan were also present, so after Mr. Wang ordered tea, Tolt inquired whether they might adjourn to his study for a chat.

Mr. Wang was all affability. "Yes, let's escape the loud chatter."

Once ensconced in the study's leather armchairs and tea served, Tolt said, "Uncle, may we speak in confidence?"

Noticing the seriousness of Tolt's expression, Mr. Wang waved away the servant standing attendance. "What is it? Has something happened?"

Looking down, Tolt's eyes filled with tears. They seemed to be choking his throat. With a quick brush of his handkerchief, he dried his eyes, swallowed and looked up to face Quentin and his father. "I'm afraid I come bearing bad news."

They looked at him, concern and puzzlement mingled on their faces.

"It is in fact, the worst news I could ever have to tell."

Mr. Wang gripped the armrest of his chair with his free hand and with quiet deliberation, placed his teacup on the desk next to him. Quentin's face appeared mystified at the serious demeanor of his normally wisecracking friend.

"It's Diana." Tolt's voice cracked.

"Diana?" Quentin asked.

"She's been in a car accident. In Tokyo."

Mr. Wang's face turned pale. Tolt plowed on. "A car struck her crossing the street."

Before Tolt's eyes, Mr. Wang's face turned stone-like. An

image of Mr. Wang's similar reaction a year earlier when the golf club head had almost killed Quentin flashed across Tolt's mind. There was no escaping fate this time; it was clear that Mr. Wang knew the answer even before another question was posed. Sharp voiced, Quentin asked, "Is she in hospital?"

Tolt's tears returned. "No. It's worse. She's... she's gone."

Quentin jumped up and gave an agonized cry. Tolt rose from his chair and crossed over to grasp his friend's shoulder. Mr. Wang compressed his lips, struggling to maintain control, his eyes red. "Tell us. Tell us what happened. Why have the Takematsus not sent word?"

"Were you there?" Quentin asked in a ragged voice. "How could there be no news?"

"No, I wasn't there." He ground his jaw, as if both compelled to speak and blocked from saying more. "My God, if only I had been, if only I had left for Tokyo with them when they wanted me to! Maybe I could have saved her, pushed her out of the way."

"But what of Tak and Sumiko?" Quentin demanded. "Do they know? Were they there? Are you...are you positive she is dead?"

Tolt then proceeded to tell them all that had transpired. Mr. Wang and Quentin sat back in their chairs, heavy with a combination of sorrow and bewilderment. Mr. Wang finally spoke. "You say this happened days ago. Why didn't Sumiko contact us? Send a telegram?"

"Her situation is... also complicated. Tak was determined that Takeda would not benefit from his actions towards Diana. He was adamant that his sister not marry Takeda." Mr. Wang and Quentin nodded in understanding.

Tolt paused, thinking how to proceed. "Uncle — sir, there's one other piece of news to tell you. In some sense, it no longer matters. And perhaps it will make you unhappy. If so, I apologize."

Mr. Wang gazed at Tolt, his expression neutral. Quentin's face again resumed a puzzled air.

"For me… for me and Diana, this was happy news we planned on sharing when she returned." Tolt took a deep breath. "Recently, I asked Diana to marry me. She consented, subject to your agreement, sir," he added quickly. "We were going to ask your permission."

Tolt waited, fearing the lash of rejection springing forth. It felt like he had cut open the protective sheath of his ribcage and exposed his heart to be hacked. Enduring Diana's loss was already awful. Losing her family's friendship would be an added torment. Quentin looked at his father, astonished. Mr. Wang remained silent, as if weighing how to respond.

Unable to restrain himself further, Tolt blurted out, "It may be you wouldn't give your blessing. The wedding of your daughter to a foreigner, to a Negro, would have been distasteful. I recognize that, but I want you to know I loved and admired your daughter. My intention was to devote my life to her happiness. It would have been my greatest honor to have been her husband, and if it would have pleased you, to have been part of your family."

Mr. Wang's answer stunned both Quentin and Tolt.

"Yes, my son, I knew all of this."

"You knew?" Quentin and Tolt exclaimed.

"How?" asked Tolt. "How could you know?"

Mr. Wang gave a tremulous smile. "Ah, you know my daughter. She is… what is that expression in English, 'an open book'? If she likes something, you know. If she detests something, you know. In recent months, I could tell she was happier than ever. So I started to observe, to see what was making her so content. And I noticed that being with you seemed to bring her happiness. One day as she was here, tidying my books and I was sitting at my desk working, we were chatting. I asked her if she was in love with you. And she told me."

"She told you? Told you what?" Tolt was truly surprised.

"She told me she wanted to marry you, but she wouldn't if it meant being cut off from family."

Quentin looked at his father with open-mouthed shock.

"What did you say?" asked Tolt.

"Well, I have to say that I was surprised things were so far advanced. I said I didn't favor her marrying a foreigner." Tolt's face fell a bit. "And you know what she said to me?"

"What?"

"She told me that I was a hypocrite."

"A hypocrite?" Quentin gasped. "She called her own father a hypocrite?"

Mr. Wang chuckled again. "Yes, Quentin, your sister is impertinent. She reminded me that I myself married a foreigner, so objecting to her doing so would be hypocritical. And she was right."

He placed his teacup down on the desk in front of him and looked at Tolt. " I thought about you, about how you are. You're the first American I have really gotten to know — as a person — not in a business setting. And of course, you're the first Negro I have ever met." He gave a rueful smile. "For an old man like myself, it's a little odd, I must admit. But as I thought about it, I realized that I like you, and I started thinking about the way you behave. The way you call me "Uncle" just like my son's Chinese friends do. The way you are respectful of your elders. And loyal to your friends. And I thought, I don't know if this is American behavior. Or Negro behavior. Or maybe it's learning about China and Chinese. In any case, it occurred to me that I quite like you, regardless of whether you're American or a Negro."

Tolt gazed at him with gratitude.

"And, then Diana. She reminded me that the reason I still

have my only son, is because of you. I thought of that. You saved Quentin. And in terms of fate, one good turn deserves another. You brought me good fortune. I ought to see good fortune in our being a family together. And so, I agreed with her. I gave her my consent."

"But why didn't Diana say anything to me?"

"You and she had agreed to ask for my permission together. She was afraid you would be upset by her telling me first. To be fair, I was the one who asked her." Mr. Wang compressed his lips. The three men fell into a silence finally broken by Quentin. "I had no idea. You know I'm conservative, but I recognize the wisdom of my father's words. I want you to know I would have welcomed you as a brother, Tolt."

Tolt nodded.

"And so," said Mr. Wang, "we must return to sad reality. We will be holding a funeral, not celebrating a wedding."

"Sir, if I may, I have a request for you."

"Yes?"

"Well, Tak fears that Takeda will use the leverage he now has through this story about Tak being the driver of the car to force Sumiko's family to consent to her marrying Takeda. He asked me to get her away from Japan, to bring her to Shanghai and then on to the United States."

Mr. Wang tapped his fingers on the desk in front of him, weighing what he had just heard. "That would be wise."

"Tak was fearful that if Sumiko traveled under her own name, she might be detained, so we left Japan with her traveling on Diana's passport."

This news elicited astonishment from Mr. Wang and Quentin. "We've all joked in the past about their resemblance," Quentin said, "but one passing for the other? How did it go?"

"It worked. But now, there is a new challenge to face. To

overcome it, I need your help."

"What do you mean?" Quentin asked.

It was Mr. Wang who answered. "I think I know. You want to apply for a visa with Diana named as your wife. But it will be Sumiko. Is that right?"

"Yes. Exactly."

Quentin's looked stricken. "Sumiko? Your wife?"

"Well, yes, legally, but only until we can get her away and figure out what to do," Tolt replied.

"Yes, but why as your wife? Couldn't she simply obtain a visa as Sumiko Takematsu? It's one thing to deceive the border guards here; it's another level of risk to enter the U.S."

"But that's just it, my son. Tolt here has told us the sensitive mission that this Takeda has been entrusted with. I can't imagine Tolt would make something like this up."

Tolt nodded.

Mr. Wang's face took on an even more serious expression. "One does not cross a man like that lightly. Your friend knew this, and that is why he was so intent on getting his sister away. In all that he has asked Tolt to do, Tak has been wise. It's too dangerous to travel under her own name. No, she must continue to use Diana's identity."

Quentin nodded.

His father said to him, "You know what this means, of course?"

Quentin shook his head.

"So, shall I bring her here?" Tolt asked.

"Yes, that's precisely what you should do," Mr. Wang replied to Tolt.

"Bring Sumiko *here*?" asked Quentin.

"Yes, but she will not be Sumiko. To protect her, she must be Diana. She will live with us for a while under Diana's name."

"You mean we will not be in mourning for my sister?"

"In our hearts, we will all be in mourning. But for now, we need to help a friend in need. As far as the rest of our family and the world are concerned, things are as they were, except for the happy news that we will be celebrating our dear daughter's marriage to your close friend Tolt, and sending the happy couple to live for a while in the United States." Mr. Wang waved his hand. "Perhaps Tolt's grandfather is ill and his help is needed. We will think of an explanation. In any case, all will seem normal. Once Tolt and Sumiko are safely on their way, there will be time for mourning."

Mr. Wang looked at Quentin. "Bear in mind what else this news warns us of: war is coming. Something far beyond the small-scale action Japan has been waging against China these last few years."

He took a somber sip of his tea. "If Japan succeeds in surprising the world, this island of prosperity we inhabit in Shanghai is going to be overrun. It will sink below the tide. So besides preparing for the wedding, you and I need to sort out what preparations need to be made for our business interests, to protect the rest of the family as best we can."

Turning to Tolt, Mr. Wang said, "Child, you must go now to collect Miss Takematsu. Tell her she comes as a daughter. While you are gone, I will speak to the rest of the household. When she crosses the threshold, she will cease to be Sumiko Takematsu and will be my daughter. She must address me as father, Quentin as brother and all the aunties, uncles and cousins who make their home here, likewise."

Mr. Wang stood and extended his arm to shake Tolt's hand. Rather than accepting Mr. Wang's handshake, Tolt slid to his knees and bent down to touch his head to the ground in front of Mr. Wang's feet, the traditional sign of filial piety. Seeing Tolt's example, Quentin did likewise. Tears streamed down Mr. Wang's face. He reached out his hands to them.

"Come, we have work to do," he said.

Ronnie Jr.'s cheeks were flushed, his eyes bright. The rare chance to challenge Tolt gave a special zest to his questioning. "What do you mean you want to get married? And even if you do, what does that have to do with getting a visa? You're marrying a girl here in Shanghai. You're here in Shanghai. What's the need for a visa to the States?"

Tolt took a deep breath, and caught himself before the irritation became audible. Do not rise to the bait. He was not going to stoop to Ronnie's level. Despite years of provocation, Tolt prided himself on the fact that he had only ever acted to defend himself against, and had never attacked Ronnie. He aimed to hold true to that commitment. As he let out his breath, he considered how much to tell Ronnie, who was tapping his fountain pen with evident impatience on the desk in front of him.

"Here's the deal," Tolt said. "Last summer America cut off oil exports to Japan. The folks I've been talking to say its stockpile of oil is enough to last six months. After that, the tank runs dry. Where is Japan going to get the fuel needed to run its economy?"

Ronnie exploded. "Gross, what is it with you? It doesn't matter how straightforward the question I ask, you can't be bothered to give a direct answer. No, you've got to quiz me. To go on the offense. Prick me with your épée. We're not fencing here. I simply want to know why it's so urgent that your cherished bride obtain a visa to the States. As the officer responsible for Snow Drift in China, it's a reasonable question."

"Of course, it is. I am giving you background, because as much as I love living here, I'm worried. There's a good chance the situation between Japan and the States will deteriorate further. Once Japan gets close to the bottom of the oil barrel, war could break out. I don't want my new wife trapped here and unable to gain admittance to our country. So, my thought is to take care of it now."

Ronnie scoffed, "You know as well as I do there are lots of girls here who want a way out. Chinese, Russians, you name it. How do we know this one isn't marrying you to get a ticket to America for a better life?"

Tolt tried again to restrain himself, this time from laughing out loud.

"Ronnie, Diana isn't a Russian dance hostess or a poor girl from the back of beyond. Her family is part of the Shanghai elite. In all likelihood, they are probably wealthier than...". He refrained from saying, "than the Planter family", instead concluding, "than the wealthiest family in Seattle. There's no need for a marriage license to a Yank."

"That's just it, son. Something here smells fishy. Excuse me for being blunt, but I'll just come right out and say it. I don't know these people like you do, but what I *do* know is that these Chinamen are more status conscious than the King of England. How do you explain the daughter of a family like hers agreeing to her marrying a foreigner? And not just a foreigner, but let's face it...a Colored foreigner. Everyone I hear tells me how they like light skin... but her pappy is letting her marry a spade?" Ronnie slapped his desk with the palm of his hand. "I may be some palooka from the Pacific Northwest, but something here's not straight up. And I don't like the possibility of Snow Drift's name being dragged into some phonus balonus."

"Sure, all the things you're saying about Chinese generally are true. But we know that what's true generally isn't always true in the specific case." Tolt gestured to the framed photo of Ronnie's parents on his desk. "Look at our families. Generally, in America, wealthy White businessmen are not social friends with Negro men. But, in the specific case of your father and my grandfather, they *are* close friends." Ronnie grimaced. "Same's true here: as a general rule, Chinese may not mix with foreigners, but in the specific case of the Wangs, we are truly close. Diana's father has given me his blessing. There's no way I would marry her otherwise."

"Hmmm," Ronnie leaned over and took a cigar from the humidor on his desk, starting to clip it. "Let me ponder it." Intent on lighting his cigar, he overlooked the tense clenching of Tolt's hands as he left.

Tolt and Quentin stood before Mr. Wang's desk, the expressions on both their faces expectant.

Mr. Wang gestured towards Quentin, "The key is to make as big a show as possible of this wedding. We cannot for any reason seem to be hiding or disapproving. Son, you must go around to the fanciest hotels and ballrooms, making a big noise about wanting the most space for the largest number of guests. Be coy. Don't say it's for a wedding, but just give off lots of hints that your father is planning the event of the year."

Quentin gave a vociferous nod. "Yes, Father. I'll pop round to the Park Hotel tomorrow."

"Good. Let's see if we can get them spreading the word." Mr. Wang turned his attention to Tolt. "Next is whether to have a wedding lunch at one of the big restaurants before you two depart for the States. Play up the fact that this is a marriage which I support. We're just waiting until an auspicious date to hold the big party."

Tolt began to answer, but as he did so, the door to Mr. Wang's office swung open and all three looked over to see Sumiko standing in the doorway with a garment slung over her arm, her face looking stricken.

Tolt walked over, and hand on her shoulder, guided her towards one of the chairs. Mr. Wang stood up and came around his desk, "What is it, my child?"

Sumiko held up the clothing she had been carrying. "Hsiao Ch'en brought this out for me to see." Tears started to pool in her eyes. She was holding a deep pink *ch'i-p'ao* with a matching fitted bolero jacket, lined with white fur. The shade of the dress matched perfectly the sapphire engagement ring sparkling on her left ring finger. "It's one of her wedding outfits."

The tears spilled down her cheeks as she dropped into an armchair. Mr. Wang, Tolt and Quentin all looked at one another.

Mr. Wang cleared his throat. "Well, as to a wedding lunch, perhaps that's not necessary." He walked back to his desk and sat down, picking up a pen, he tapped it on the desk, then popped up. "Daughter, please ask Hsiao Chen to arrange a hat to go with this outfit. One with a veil."

Sumiko looked up at him, puzzlement apparent.

"Not a voluminous veil like Westerners wear for mourning. Something chic, something a French lady would wear to a luncheon or a race meet. Now, Quentin, I have another task for you…"

Three days later, as Mr. Wang led Sumiko and Tolt out of the wedding registrar's office, a flash bulb went off. The three of them, plus Quentin following behind, all reflexively raised their hands to shield their eyes. A young man with a notebook and sharpened pencil strode up to the group.

"Good morning! Tan here, society reporter for *Modern Shanghai*. May I get a quote?"

Beneath the closely-fitted veil, Tolt could see Sumiko was stricken. Before he could think of what to say, Mr. Wang gave a booming laugh, "Ah, you're too tenacious Mr. Tan. Here I thought we could slip in and out of the wedding registrar's office with no publicity!"

The reporter stood taller, an expression of pride evident on his face, "Well, at *Modern Shanghai* we take our work seriously, Mr. Wang. How about a quote on the marriage of your daughter? A marriage to… a foreigner?"

"Certainly!" Mr. Wang put his arm around Tolt's shoulders, "Mr. Gross here has long been a close friend of our family. Why, he and my son Quentin studied law together in America! We are delighted that he will now be part of the family."

He shook his finger at the reporter. "Today's just a formality, mind you. The official wedding ceremony will be after the Lunar New Year, when Diana will be able to bring my closest sister home to join in the celebration. Then, we'll have a big party… the biggest Shanghai has seen for some time. Who knows, if you get this story right, you might even get an exclusive interview and pictures from the newlyweds."

"Yes, indeed, sir! I've taken down everything you said. Would it be all right to get another shot of the happy couple?"

Mr. Wang gave an affable nod, as Tolt and Sumiko held hands and smiled. Noting the tears glistening behind her veil, the reporter exclaimed, "Tears of joy on this happy occasion!"

Mr. Wang waved goodbye and hustled everyone towards the waiting car. It was done.

The interview room at the new U.S. consular offices on Kiangse Road was painted bright white and the furniture was still glossy, but the place had a sterile, oppressive feel. Tolt and Sumiko sat on one side of a table, awaiting the visa officer. Sumiko held her gloves, the ring finger on her left hand dazzling. With the thumb and forefinger of her right hand, she was twisting the ring back and forth. Tolt sat next to her, one leg over the other, jiggling his dangling foot.

The sound of the door opening made them both start. A man who looked as if he enjoyed Shanghai's delights to the detriment of his waistline and liver, entered holding a file. He walked around the table, placed the file on it and took a seat, giving them an intense gaze. "Good morning, Mr. and Mrs. Gross."

Sumiko and Tolt both nodded and murmured greetings in return.

"I'm Bill van Asselt, senior visa officer, and this morning we'll be reviewing the request that you've filed for an expedited spousal visa."

Van Asselt pulled several documents from the file. Tolt could see the application, the marriage certificate, as well as some snapshots from UW days showing him and Diana. The certification letter Ronnie had finally signed was in the pile, too, as well as some other items he couldn't see.

"The paperwork you submitted looks to be in order," van Asselt observed. Tolt felt a sense of relief flow through him. "We did receive some additional information, however, which I want to ask you about."

"Additional information?" asked Tolt.

"Yes, given the current international situation, we've seen an uptick in falsified filings. Jewish girls from Vienna hoping to find a new home by way of marriage to a U.S. Marine. Chinese girls wanting to escape Japanese occupation by marrying an American. So, we have to keep our eyes out for supplemental information, to make sure there's nothing fishy going on."

"I can easily imagine that might be so, Mr. van Asselt, but as you can see from the materials we have submitted, my wife and I have known each other since our student days in Seattle."

"Sure, as I said, everything you submitted looks to be in order." Tolt thought he heard a slight emphasis on the word '*you*' and wondered if that signified anything.

Van Asselt rested his wrists against the edge of the table, steepling his fingers against one another, as he added in a sterner tone, "You'd be surprised − or maybe you wouldn't − at the creativity of the schemes we see. We're aware of at least one Negro musician here with his band who was running a side deal marrying off girls wanting a ticket to the States to his various bandmates and applying for visas to be issued before their gig ended."

Van Asselt looked Tolt up and down with a speculative expression and picked up Ronnie's letter. "Says here you're a manager at Snow Drift; Assistant GM, in fact. Quite a responsible position for one as, well, as...well, someone as...young as you are. Did you have any business experience before coming to Shanghai?"

Tolt willed himself to stay calm. "As you'll see from my resume, I graduated from law school not long before coming here. The owner of Snow Drift, Ronald Planter Sr., he's known me since I was small. He figured with my language skills, I'd be able to help Ronald Jr. with things here."

"Hmmm. Certainly." Van Asselt picked up Tolt's resume and gave it a scan, a mistrustful expression on his face.

Placing the resume back on the table, he continued. "Well, some of the latest schemes are based on the idea that we at the Visa Section are susceptible to the fallacy that all Orientals look alike. The fraudsters are borrowing, stealing − who knows the arrangement − documents from girls who have some legitimate tie to the U.S."

At this van Asselt, raised his eyebrows and looked at Sumiko. A small smile played on his lips, but van Asselt's eyes looked cold as they inspected Tolt and Sumiko, "Maybe the girl studied in the States or had family reasons to spend time traveling in

North America. In any case, these documents get used by some other girl. Some other girl with a passing resemblance to the documented girl. And presto — an imposter transforms into a new person."

Tolt struggled to decide whether to appear sympathetic regarding the frauds being perpetrated, indifferent, or outraged at the implication he might be involved in such an arrangement. Van Asselt continued.

"We're still trying to sort out the driver behind such schemes: is it a mere money-making venture such as your Negro musician compatriots have finagled? Is it a variation on the desperate girls seeking a home? Or, is it part of some intelligence effort?"

Van Asselt looked at both Tolt and Sumiko. Without turning to look at Sumiko, Tolt could sense tension emanating from her.

"I'm sure you've seen it all, Mr. van Asselt," he answered in an even tone. "But my wife and I, well, we're just garden-variety newlyweds." Tolt picked up Sumiko's hand and gave it a squeeze. "I'm hoping to get her back to the States with me before Christmas, holidays with the family and all that. And if I may say, does this ring look like the sort of Woolworth's trick a fraudster would use?" Tolt tipped his head in the direction of the sizable stone sparkling on Sumiko's hand. He laid a clipping on the table. "And here's a magazine story about our marriage. Do the kinds of couples you're describing get written about in the Shanghai society magazines?"

Van Asselt tapped his fingers on the table, considering. Then with a quick motion, he pulled another document out of his file and laid it on the table between them. "Point out to me the names of the people in this picture," he said.

Tolt and Sumiko both frowned. It wasn't one of the photographs they had submitted with their application. It was the picture taken at the Fairy Tale-themed ball, showing Tolt, Tak and Quentin as the Three Blind Mice, and Diana and Sumiko as Fairy Maidens.

Diana's smiling face was gleaming up at Tolt. How had van Asselt gotten this picture? Time seemed frozen as he considered how to answer. Then he realized Sumiko had taken control.

"That is me, and of course, my husband is in the center row behind us girls," she said. "Besides us, the others are my brother, Quentin, and our friends Saburo and Sumiko Takematsu."

"Your resemblance to her is striking," van Asselt answered. Pulling out the pictures of Tolt and Diana from her Seattle days, he continued. "In fact, in these pictures, Sumiko looks more like you than you do yourself."

Tolt felt his stomach heave. Before he could conceive of an answer, he heard a soft giggle from Sumiko, the sort of breathy, self-effacing laugh that a girl might use while batting her eyes.

"Ah, you sound just like my father!" she said. "When he met Sumiko, he started a joke that she looked more like me than I did. But he would always claim that as my father, he could tell who was who. So, one day, Sumiko and I decided to turn the joke on him. You know what we did?"

Van Asselt appeared intrigued. He leaned forward, looking at Sumiko as if he were a child listening to a fairy story. "What?"

"Well!" She placed her hand in front of her mouth, hiding a giggle. Tolt had never seen her so coquettish. "One day we switched roles. Sumiko had spent the night at our house and when morning came, she went down to breakfast as me and I as her. She did everything just as I did: sat in my seat, poured my father's tea, handed him his newspaper. Finally, my brother came down to join us. We hadn't told him of our plan. Once he sat down, he looked around the table and asked, 'What's Sumiko doing dressed in Diana's clothes?'"

"What did your father do?"

"He put down the paper, took a good look at the two of us and burst out laughing." Sumiko cocked her head and asked van Asselt, "You know how Quentin knew?"

"How?"

Sumiko smiled widely, showing her teeth, "See? No gap." Pointing to Diana's face she added, "But Sumiko, she has a gap between her front teeth."

Van Asselt laughed appreciatively. "I have to say, that is quite the story, Mrs. Gross. Thank you. But be that as it may, given the prevalence of the deception schemes I mentioned, to be on the safe side, let's have you bring in this Miss Sumiko. That will dot the i's and cross the t's. As soon as that's done, the visa's yours."

Van Asselt smiled a smile that managed to combine joviality and smugness. Tolt felt hate rising up his throat. Hate for this smug bastard who thought of Negroes as tricksters running sex slave operations. Hate for Ronnie Planter, for it had to have been Ronnie who had provided van Asselt with a copy of the picture.

But Tolt's voice remained calm. "Normally that wouldn't be a problem, Mr. van Asselt, but at present, Sumiko and her brother are in Tokyo."

"Of course they are," van Asselt said in a bland voice, condescension ever more apparent as he started to gather the materials in front of him and replace them in the file folder.

"No, really! Diana — Mrs. Gross — was just there on holiday. While there, Tak had a car accident and suffered some injuries. At present he can't travel. He and Sumiko don't know when they'll be able to get back to Shanghai."

"Well, when they *do* make it back, you just bring her here. I promise you I'll issue Mrs. Gross her visa that same day." Van Asselt stood up, his folder tucked under his arm.

"But, sir, that could be months; it could be into the new year before Tak is declared fit for travel. There's no way we can get home to Seattle by Christmas if we have to wait for their return to Shanghai to get Diana's visa!"

"An accurate précis, Mr. Gross. I can see why your employer deems you capable. Now, excuse me, I have another interview."

As he strode out of the room, Tolt and Sumiko were left looking at each other. How could van Asselt's demand be satisfied?

16

LATE OCTOBER/NOVEMBER 1941

"What the hell are you doing?" The reverberation of the slamming office door still echoed as Tolt stood in front of Ronnie's desk.

"Happy almost-Halloween to you, too. Is this how folks do trick or treating around here?" Ronnie looked up from the newspaper laid out on his desk.

"Why'd you do it?"

"You're going to have to be a tad more explicit. Never have been much for riddles."

"The picture. Why'd you give a copy of this picture to van Asselt?" Tolt shook the framed picture of him and his friends at the Fairy Tale ball in front of Ronnie's face.

"Oh that." Ronnie's face took on a reflective expression, as if he were recalling some distant event. "Yes, well, old Van and I happened to be having a toddy. Around the time I sent in that letter you were hounding me for. He mentioned some cases he was working on with some dodgy types — some of them Negroes, if you must know. I told him that wasn't you. No siree. Told him you're a shining light of the community, involved in charity balls, community activities and such."

Ronnie gave what he must have thought was an angelic smile, but the glint of hate shone through his eyes. "What better way to prove your bona fides than to provide old Van a copy of this photo?"

Ronnie slowly rose from his chair, hooking his thumbs into the pockets of his vest, as he surveyed Tolt. "Why? Is there some problem?"

Anger exceeding what he had ever felt towards Ronnie boiled inside Tolt. He gritted his teeth, answering in a terse voice, "Yes, there damn well is. Van Asselt has taken it into his head that I'm one of the con artists he's dealing with and won't give Diana a visa unless Sumiko can appear to prove she and Diana are two different people."

"Well that's not so bad, is it? Just haul in little Cio-Cio-San, and have done with it," observed Ronnie shrugging his shoulders.

"If it were that simple, don't you think I would have done it already?"

"What's so complicated?"

"She's not here. Sumiko and Tak are still in Tokyo. He was in a car accident and can't travel. Not sure when they'll be back."

Ronnie nodded. "Well that *is* a shame, isn't it? Guess you'll have to wait."

"Damned if I'm going to wait! I'm getting her out of here." Tolt turned around to leave, but Ronnie's next words caught him as he headed toward the door.

"Be careful what you say. Coming from someone other than the upstanding Tolt Gross, that'd sound dodgy. Might make me think I owe it to warn Van of a plan to subvert the laws of our good ole' U.S. Of A. What's so urgent anyway? Christmas in Shanghai is lovely."

Tolt narrowed his eyes but said nothing as he opened the door.

It was Thursday and Quentin, Mr. Wang and Tolt were again

in Mr. Wang's study, this time to discuss progress on van Asselt's demand that Tolt and "Diana" produce Sumiko for an interview. All wore glum expressions.

"I asked a fellow who has handled sensitive matters for me before," Mr. Wang said. "He's skilled at uncovering secrets. You Americans would call him a detective. He says this van Asselt is clean. No girlfriends on the side, doesn't visit prostitutes, no drugs, doesn't seek bribes. Nothing."

Quentin frowned. Tolt tapped his fingers on the armrest of his chair.

The door opened and Sumiko slipped in. "No luck I see," she said, taking in their despondent faces.

Tolt shook his head and grimaced. She replied, "Then the choice is clear. November is almost here. Time is drawing tight. You must book passage on the next available ship. With Father Wang's permission, I will stay here. Who knows, once you are back in the States, another option may present itself. And if it doesn't…"

"Absolutely not.." Tolt sat up and leaned forward. "I promised Tak I would get you away. *That* promise I'm keeping."

"Getting you two *away* from China is not so hard," Mr. Wang observed. "Those arrangements I can make. You could go south. Remember, we have family operating branches of the Wangfu business in Malaya and elsewhere. You could try there for a visa to the States."

"Thank you, Father Wang. But from what Takeda has said, once the wheels are in motion, Japan is likely to head south as quick as quick can be. There's a risk we could get stuck there too."

Mr. Wang nodded. Tolt shook his head. "There's no way for it. I'm just going to have to go in to see van Asselt tomorrow."

Sumiko reached out and touched his arm, "I will go with

you."

He smiled at her, "No. Thank you. This time, I need to see him alone."

"Mr. Gross, I thought I made myself clear. Once your Japanese friend can present herself, I will issue Mrs. Gross a visa to enter the United States."

They were standing in one of the consulate's meeting rooms. Tolt had managed to talk his way in, but this was no sit-down affair. He plunged into the matter at hand. "Thank you, sir, for seeing me. I've checked, and the Takematsus still don't know when they'll be able to travel. Mrs. Gross and I can't just sit around waiting. We need to get to the States as soon as possible. Please, won't you give us the visa?" Tolt had rehearsed this speech multiple times. It cost him a great deal to adopt such a supplicating tone.

"We've covered this ground before. As I told you, there are plenty of schemes afoot whereby double identities are being used by con artists to secure U.S. visas. Who's to say you're not one of them?"

"With respect, Mr. van Asselt, I work for a reputable company with an established history both here and in the States. Would I really put the company and my job at risk with a scam?"

"You'd be surprised at what goes on here. Why just a few years ago, Frank Raven, one of the most admired businessmen in the American community, turned out to be a fraudster. Went banko. Thousands of his investors left destitute. A pillar of the community! In Shanghai, who's to say what's legitimate and what's a scam?"

Tolt looked away from van Asselt. "Like I said, my wife and I need to get away..."

"Yes, your desperation is apparent." Van Asselt rapped his

hand on the back of the chair next to where he stood. "Frankly, that's part of what's got me pondering what no-good you may have been up to. Why so hell-bent on getting away from here?"

"It's nothing *I've* been up to, sir. It's the situation. With Japan, that is."

Van Asselt gave him a probing look, but didn't interrupt. "The fact is, well, the Japs... they're planning to attack the United States."

Van Asselt's eyebrows shot up. Said like that, it sounded so bald. Before van Asselt could say anything, Tolt hurried on. "I heard this news direct from a cousin of Tak and Sumiko Takematsu. A Japanese naval officer. He's the chief planner. It will be against the U.S. forces at Pearl Harbor. Once America is at war, there will be nothing holding Japanese forces back from attacking all over Asia. That's why it's so urgent to get a visa, so my wife and I can get away."

Van Asselt's eyebrows could go no higher. He burst out laughing, and leaned on the back of the chair next to him for support as guffaws shook his body.

"Sir, this isn't a joke. I can share more details, but the bottom line is this: Japan has limited reserves of fuel, the U.S. has cut off access to resupply, and Japan is going to seize control of resources elsewhere in Asia."

Van Asselt took a deep breath. "So, you mean to tell me that you — an American, a civilian, a... a Negro, *you* have intelligence about a top-secret Japanese plan to attack the United States?" He shook his head, grinning all the while. "I have to give you credit, Gross. This is the most creative yarn I've yet heard arguing for a visa. And that's saying something…"

"Mr. van Asselt, I assure you, I am not joking. This is deadly serious. I've tried raising the alarm with the U.S. authorities when I was in the States over the summer and…"

"Did they agree with you?"

"Unfortunately, no. But…"

"What about your employer? Mr. Planter, does he agree with you? Why isn't he evacuating?"

"I've not told him of the plan."

"You've not told him?" van Asselt raised an eyebrow.

Even as Tolt could perceive that each word he uttered sounded more preposterous, he pressed on. "No, I haven't. Frankly, given how hard it is to keep information confidential in Shanghai, I have been afraid to speak to anyone here about this matter for fear that my Japanese friends, the Takematsus, would be implicated by their government."

Van Asselt looked perplexed at this.

"As spies," Tolt explained.

"Ah, yes. As spies. Well, in these days of assassination and intrigue that is a convenient catchall, isn't it?"

"Sir, this isn't a scam. I love living here. Truth to tell, being a Negro here is a hell of a lot simpler than in America. I've no wish to leave Shanghai. Be that as it may, the Japs *are* coming. And it'll not go easy on Americans. I don't want to stick around to find out, and I definitely don't want to leave my wife behind. She and I have to leave together."

A glimmer of concern, perhaps even of apprehension, flitted across van Asselt's face, but in an instant it was gone. "Were the situation as you claim," he blustered, "State would be in the midst of evacuating us diplomats and the War Department would be reinforcing the Fourth Marines. But I don't see anything like that happening."

Tolt started to interrupt, but van Asselt raised his hand. "Play the terrified fool all you want. I'm not convinced."

Tolt felt he was sinking. What option was now left?

"Your story that the Japs are going to descend like the

Mongolian hordes may not be convincing, but I'll give you credit for creativity," Van Asselt continued. "It's the best damned scam I've heard. Haven't laughed so hard in months. And a good minstrel show is worth a payment." Van Asselt grinned in a way that combined both odium and false good humor. "So, have you got your wife's passport with you?"

Tolt took a deep breath and pulled the passport from his pocket. Why did getting what he wanted feel like degradation?

"You got it?" Sumiko asked with astonishment, as Tolt entered Mr. Wang's study with her passport open to the page with the visa. Tolt smiled and nodded.

Quentin was with her, but Mr. Wang was nowhere to be seen. In the days since the visa interview, the friends had taken over his office as a sort of command center, trying to figure out how to overcome the challenges of the two exiting China for the States. There was no other place in the house where they could discuss the matters at hand. They continued to apologize each time they saw Mr. Wang for invading his private sanctum, but he urged them not to worry about that. There were more important affairs to attend to.

Quentin had spread passenger steamship brochures on the round table to the side of the room. With the restrictions on U.S. trade with Japan in place, fewer ships were now traversing the Pacific. Quentin was examining alternative routes, trying to assess whether there was a safe one that would avoid the European war. It didn't look like any ships departed until December.

Tolt dropped down onto one of the stools arranged around the table, picked up some of the timetables and shook his head. "December won't work. We need to put on the gas."

Quentin put down the brochures. "Well, what do you suggest?"

Tolt drew out a brochure of his own from inside his jacket. "This..."

The cover showed a bright blue plane next to an image of a globe. Quentin read aloud the copy. "A journey of 8,000 miles in five and a half days!" He placed the brochure on the table. "You're going to *fly*?"

"Why not?" Tolt said. "We got the visa, but talk to the steamship lines about getting passage? All full. So I got to thinking. There's the Clipper service that operates out of Hong Kong. They have a flight to San Francisco once a week. The next one departs this Wednesday."

Quentin grimaced. "That's all well and good, but how do you propose to get to Hong Kong by then?"

"Take the flight service from here to Canton, then take a shuttle boat from Canton down to Hong Kong."

"Are you nuts? Don't you remember last year one of their planes was shot down by the Japs?" Quentin exclaimed. He looked at Sumiko, and then appeared to regret his vehemence. "Not a usual event, but still, but a risk," he added.

Sumiko said nothing.

"You've got the calendar right there and know the variables," said Tolt. "It's not like choices are thick on the ground. If the Japs don't attack until after Christmas, fine, there's likely to be steamship passage we can wrangle. But what if the plan is to attack before the Yanks are eating Thanksgiving turkey?"

Quentin nodded.

"That's why I think we have to take the risk of flying. Plus, everyone we know travels by ship. Via air, it's less likely that we'll see someone who knows her as Sumiko, not Diana."

"Fair point," Quentin conceded. "So, when do you propose to leave?"

"Monday." Tolt again reached into his pocket, extracting an

envelope. "Tickets down to Hong Kong are already booked."

Quentin's face was solemn. Sumiko gripped her hands together. "So, I am going to America after all." Tears filled her eyes. "I know what you are doing is intended for the best, but still I feel like a traitor. The only thing that keeps me from returning to Tokyo is the knowledge that I'm doing what my brother asks." With that, Sumiko rose. "Please excuse me."

Their farewell from the Wang household was moving, and certainly not happy. Mr. Wang rose early to send them off, before the rest of the family were up. As they were standing in the hallway about to put on their coats, he gestured for Tolt, Sumiko and Quentin to join him in the alcove off the main living room where the family's ancestral altar was arranged.

They stood behind him as he lit incense and made three bows to the altar, seeking blessings from the ancestors for their journey. Quentin had previously told Tolt of this tradition observed when a Wang family member went on a long trip or took some eventful action.

Having placed the incense sticks upright in the dish of sand before the candles burning on the altar below an elegant silver Buddha seated in the lotus position, Mr. Wang turned to face them. "Children, may your journey be peaceful and the winds smooth."

Tears streamed down Sumiko's cheeks and, abandoning her identity as a Chinese girl, she gave a deep bow. Tolt started to kneel down, preparing to kowtow. Mr. Wang hastened over and held his elbow, preventing him from doing so. "No, no, my son, there's no need."

Tears sprung into the corners of Tolt's eyes as he looked into Mr. Wang's face. The two men grabbed each other's arms, almost embracing, but not quite. Mr. Wang said, "Stay strong, my son." Tolt nodded.

"All right, sister; it's time," Quentin spoke to Sumiko in an encouraging tone, his hand on her back. And suddenly, there was a bustle of coats, collecting of hand luggage, confirmation that tickets were where they were supposed to be and hustling into the car. Mr. Wang stood under the portico, waving to them as the car drove out of the gate. Tolt felt a wrench. Would he ever return? Would he ever be quite as happy as he had been during this Shanghai interlude?

Tolt turned to Sumiko. "You're shaking," he observed with concern.

She gave a faint smile. "Nerves."

"You weren't this nervous the day of our visa interview!" he tried to joke.

"I suppose I wasn't. Somehow that didn't seem real. But today, well, this does."

Quentin sitting up front next to Driver Li, looked back with a sympathetic smile.

Tolt patted Sumiko's gloved hand. "It's all going to be fine. Just remember what we discussed. You're a new bride, in love, but shy."

Sumiko nodded, her expression tense.

"Try to look happy, but sort of embarrassed or overwhelmed. I'll be the proud husband who speaks for his wife. That way, we'll limit the likelihood of someone noticing that your Mandarin has a Japanese accent, or that you don't know Shanghainese."

"Right." Sumiko took a deep breath and sat up straighter, trying a small smile.

"And try not to bow, unless there are Japanese guards at the airport in which case... well, try to bow as if you're not Japanese."

She took another steadying breath and nodded. "No bowing."

Tolt gave her a reassuring smile, then looked out the car window at the crowded kaleidoscope of Shanghai whizzing past, buildings jumbled together so densely that the whole facades at times seemed about to topple onto the crowds.

This was it. A last look at the place where he had been the happiest. The person he loved best was lost to him, and now the city where he had been so alive would be lost to him too.

Soon, they were pulling up before the semicircular terminal of the Lunghwa Airport. No Japanese military guards were visible at the entrance, but local police were checking people's papers. Abandoning Western etiquette, Tolt went ahead of Sumiko. Wordlessly, he handed over their papers. As the policeman finished reviewing them and was handing them back, the clutch-style handbag Sumiko carried under her arm, slipped and landed on his foot.

Mortified, Sumiko bent down to pick it up, saying in Japanese, "I'm so sorry."

Both Tolt and Quentin froze. As soon the words were out of her mouth, Sumiko flushed, realizing her error. When she stood up, holding the handbag, she gave a bob of her head, saying in Chinese, "Sorry!" and endeavored to appear a Chinese girl who knew only a few Japanese phrases.

"Sister, you are so clumsy! Pay attention," scolded Quentin in Chinese. A faint smirk showed in the policeman's eyes.

She, Tolt and Quentin walked to the terminal with the porters trailing behind bearing their luggage. Sumiko tucked her arm into Tolt's, and he could feel her trembling more than ever. The check-in procedures went smoothly, however, and soon it was time to say farewell to Quentin.

The three had previously agreed that the story they would follow was that Tolt was taking his new bride to the States to visit his family and spend the Christmas and New Year holidays, with the plan to return to Shanghai in the spring. The tone of the send-off would be celebratory and expectant of a speedy return.

Standing not far from the gate leading out to the tarmac, Quentin slapped Tolt on the back and said in a hearty tone, "Well brother, have a good trip and we'll look forward to your return and the big party in the spring!"

Putting his arm around Sumiko he said in a smiling voice, "Sister, enjoy your visit to your new family!"

Both Tolt and Sumiko endeavored to maintain broad smiles and respond in kind. Tolt tucked Sumiko's arm under his and they started towards the departure gate where an agent stood collecting tickets., Both looked over their shoulders to wave to Quentin. He stared at them with fierce intensity, then strode towards them. Sumiko and Tolt stopped, dropping their arms and turned around as Quentin reached out to embrace them.

"Stay strong," he said in a low tone, then released them. "Until spring!"

Tolt gave a nod as they broke apart. He moved towards the gate and didn't look back again. He couldn't look back. His heart was breaking.

17

November 1941

AFTER THE NOVELTY of being on an airplane had subsided, the journey to Canton passed without event. The plane made its hops down the coast, and by the end of the day, they had transferred to a swift boat that carried them down to Kowloon, where they checked in at the Peninsula Hotel. After the bellboy had left, they looked at each other with weary smiles.

"So far so good."

"Yes," Sumiko agreed.

"Look, given that we're man and wife…" Tolt nodded to the rings on Sumiko's left hand. "It would attract attention if we took separate rooms, just know that on this journey, I'll be sleeping on the sofa or the floor."

Sumiko gave a wan smile. "That's thoughtful of you."

Tolt grinned. "A considerate husband is what I aim to be. So, how about we freshen up and go down for some dinner?"

"Being out of China, away from the Japanese army presence, I already feel better. Less nervous. Yes, let's go have dinner and then tonight we'll get a good sleep."

"That's the spirit!"

The next morning was spent at the bank obtaining funds for the Clipper tickets and then on to the Pan American office in the Peninsula lobby to pay for and collect them. After taking care of business and eating a quick lunch, they decided they would each get tidied up before their big trip. Tolt headed off to the Peninsula's barber shop for a shave and Sumiko repaired to the beauty salon for a manicure and to have her hair set.

When they reconvened later in the lobby over the hotel's famous afternoon tea, they admired each other's fresh appearance. "Most elegant, Mrs. Gross. You're a sight for weary eyes."

Sumiko gave a rueful smile, and poured a cup for each of them. "The last few days were so rushed, we haven't had a chance to discuss what happened with Ronnie. What did he say when you told him you had managed to get me a visa and would be leaving for the States?"

"Ah, well...*that* news set off all sorts of gum-flapping. Young Mr. Planter was convinced he had managed to put the kibosh on any idea of my taking you to the States."

Sumiko raised an eyebrow over her teacup. The Clipper was scheduled to depart at 8:30 in the morning, so they retired early to take the coach from the Peninsula to Kai Tak Airport, where they would take the tender out to board the Clipper. Riding to the airport, Tolt sensed that Sumiko was indeed more relaxed than the day before, and he noticed that he was, too. Excitement at the prospect of heading home began to swell in him.

At the airport, they dismounted from the coach with the others who had stayed at "the Pen." They noticed Pan Am officials were speaking to several passengers clustered around them. As they drew near, they caught him saying, "So with our apologies, the Clipper will not be departing today." Tolt and Sumiko gave each other anxious glances.

"What's that?" an older American businessman called out. "I've got an appointment in Honolulu I need to make! The forecast is for fair weather. Why the delay?"

"It is a request from Washington, sir. Our headquarters in New York wired us this morning. Apparently, a senior official is on his way to Washington and we have been told to hold the Clipper to allow him to make the connection."

"Well, where's he coming from? From the hinterlands of China?"

"I'm afraid we cannot say, sir. But later today we'll know whether we'll be taking off tomorrow or the plane will be further delayed."

"Further delayed?" Tolt exclaimed.

"Yes, we're not sure if the official will arrive tonight or not. As soon as we know, we will send word to your hotel."

There was nothing for it but to re-board the coach and return to the Peninsula. The sensation of deflation and anticlimax was overwhelming.

That evening a knock came at the door to their room. Opening it, Tolt found a bellboy bearing a small silver tray with a note. The Clipper would not be departing on Thursday. A thought occurred to Tolt, and he dug into his pocket for some coins. "Here, see if any of today's papers are still available."

After the bellboy departed, Sumiko said, "I'm afraid I don't much feel like going down to dinner. Do you mind if I have something brought up?"

"That's fine. We can have a quiet meal and then if we feel like it, go for a walk."

She smiled wanly. Tolt could tell her earlier anxiety was returning. While she was reviewing the menu and preparing to ring the bell for the floor butler to take their order, the bellboy came back with the *South China Morning Post*. It was a bit wrinkled.

"Sorry, sir. There weren't any fresh ones, but the shoeshine stand had this one left over." Reaching into his pocket, he retrieved the coins Tolt had given him.

Tolt told him to keep them and sat on the sofa while Sumiko conferred with the room service butler. A headline caught his eye: "Japan and US Near Final Showdown: Kurusu Mission May Decide Pacific Issue." The article reported that one of Japan's most respected diplomats, in fact, the man who as ambassador to Germany had signed the Tri-Partite Agreement, was being dispatched to Washington to pursue the withdrawal of trade sanctions. He would fly by Clipper to the U.S. West Coast and then travel to Washington by train.

Tolt set down the paper. A senior Japanese diplomat, perhaps with an entourage, would be flying with them. A multi-day journey cheek-by-jowl with Japanese officials. He wracked his brain trying to remember whether Tak had ever mentioned them having relatives or ties in Japan's diplomatic corps. Would the Takematsus know Kurusu?

"Are you all right?" asked Sumiko.

"Fit as a fiddle," replied Tolt in a somewhat mechanical tone.

"Suddenly you look like you're not feeling well. Do you want to lie down?"

"Well, I may just take a rest. Finish the paper before dinner arrives." Tolt stretched out on the bedspread of the bed in the adjacent room and lifted the paper as if to read it, but in reality, he was contemplating various scenarios that could arise while flying with the Japanese delegation to the United States. He decided to dispose of the paper without Sumiko seeing the headline.

Another day of tedium passed, and on Thursday evening they received word that the long-awaited official had arrived in Hong Kong and the Clipper would depart the following morning.

As they took their seats on the Peninsula coach in the early hours of Friday morning, the same cantankerous American businessman was across from them, complaining in a loud tone to the fellow behind.

"Damned Japs," he said. "It's all fine and well that they want to talk peace, but hell, the wait for this blasted Jap diplomat has blown my schedule to bits."

Sumiko gave Tolt an anxious glance. "Did I understand him correctly? The official who's going to be on the plane with us isn't Chinese or American... he's Japanese?"

Tolt gave a grave nod. "Yes, that's right. The Takematsus don't have any relatives in the foreign service, do they?"

"No."

He gave her gloved hand a squeeze. "Well, that's good then. And remember, we're not in Japan-controlled territory." He looked at her with what he hoped was an encouraging expression. "We'll be traveling on an American plane. And you're a Chinese girl."

In a whisper Sumiko replied, "Yes, but if somehow they realize I'm..."

"Not going to happen," he answered in a low tone. "Let's stick with our plan, Mrs. Gross." Falling back into character, she lowered her head to his shoulder and aimed for a relaxed air of sleepiness.

The coach arrived at Kai Tak aerodrome and they passed through customs and immigration procedures, then their luggage was whisked away by boat to be stowed aboard the plane. Soon the flight crew arrived and they walked along the jetty to see the aircraft bobbing in the water. Tolt and Sumiko scanned the waiting area for Japanese officials but saw only a scattering of mostly Western businessmen. As they walked down the jetty, Sumiko gripped Tolt's arm and he patted her hand.

Waiting for their turn to board, they saw a group of people arriving behind them. They were led by an Asian man in his fifties, dressed in a dapper but conservative manner, and accompanied by a younger man who appeared to be his assistant. Several men in suits, whose bearing suggested they were military trailed behind. Tolt looked down at Sumiko who had turned as pale as the white handkerchief in Tolt's breast pocket.

"What is it?"

She shook her head, pressing her lips together and casting her face down. Tolt figured it must be nerves. As it happened, only two men boarded the Clipper, their escort remaining behind. Tolt and Sumiko boarded the plane, and a steward showed them to their loveseat-width places. On the other side of the cabin the Japanese diplomats were occupying two single seats facing each other across a table. The elder man nodded in their direction and Tolt nodded back, but Sumiko's face was so downturned that he doubted she had even noticed the courtesy by their fellow passenger.

Through the first couple of hours of the flight, Sumiko remained sunken into their seat, her eyes and face focused either straight ahead of her or downward. She wouldn't even look at Tolt. When the steward came around to offer refreshments, he inquired whether Mrs. Gross was feeling ill. She shook her head, but her demeanor didn't change. Eventually, the steward called the passengers to take lunch in the adjoining cabin. Tolt counted fourteen passengers. Fortunately, they were given the only table for two and the Japanese were seated at the table farthest from theirs. Sumiko ate little, but Tolt found the food quite tasty. After lunch was cleared away, a steward showed passengers wishing to take a rest to a rear cabin fitted with Pullman rail car-type sleeping berths. Tolt and Sumiko returned to their seats, while the senior Japanese diplomat availed himself of the washroom. His assistant took the opportunity to stretch his legs, walking back and forth along the length of the plane's central aisle.

Taking advantage of their absence, Sumiko gripped Tolt's hand with an intensity that surprised him. In an urgent tone, she whispered, "It's Ambassador Kurusu!"

Tolt nodded. "Yes, he's the diplomat the Japanese government is sending to Washington."

"You don't understand. I met him once."

"What?"

The roar of the engines made holding a quiet conversation difficult. Sumiko strove to speak so as to make Tolt understand her while not alerting their neighbors.

She leaned on his shoulder as if sharing affectionate words. "In Berlin. I visited family friends on my way back from Switzerland. While I was there, the embassy held several receptions and luncheons welcoming him, and I was invited."

"Did you speak with him?"

"Yes, several times. Including at a small luncheon where I was seated across from him."

She looked at Tolt with fear in her eyes. "What if he..."

"Don't think of it. Just be Diana. Act how she would act."

Sumiko nodded. The steward walked past them, and she called out, "Steward, please! I'm feeling much better now. A little tomato juice, thank you."

Tolt grinned at how the mandate to behave like Diana was acted out. The two men, returning to the cabin gazed at the steward addressing the lady's request, but seemed to find it unremarkable.

After they had retaken their seats and were settled, Sumiko again leaned into Tolt's ear. "Did you know it was Ambassador Kurusu we were waiting for?"

Tolt nodded. "Yeah, the newspaper mentioned his name." Sumiko compressed her lips, but said nothing, as she accepted the glass of tomato juice from the steward .

During the long and tedious flight from Hong Kong to Manila, then on to Guam and Wake Island, Kurusu was mostly preoccupied by his briefing materials and ignored the passengers around him. Again and again, Tolt reconsidered the various discussions he and Takeda had had, trying to weigh whether and when the plan for attacking Honolulu was likely to be activated.

He hoped the fact that Kurusu was on the plane meant it would not be, but also recognized that Kurusu's mission might simply be a diversion. He wondered if Takeda had surmised what had happened to Sumiko. If so, was he looking for her or, preoccupied by his duties, had he given up? He shied away from thinking of Tak, hoping he was all right. His head ached with the incessant roar of the plane's engines and the thrum of his thoughts.

As the plane bounced down upon the light blue waters inside the reef at Wake, Sumiko whispered, "What a relief! We're getting closer."

Tolt squeezed her hand. "Can't wait to be on the ground in Honolulu," he whispered back.

Before disembarking, the captain stood at the doorway of the cabin and with a sober expression announced, "Folks, sorry to tell you this, but we need to have some work done on the plane before we can head onward. The control tower has also advised that a weather system is approaching. If it doesn't veer off before our repairs are complete, we may need to wait awhile."

"How long, Captain?" asked Kurusu's aide.

"I'm afraid we really don't know. But not to worry, the Pan American hotel here is quite comfortable and the water makes for pleasant swimming. So, enjoy the break and we'll update you as we know more."

Sumiko and Tolt looked at each other in dismay. They followed behind Kurusu and his aide as the passengers made their way onto the dock where the Clipper was tied up.

A day passed. And another. The stress of being cut off from the world, stuck on a tiny island in the middle of the Pacific Ocean weighed heavily. Finally, on the third day they departed for Midway, near to which they would cross the international dateline. As the Clipper gathered speed and prepared to take off from Wake, Tolt could feel his stress easing a bit. Hours later upon approach to Midway, the steward moved around the cabin instructing the passengers to close the shades on the Clipper's passenger windows.

"What's with the hocus-pocus on the curtains?" asked the businessman who had complained about the delay in Hong Kong. "You got a magic show planned for us?"

"No, sir. No magic show today, I'm afraid. The Army and Navy have installations on Midway. We're required to maintain black-out as we approach and take-off."

"Well, that's good to know, my man. Good to know our military has us protected in case of, in case of…" The passenger looked over towards Kurusu and seemed to rethink how to formulate his comment, "any need."

Upon disembarkation, the passengers were shown to the Pan Am hotel, whose lobby was furnished with comfortable rattan armchairs and sofas. The hotel manager explained they were free to swim in the water in front of the hotel, but could not go beyond the fence that had been installed around the hotel's rear and sides. The ten-hour wait was tedious, but Tolt felt grateful that at least this time there was no delay. They set off for Honolulu without incident and landed late on the following day, November 12.

While at Midway, Tolt had arranged for a telegram to be sent ahead to Jimmy. As the plane circled the blue waters of Waikiki, Sumiko sat up in her seat peering out, exclaiming at the beauty of the scene. From the glimpses Tolt could catch, he agreed with her. Immediately to the west of downtown lay the huge naval yards of Pearl Harbor, occupied by an array of vessels. The plane landed farther to the west on the waters of the Middle Loch of the Pearl City Peninsula.

An extensive web of docks jutted out from the land and the Clipper bobbed gently towards them. Once tied up, the air ship's passengers disembarked for customs inspection. That procedure completed, they could walk across the docks to the landing where the press corps were waiting in full force to greet Kurusu, eager to ask about his plans to break the diplomatic impasse. Tolt, holding onto Sumiko's hand, slipped behind Kurusu, and past the reporters to where he saw Jimmy waiting.

Jimmy reached out his hand to shake Tolt's, and grabbed Tolt's other arm. "Man, is it good to see you!"

Tolt wanted to reply, but found the words clogging his throat as his eyes suddenly teared up. Sumiko smiled as she stood next to them.

"Manners, son," Jimmy teased. "What would Ping say? Do the introductions!"

On the long flight, Tolt had already decided that to lessen the risk of betraying Sumiko's identity, even with Jimmy he would introduce her as Diana Gross.

Maintaining a happy demeanor was a challenge when he thought about who should have been traveling with him as Diana Gross. But Sumiko had just spent several days pretending to be a different person and a different nationality, enclosed in a tight space, just four feet from a man who had known her as a Japanese citizen. His acting efforts ought to at least match hers.

"Jimmy, I'm pleased to present my wife, the beautiful Diana Gross. Diana, this is my oldest and best buddy, Jimmy Johnson."

Sumiko reached out her hand to shake Jimmy's and he gave

hers a hearty shake. "Welcome, Mrs. Gross! You're going to have your hands full with this fella, but we'll have plenty of time to talk about that!"

Sumiko smiled. "It's a pleasure to meet you, Jimmy. Tolt has told me about your adventures when you two were small."

"Well, let's hope he hasn't told you too much!"

"Partner, self-interest has preserved your good name!" Tolt replied.

"Let's get your bags and get you to your hotel for a rest. You must be tired and hungry," Jimmy observed, waving to a porter. "Where you staying, anyway?"

"The Royal Hawaiian."

Jimmy let out a low whistle. "You're doing things up right!"

Tolt put his arm around Sumiko and smiled. "I hope so."

Jimmy walked over to a woman whose arms were laden with a variety of leis. "Gotta get you welcomed proper," he said over his shoulder. He slipped the vendor some money and took a lei for each of Tolt and Sumiko. Sumiko bent her head down for him to put it around her neck, breathing in the flowers' fragrance.

The two friends grinned at each other as Jimmy prepared to put Tolt's lei around his neck.

"Man, it's good to see you. And I never expected you'd be giving me flowers!" Tolt joked.

"It's so's when we old codgers, you can rib me," Jimmy replied.

By the time they left the Clipper's moorage site, darkness had descended, so views were limited, but it was clear they were in a different world. As they drove towards downtown, the combination of the sea air and the fragrance of the tropical flowers made a potent and attractive welcoming perfume. Tolt felt some of his anxiety dissipate.

With the new cars, big buildings, wide roads and bustling

downtown, they could have been in Los Angeles. Honolulu looked and felt like America and that was a relief. He was also reunited with his oldest buddy. Tolt resolved to be positive.

At the Royal Hawaiian's registration desk, the clerk asked, "You're with the Clipper, correct? Just one night."

"Yes, just landed on the Clipper, but not sure just yet how long we'll stay. Can we keep it open-ended?"

"Yes, certainly, Mr. Gross." Sumiko's forehead wrinkled with surprise at this exchange, but she refrained from comment until they had bid goodnight to Jimmy and been escorted by the bellboy to their room.

As Tolt was shrugging off his jacket, she asked, "Why aren't we checking out tomorrow to join the Clipper?"

Fiddling with the room key in his trousers pocket, Tolt considered how much to explain. "Let's sit down and talk," he said, gesturing to the sofa.

After both were seated, Tolt looked at Sumiko and smiled. "We made it!"

She gave a tentative smile.

Tolt rushed on, "I mean, we're not yet on the mainland, but you saw the cars, the street signs, the people — we're in the good ole' U.S. of A.!"

"It doesn't yet seem real." Sumiko paused. "Do you... Would it be all right... now that we're in Honolulu... tomorrow can we send a telegram to my parents to let them know I'm all right? And, and... maybe they will reply with word on how my brother is."

"Sure! First thing in the morning," Tolt answered with what he hoped was reassuring confidence.

"But the Clipper leaves tomorrow, and they said they're temporarily on an every-other-week schedule. I thought we were trying to get to Seattle as soon as possible?"

"I don't know. Seeing Jimmy, the fresh air — it occurred to me that we don't have to be in a rush. Now that we're here in U.S. territory, that is." Sumiko still looked perplexed. "It's been a tough few weeks. Maybe it would be good to relax a bit, just take it easy."

"So, we're going to be tourists?"

"Yes, that's the idea. Just a couple of young, honeymooning tourists, taking in the tropical scene."

"It certainly is a lot more peaceful than either Tokyo or Shanghai. And sitting in front of Ambassador Kurusu all those hours! Awful." She tightened her shoulders as if feeling a wave of chill. "I feel so much safer away from them. Maybe not being on the plane with them tomorrow is a good idea."

"Good! Then let's get some rest tonight. Tomorrow we'll send that telegram and then explore."

"Man, you hold your cards tight. Could have toppled me over with a feather when I found out you got hitched."

Tolt smiled. He and Jimmy were talking in low tones so as not to wake Sumiko who had turned in to sleep after dinner, while they sat out on the balcony overlooking the moonlit beach, listening to the surf as they sipped their beers.

"You next?" he asked.

"Not me, son. I've got things to do, places to see. Got to get some labels slapped on my traveling trunk 'afore I sign up for that duty." Jimmy took a swallow of his beer. "How long it take you to make the decision to take the plunge anyway?"

Looking over his shoulder, to confirm the light was out in the bedroom, Tolt spoke in a low voice. "If you only knew..." Taking a deep breath, he recounted the whole story.

As he surreptitiously wiped the corners of his eyes upon finishing the tale of Diana's death, Jimmy gave him a probing look. "Any other fella sitting here telling me this tale, I'd be saying 'mister, there's nothing to the bear but his curly hair,' but damn, we go back. I know you ain't sending me." He gave a snort, shook his head, puzzling over what he had just heard.

"Yeah, well, I gotta say, when Takeda first laid his Pearl Harbor scheme on me, I figured I'd leave Uncle Sam to his own devices. Why stick my neck out for him and his nephews?"

Jimmy guffawed, then took a swallow of his beer.

"But then Papa forwarded a postcard from you."

"From *me*?"

"Yeah, announcing you had done signed up. And been posted here. Well, that changed the game." Tolt took a swig of his own beer. "Made it personal." He set down the bottle and looked at Jimmy. "Couldn't leave my buddy hanging in the wind, without at least trying to sound the alarm."

"Yeah, well, how's that working?"

"Not so good. In August, I thought I had a chance, but no dice. As recently as last week in Shanghai, it was more of the same. Does the Navy seem to be getting ready for something? Is security tighter?"

"I'm in the Navy, but that likker you drinking makes you forget. To them we's just zigaboos. Me? I'm in the galley cooking for the Man. Only thing he's telling *me* is how he likes them thousand on a plate. Military strategy ain't in the mix."

"Sure, but I also know you're smart. Besides ladling out the baked beans, what d'ya see going on down at the base? Are they practicing maneuvers? Getting stricter about granting leave?"

"So far's I can tell, it's business as usual. Officers playing their golf. They've got us cooking up fare for their parties. They planning a Christmas party. Sure, they got their war games and such, but it's no different now than it was."

"What's the highest rank of an officer you know?"

Jimmy guffawed.

"Shhh!" Tolt looked over his shoulder.

"Sorry, man. It's just that that time in Shanghai — well, it really must have turned your head. The Man ain't interested in talking with some jarhead like yours truly. You done forgot about that when you was over there?" Jimmy chuckled, then tilted his beer bottle back for a swig.

"Nah, I know how things rate. I also know *you*. And knowing you, you've probably sized up some high-ranking Mister Charlie and figured out how things work in his outfit."

"Well, now's you mention it, there is this one fella…"

Tolt's eyes crinkled with a smile as he asked. "What about him?"

"Well, I heard tell he was born in Peking, his daddy was a missionary or some such. So, one day, he comes through the galley, talking to the chief of the mess, going on about how he wants to serve a special Chinese meal for some holiday. When was it? Oh, yeah… last winter, for Chinese New Year. Yeah, so, he's saying he wants to do a special supper, and asking the chief who he's got on the staff who could cook some Chinese chow."

Jimmy grinned and tossed the cap from his beer bottle in the air, drawing out his tale. "Well, the chief, he's scratching his head and looking around, eyeing all them Filipinos we got in there and figuring out how he's going to come up with a Chinese meal. So, me, I go ahead and says, "Sir, I know how to cook some Chinese dishes.""

A grin suffused Jimmy's face at the memory. Adopting the deep disapproving voice of the mess chief, he continued, "Boy, I'm talking to Captain Foster here. Don't be acting the fool."

"But see, that Captain, now he's kinda curious. After all, what kind of fool Negro is gonna claim he know how to cook Chinese? Mighty risky to be soft-soaping an officer. So, he says, all somber, but kind of fatherly like, 'Son, you want to tell us what you're thinking?'

Jimmy started guffawing at the memory of his triumph. "I took on my best handkerchief-head voice and says, 'Captain, sir, I ain't bull-skating. An old Pekingese I knew coming up taught me how to make them Chinese dumplings.' Well, he basically let it be known that I best not be peeping through my likkers, or he'd send me to the back side of Beluthahatchie. Then he said he wanted some for dinner that night!"

"And?"

"What do you mean 'and'? I made 'em. 'Course I got Ping's recipes down cold, man. You know that!"

"So, what'd the captain say?"

"Say? He didn't have to *say* nothing. Too busy scarfing them things down, in between swallowing his beer. 'Rounds about the second plateful, he finally got to saying how's he hadn't had something that good since the last time he went to China. I ain't woofing man, he was seriously happy."

Tolt shook his head, smiling at the vision of Jimmy's telling a naval officer he knew how to make Chinese dumplings. "Wait 'til I tell Ping his dumplings are making friends all over the world."

In a more serious tone, Tolt added, "Best would be if you could get leave and head back with me to Seattle."

Jimmy grimaced. "How much of these suds you been sucking down? The chances of my getting leave on short notice are even lower than Veronica Planter giving you a welcome home party!" He rubbed his chin. "Say, what does Diana — or is it Sumiko? What does she say about all this?"

"Diana — stick with Diana." Tolt looked down at the dregs in his beer. "This part, well, she doesn't know about."

"What part?"

"About the plan to attack Honolulu. About Takeda. She knows

he was the one driving the car that hit... hit Diana. And that Tak tried to stop him, but she thinks it's because Takeda wanted to marry her and her brother refused that these things happened. She doesn't know that Takeda was working on an operation to attack U.S. and her brother and I were trying to stop it."

Jimmy gave a low whistle, took another swallow of his beer, but said nothing. Knowing his friend, Tolt sensed a critique in Jimmy's eyes. "What should I have done? Here things still seem normal and this sounds all crazy, I know. But Americans don't understand how powerful the military is in Japan. If I had told her..."

Tolt struck the arm of his chair. "People are terrified of being seen as disloyal over the least little thing... hell, women in Tokyo don't even dare to wear their nice clothes anymore because they want to seem like they are sacrificing for the country's war effort, much less openly discussing anything critical of the government or the military."

Jimmy listened, his face impassive. "Attacking a member of the military, let alone trying to kill a respected officer, a war hero — well, that doesn't just doom the fool who dares, it screws his entire family as well. Poor kid. She's lost her family, her country, her name. Telling her about Takeda's plan just seemed like one more burden."

"Fair enough," Jimmy shrugged. "You the one there." He set his bottle down on the side table and stood up. "But you tell me she converted to Roman Catholic. Them Catholics got this guilt thing down. If she thinks her brother and Diana bought the Big Sleep on account of her, that's some heavy load she's carrying."

He stretched, looked at his watch. "Time to be shoving off."

Tolt took in Jimmy's observation about Sumiko but didn't address it. "Today's the thirteenth. Thanksgiving is in two weeks. It wouldn't surprise me if the attack came then." Tolt stood up too. "Yamamoto, he's the top guy who put Takeda to work on this project, he lived in the U.S. for a while. He'll know that's a big holiday for us. If they're going to use surprise, what bigger surprise could there be than to attack while we're tucking into our turkey?"

After seeing Jimmy off, Tolt returned to the sitting room and found Sumiko, standing with her arms crossed over her chest and an angry glare on her face. "I'm sorry. I didn't mean to wake you," he offered.

"What have you not told me?" she asked.

"We tried to be quiet, but I guess it got louder than I thought."

Sumiko shook her head, impatient. "I want to know what you meant about my cousin, about Japan. You said something about an attack." She pulled her robe closer around her, re-crossed her arms and glared, waiting for a response.

"It's late. Let's rest. In the morning I can explain."

She shook her head. "You can't mean Japan intends to attack America? That can't be true, can it? You told me we were going to stay here for a few days to rest. What's really going on?"

Tolt took a deep breath, trying to think of how to respond, what to say. He closed his eyes for a moment, seeing Tak in the hospital, the anguish in his eyes. "Let's sit down," he said in what he hoped was an encouraging tone, and gestured towards the sofa. With a wary expression on her face, Sumiko sat.

Tolt sat angled towards her, his hands pressed on his knees, his head turned down while gathering his thoughts. "I'm not sure where to begin." Looking up, he said, "How to explain without sounding crazy. I'll try. If it does sound crazy, please know that your brother knew all of this and we shared the same conclusions."

Sumiko waited. There was nothing for it, but to retell the story he had just shared with Jimmy. By the time Tolt's tale had been told, the moon was low in the sky. The litany of losses left him feeling empty.

Still on the sofa, Sumiko looked at him, tears streaming down her face. "My poor brother." Then anger flashed again in her eyes. "But I am still angry with you. *And* with him."

Startled by her vehemence, Tak asked, "Angry at Tak? Why?"

"Because you two treated me like a child. You didn't tell me these things as we were leaving Japan. You didn't tell me them when we were waiting in Shanghai. You didn't tell me Kurusu was the diplomat who was going to be on the Clipper. Even now, you wouldn't have told me about Takeda's attack plans, here on this silly pretend honeymoon, this... pretend happiness, except I overheard you speaking of them." Her face reddened.

Tolt was silent, but finally conceded, "That's true." Feeling defensive, he added, "But what difference would it have made? What could you have done to change the situation? It's not like anyone would have listened."

Sumiko's eyes flashed and when she spoke, her voice had a harsh vehemence that Tolt had never before heard her use. "Listen to the words coming from your mouth! It's the same way people have been treating you: because you're Negro, no one will listen. And yet you and my brother decided no one will listen to *me* because I'm a girl. But how do you know your assumption is even true? You never gave me the chance."

"Well, what could you have done?" he asked. "How could you — a civilian, a woman — have stopped Commander Hajime Takeda of His Imperial Majesty's Navy?"

Sumiko twisted to her mouth in an expression of disgust. "I'm not so foolish as to think I could have stopped my cousin from fulfilling his duty as an officer."

She took a deep breath, as if to calm herself. "But that day, the day that Diana died, if at my parents' house you had told me all of this, I would have suggested a different path. I would have offered to go to Takeda, to tell him that if he agreed to protect my brother, to say it was all an accident, I would have married him."

"But that's exactly what your brother *didn't* want to have happen! He didn't want you to sacrifice yourself."

"I will explain," she said with a level gaze.

Tolt pressed his lips together, holding back the words crowding to spill out. Sumiko continued in the same calm, analytical tone she used explaining how to select winning greyhounds. "I would have told my cousin I would marry him if my brother went free. And after he was free, I would have urged you two to flee — to come to the United States. For you to bring my brother here instead of me." Tolt's face took on a puzzled expression, but he didn't interrupt.

"If the two of you together went to speak to the U.S. government, with Tak explaining our family's background, our business interests and reputation, our relationship to Takeda and Takeda's plans, surely, someone would have given the matter some serious consideration."

Tolt continued to hold his tongue as Sumiko went on. "We can't know the outcome, but between the two of you, I suspect you could have persuaded them to think about defensive measures."

Tolt knew there was logic in her analysis. He had forgotten his pronouncement at the Canidrome. "If we take Sumiko's advice, we can't lose." Now it came back to him, bringing with it an encircling blanket of cold defeat.

He looked into her eyes, this time with tears streaming down his cheeks. "You're right. We should have confided in... forget it. I'm not going to drag Tak into this. *I* should have told you. What a fool I've been." Tolt frowned. "But now that you know, now that you are here, what do you suggest? What do you think we should do?"

It was Sumiko's turn to pause, then said in a slow but steady voice, "Here, there is nothing we can do. You saw the streets today, so tidy, clean and peaceful."

She gestured above. "The sky so blue, everything filled with light, the trade winds making life feel fresh and comfortable. The news you bring is like a horror story. It will seem fantastic, unreal."

"But Jimmy — tonight I spoke with Jimmy. There's this senior captain he knows. I...."

Sumiko shook her head.

"At this point, the best choice is for me to go back to Japan, to say you forced me to go with you, and try to appease Takeda so as to protect my family. Tomorrow we must check the schedule for the next west-bound Clipper."

Tolt marveled at Sumiko's calm dissection of the situation. As much as he disliked the solutions she offered, he found he couldn't devise an argument to challenge them. They were back at the dog track with her placing winning bets based on factors no one else could see.

Sumiko's analysis was right. What had he done? Recognizing he had been outclassed, he answered, "All right. Write out what you want to put in the telegram to your folks and I'll get it sent tonight. Then let's get some rest, and in the morning, we'll look into booking your ticket."

The next morning, Tolt woke before Sumiko. Letting her rest, he slipped downstairs for a walk on the still-quiet beach. By the time he had enjoyed a coffee at the hotel's coffee shop, the sun was up and bright. He figured Sumiko was sure to be awake and entering their room, he saw her sitting outside on the balcony. He dropped his jacket over the sofa, taking in the crystalline blue sky framed by palm trees, with wafts of balmy air gusting cotton-like comforting warmth. A telegram lay on Sumiko's lap, and he noticed her eyes gazing out to the ocean, seemingly not registering what was before her. Tolt picked up the telegram, which bore handwritten *katakana* script over the dots typed onto the paper.

"Your folks have already replied! What did they say?"

Taking the telegram from Tolt, in a toneless voice Sumiko read aloud, "The third gallery has been destroyed by fire. The loss of our treasures is devastating, but a relief your luggage is safe. No need to hurry back."

Tolt was bewildered. "What gallery?"

Saying nothing, Sumiko picked up a pencil resting on the newspaper crossword Tolt had been working on, which he had left on the small balcony table. In the margin, she wrote four *Kanji* characters: "三郎" and "三廊". Pointing to the first two characters, she said, "These are the characters for my brother's name Saburo. The second character means young man." Gesturing to the second pair of characters, the pencil circled the '廊' character. "This character is pronounced the same way but is written slightly differently. It means gallery, as in corridor."

She pointed to the telegram. "My parents mean my brother is dead, but they dare not say so by his name."

She slumped back in her chair, tears rolled down her cheeks. Tolt lowered himself into the other chair, still clutching the telegram. Now it was his turn to turn unseeing eyes to the sea. He thought back to when he had taken leave of Tak at the hospital. A wash of other memories then cascaded in — Tak greeting him on the first day of law school, jitterbugging at the UW's Asian Student socials, competing with Quentin and Tolt to see who could eat the most of Ping's dumplings, smiling at Tolt while he made sushi.

How could he be gone?

When Tolt had left the hospital, Tak had warned that stopping Takeda was impossible, and that they should simply focus on saving those they loved. It was too late for Sumiko's return to save Tak. Diana was gone. Japan could attack at any time. Had he erred in lingering in Hawaii?

He took her hand, which was cold to the touch. "Your parents are telling you not to return. If you do, it will only add to their pain."

She shut her eyes, and tears continued to seep out of them, tracing down her cheeks until they dropped onto the collar of her dress.

"I know you want to be with them, but your brother would want you to escape. I think that's what your parents want too."

She compressed her mouth, her shoulders shook.

"Please don't go back to Asia yet. Come with me to the mainland."

Sumiko nodded, rubbing her cheeks with her free hand.

Trying to sound resolute, Tolt said, "Good! I'll book us passage." He went inside, phoning the front desk to make the necessary adjustments.

After hanging up, Tolt lay down onto the sofa. A heavy, heavy weight was crushing his chest. Tak was gone.

Had this all been for nothing? Tolt admitted to himself that by now, he feared the absence of attack almost more than what the attack he believed was coming. What if he had led Sumiko down a path of increased danger for nothing? What if Tak had died for naught? What if Sumiko had sacrificed all for a phantom risk? Diana dead, Sumiko's parents alone without either of their children. What misery had he wrought?

He reminded himself that Diana's death came at Takeda's hand, and now Tak's death was a further indication that the risks were not imagined. Still, doubt nagged at him. After all, wasn't Kurusu now on the scene in Washington? Would political considerations calm the military tensions? He yearned to be back at Our House. The comfort that had once seemed stultifying now beckoned urgently. He couldn't wait to board the Clipper for San Francisco.

18

LATE NOVEMBER 1941

"Are you certain about staying?" Sumiko asked one last time as they stood again on the Pan Am pier. This time there was no scrum of journalists, only passengers accompanied by family, or a few tourist visitors being escorted by hotel staff. "You said you were done trying."

Tolt picked at a loose flower petal that had dislodged from the lei around Sumiko's neck onto her jacket, "Yes, I did. But then... well, there's Jimmy."

He grimaced, and she took his hand. "I'm going to see if he can get me a meeting with his captain. I showed you the news that the Fourth Marines will withdraw from Shanghai; maybe that means they'll be more willing to listen to what I have to say."

She nodded. Tolt's was a dilemma she knew only too well. He smiled encouragingly. "Now when the train finally drops you in Seattle, remember that Ping isn't nearly as fierce as he looks. You'll have Sato eating out of your hand in no time, and Papa... well, he's going to love having a granddaughter."

They embraced, then Sumiko turned to head down the pier, towards the bobbing silver Clipper, waiting to whisk her to San Francisco. Tolt stood staring until the Clipper had taken off, remembering Tak, pining for Diana, heart aching at the loss of two so dear. If he really believed what Takeda had told him, he had to try one last time. Not for the government, not for his fellow citizens, but for Jimmy. November 17, ten days until Thanksgiving. Could he get the Navy to take the risk of imminent attack from Japan seriously?

***

"Whaddya say? Whip up a pot of dumplings, then ask him if he'd be willing to speak with a buddy of yours who's just returned from China and Japan?"

Jimmy shook his head. "You don't quit, do you?" Tolt grinned and shrugged his shoulders.

Jimmy frowned. "Didn't I tell you to get on that silver bird winging its way to San Fran? You really do think you are that Chevalier de Saint-whatever, and I'm some damsel you're going to rescue? Shit." He shook his head.

"C'mon. There's got to be a way for me to talk to someone with some rank. Someone who could get the top brass's attention. What've you got?"

Jimmy sighed. "This evening I'm on duty. I'll go in early, make up a mess of Chinese dumplings for Captain Foster. Don't know that he'll take the bait, but I'll try."

Foster surveyed the well-dressed, poised young man standing before his desk. A Negro telling him as if it were the most natural thing in the world of a secret plan by Japan to attack the naval base at Pearl Harbor. Sure, he sounded convincing, but it was so incongruous. Top secret intelligence coming from a person of a type usually associated with the most ill-educated laboring forces? Was he on the level? He appeared sincere. His explanation that he had recently returned from working in China and Japan as a result of long-time family connections, was believable. It seemed possible that he might have had access to such on-the-ground information. Of course, the Navy was worried about the deterioration in Japanese-American relations. They were already identifying reliable citizens in the community who could assist if a military emergency arose. But still — the idea that an officer in the Imperial Navy would leak such sensitive data to a civilian, much less a foreign national? It stretched credulity. Perhaps the young fellow was genuinely well-intentioned but had misapprehended what he had heard. Captain Foster reflected on all this as he twirled his fountain pen in his hand, his expression neutral as he listened.

Finally, Tolt paused and Foster asked, "So, you and young Johnson grew up together, eh?"

"Yes, sir. We've known each other since we were in elementary school."

"Johnson tells me you speak Chinese and Japanese, but you were born in America, correct?"

"That's right, sir. I was born in Seattle. There was a handyman from Japan and a cook from China at the hotel my grandfather runs. They were both proud of their heritage. Teaching me about their country, language and culture was the arena in which they competed, so I had teachers eager to make sure I learned."

Foster rested his elbow on the arm of his chair. "As Johnson has probably told you, I know something of China myself." He pointed to a photograph of a man wearing clerical garb, on a bookshelf next to the desk. "My father served as a missionary in Shantung; I was born in Peking and lived in China until my parents sent me home for high school. Was last there in 1930, when I served the naval attaché to our embassy in Nanking. Damned shame what the Japs have gotten up to since '37. But try as they might, they don't seem to be making much progress."

He settled deeper in his chair. "Fact of the matter is, the last several years, they've been pretty bogged down. Of course, they are now allied with the Huns and the Italians. With Germany occupying France, they've thrown some crumbs to the Japs, given them right to station troops in French-Indochina, so I suppose that's to the good as far as the Jap view of things goes." he continued twirling his fountain pen. "Given all they've already got on their plate tho', it's hard to believe they'd be fool enough to start a war with *us*," he said in a reflective tone. "But perhaps that Kurusu fellow who's just come through on the Clipper is meant to try to convince us of that possibility. Give 'em some negotiating leverage. Maybe Mr. Roosevelt would change his mind and allow oil and such to be sold to them."

Foster set the pen down and looked at Tolt.The phone on Foster's desk began to ring. He pressed a button, the sound stopped. Tolt tried to ignore the interruption. "...when I asked Takeda how he could dare to tell me — a civilian, a foreigner — about such a sensitive plan, he laughed. He said he knows that in America, Negroes are not respected, so even if I tried to tell, no one would believe me."

Foster gazed at Tolt with a raised eyebrow, but did not interrupt or contradict him. It occurred to Tolt that this detail was validating to Foster, which was both reassuring and depressing.

He plowed on. "As of March, Takeda made clear the attack wasn't a foregone conclusion. Continued access to key industrial materials like fuel, was vital and with those things secure, Japan would have no need to attack. But if Japan's strategic supplies were threatened, then his plan would be invoked."

Foster's face assumed a thoughtful expression. Sensing he was making an impression, Tolt carried on. "Over the summer, after trade sanctions were imposed by the U.S., I saw Takeda again and he told me it would be wise to leave Asia and head home. In August, the oil embargo began. Now it's almost December, and Japan's has probably used up over eighty per cent of its oil supplies. That suggests an attack is likely any day, almost surely before year's end."

"Hmmm, perhaps."

Foster stood, signaling the interview was over.

"Let me run this up the flagpole, see if it is consistent with any other intel coming in. If I need more, I'll come back to you. Staying at the Royal Hawaiian, are you?"

Tolt confirmed that was the case and withdrew, hoping the discussion would do some good.

Tuesday passed. Wednesday came and went. Nothing. As the sun rose on Thanksgiving morning, Tolt woke feeling tense. He listened for any unusual sounds. Only the waves and birds; all seemed normal. Was this going to be the day? The hours passed with Tolt so on edge that the act of chewing his Thanksgiving dinner felt like prying open a stiff can. When after dinner, someone set off fireworks down the road from the Royal Hawaiian, he just about jumped out of his skin. By the time Friday rolled around, Tolt's fingernails were ragged from his nervous gnawing and his foot had been tapping so hard it seemed likely he'd worn down the leather on his shoe.

All week, Jimmy had been on duty on the *West Virginia*, unable to take calls. It was Saturday morning before he was able to get away to meet with Tolt. Almost before Jimmy took his seat at the drugstore where they had agreed to meet for lunch, Tolt asked, "Foster said he'd follow up. Have you heard anything?"

"Hold your horses. My stomach's flapping so hard I can't hear myself talk. Let's get some chow coming!" After placing their orders, Jimmy turned to his friend. "As a matter of fact, yesterday Foster did call me in to discuss an idea." Jimmy's voice took on an amused tone. "Damned Chief of Mess almost wet himself when the sailor came down to the galley with a message for me to visit the Captain!"

Tolt's fingers perched on the edge of the formica table, his expression expectant. Jimmy laughed so hard he started to cough. When Jimmy regained his breath, he continued, "'Course I went right up. When Foster was done telling me what's what, he dropped a nugget about my buddy, 'that young Tolt Gross.' Yeah, you made quite the impression, son."

Tolt's hopes surged. "What'd he say?"

Jimmy made an attempt at imitating Foster's voice. "Well, Johnson, I passed your friend Gross's concerns on to the State Department and to ONI."

"What's ONI?"

In Jimmy's normal voice, he answered, "Office of Naval Intelligence."

"Oh yeah. Those guys."

Resuming his Foster impression, Jimmy continued in a pompous-sounding tone. "Got a couple of messages back. The State Department says the Sino-Korean People's League has informants here, including a Korean working in the Jap consulate. That Korean told the League he's seen blueprints of the above-water and below-water installations at Pearl Harbor, spread out on the consul's desk. The League's been saying the Japs are preparing to attack. This League agent keeps pestering the State Department, but they've concluded it's just a bunch of worked-up colonials, trying to engineer the overthrow of their masters."

"What? He said that?"

"You think I'm making this mess up? Then Foster, he picked up a piece of paper from his desk and says to me…" Here Jimmy used a menu as a prop and resumed his Foster voice. "Both ONI and State indicate part of the Kurusu mission and the Japs' diplomatic initiative is to spread disinformation and generate anxiety about imminent war, so as to get American public opinion to urge the President to accommodate Japan's demands."

"Yeah, sure. But still..."

"Hold the phone. Then the Captain started to get all red in the face. Won't look at me; just lookin' down at his notes, and says that 'according to ONI, for some years now, the Japs have engaged in propaganda efforts directed at your people, the, uh, Negroes to... uh, well, prey upon your sympathies, your potential dissatisfactions with your status, to support Japan's positions about overthrowing Anglo-Saxon dominance.' How d'you like them beans?"

Tolt was too angered to say anything. Jimmy finished with, "So, then the old man ends up telling me that State and ONI think my buddy Tolt Gross may have been manipulated by Japanese disinformation efforts. Nice, clean-cut fellow. Well-spoken. But after all, Coloreds... so gullible. Foolish Negroes. Yeah." Bitterness seeped into Jimmy's voice.

The friends sat in silence, which made the drugstore radio's blaring Bing Crosby's "A Song of Old Hawaii" all the louder. Tolt no longer saw the Coca-Cola advertisement that hung above Jimmy's head. An idea was taking shape.

"And we're back! It's been a pleasure having Tolt Gross of Snow Drift Flour with us at KTU for this Saturday afternoon's Week in Review. Those of you who have visited Seattle are familiar with the delicious Snow Drift flour scones. Hearing how Snow Drift is spreading beyond the Pacific, well, it's pretty darned exciting!"

"Thank you, Mr. Jones. It's my pleasure to have been with you today." Tolt had parlayed an evening's chat in the Royal Hawaiian bar over whiskey with the presenter of Honolulu's weekly local news program into an interview. Some days ago, Jones had made the offer, but being so focused on passing on intelligence to the Navy, Tolt had not accepted. After his meeting with Jimmy, a call from the drugstore phone resulted in a hearty welcome to drop by that afternoon for an on-air interview.

"Well, wishing you smooth travels on Monday's Clipper! Any final thoughts?"

"As a matter of fact, there *is* one last point I'd like to touch on."

"By all means..."

"As I mentioned, Japan's presence in the Asia-Pacific region is growing. Well, frankly I've heard directly from an Imperial Japanese Naval officer word of a plan that leaves me pretty concerned, and I think your listeners would be too, if they knew of it."

"Concerned? For China?"

"No, Mr. Jones. For America. Specifically, for these beautiful islands."

"Well, you've certainly piqued my interest, Mr. Gross. What've you heard?"

"Well, earlier in the year, this officer told me he was tasked with planning how Japan's forces could attack the Pacific Fleet here at Pearl Harbor, and last time I saw him, he said the plan is going forward."

"Some late-night shenanigans and glasses of spirits greasing men's tongues, Mr. Gross? Sounds like there could be a story behind the story, if you catch my meaning."

"Given the peaceful surroundings here in Honolulu, I'm sure this does sound fantastical, Mr. Jones. But it's not a joke, and..."

A flashing red light went off above the announcer's head, and the producer popped his head inside the booth, "Jeff, just heard from the management. Switchboard's lighting up something fierce, including from the brass from Pearl Harbor. They're none too pleased. We've gone to commercial, and word is, Mr. Gross needs to vamooski."

Tolt smiled. Things were going as hoped.

A sailor was waiting outside a Navy car when Tolt emerged from the Advertisers Publishing Company Building. He drove Tolt to Pearl Harbor, where Foster was waiting in his office, steam almost visibly emanating from his reddened ears.

"What in Sam Hill are you playing at, Gross? You trying to get the civilian population here in a full frenzy?" Foster pounded on his desk for emphasis.

Tolt stood in front of Foster's desk, right where a week and a half earlier the two had cordially discussed Tolt's warning. Foster's anger was volcanic. "And how you thought going on the Island's most listened-to local news program was going to be to your credit is beyond me! Didn't Johnson relay the message I gave him? What kind of fools are you two?"

Tolt felt his spine stiffening. Anger at him was one thing, but Jimmy shouldn't be dragged into this.

"Sir, with respect, Jimmy did relay your message. ONI discounts the possibility a Japanese surprise attack is real because it believes the rumors are merely the work of disgruntled Korean nationalists trying to stir up trouble."

"Damned right! And civilians like yourself shouldn't be interfering in matters above your pay grade." Foster jerked his head in the direction of the window. "You may think that my authority extends only to the MPs and the brig here on base. Hell, only reason I didn't have the County Sheriff put you in *his* brig is that I know he's out on the golf course this afternoon." Foster snapped his fingers with a loud pop. "But mind my words, boy, another word about this Jap attack nonsense and your sorry ass will be locked up just as tight as Johnson's will be."

A frisson of fear cooled the anger surging through Tolt. "Sir, respectfully, American citizens do hold rights of free speech in Hawaii even if it's not a state."

Foster banged his hand on the desk. "Don't come in here talking to me about free speech! No one... hell, not even FDR himself has a right to gin up a riot. And, that's what you're doing, by God. It needs to stop! Now, I understand you are booked on the Clipper departing on Monday."

Tolt gave a curt nod.

"Well, between now and then, I want no public comment from you on these matters. None. Do you hear me? Because if there's one peep — even one — in the papers, on the radio, on the street, Johnson is going in the brig and you in jail. You got me?"

"Sir, Jimmy has nothing to do with this. Any problem you have is with me. But since we're talking about Jimmy, may I make a request on his behalf? A request for leave."

An incredulous expression suffused Foster's face, and he started to guffaw. "Request a leave? What sort of outfit do you think we're running here?

Tolt thought fast and responded in his best tone of respectful subservience, "Well, I'm sorry to say, sir, yesterday I received a letter from my grandfather in Seattle. He wrote that Jimmy's mother is poorly. She was admitted to the hospital and the doctors don't think she's going to see the New Year."

Foster shook his head in disbelief. "Johnson can't just take off."

"Of course, sir. It's just, well, by the time he goes through the usual channels, it may still be another week before he can catch a ship to the Mainland. It may be too late. If you could approve a leave now, Jimmy could take the Clipper with me on Monday."

"Be that as it may, Gross, the wellbeing of one mess man's

mother is not my primary concern. If you haven't noticed, we are running a sizable outfit here. Hell, there are over 1,400 sailors on the *West Virginia* alone. If every time a sailor's mother took ill he decided he needed to hop home to be by her bedside, where do you think that would leave the defenses of the country? The subject you claim to be so worried about!"

"Sir, certainly I appreciate the need to maintain order and defensive readiness, but Jimmy, he's merely a messman. If there were any way you could help him out..."

"No," Foster cut him off. "That's not going to happen. Not only is there not a chance in hell Johnson is going on leave, if you keep this up, he's going to be in the brig. Now, I have other matters to attend to, but mind what I said: no more about these fantasies of the Japs descending from the skies!"

Back at the Clipper pier once more. With each visit, he was liking it less and less. Jimmy had come to see him off. Looking at the plane bobbing in the sunlight at the end of the pier, Tolt urged, "Come on! Look, the plane's not going to be full. I'll buy you a ticket! We'll sort out the Navy once we're back in Seattle."

Jimmy shook his head, whistling. "Boy, what'd life over there do to you? You sneaking puffs of opium behind my back or something? I hop aboard with you, and by the time that bird bounces up to the pier in San Fran, Foster'd have a couple of MPs there to greet me. No, thank you!"

Tolt frowned, trying to think of a final witty thing he could say that would persuade Jimmy to come with him. Nothing came to mind. The end of the line, and he was standing empty-handed.

Jimmy gestured for emphasis. "Stop looking all sad sack. I believe you, man, but fact is, there's not much we can do. It's not like that Takeda's sending a telegram along to the Captain, telling him you're on the up and up." Jimmy shook his head. "We've just got to hope for the best."

The Pan Am staff were gesturing to the passengers to start making their way down the dock. The friends turned to one another to shake hands, their free arms each reaching out to grasp the other, as close to an embrace as possible without actually hugging.

With a wry smile, Tolt urged. "Stay out of trouble!"

"Me? Always! Always, son. Give your Granddad my regards, and to Ping and Sato, too."

As Tolt walked down the pier towards the Clipper, he turned to take one last look at Jimmy. He could see Jimmy had been watching him with a grim face, but when he caught sight of Tolt turning to look at him, he lit up with a brilliant smile. "Go on, you. Time's a-wasting!"

God, he wished Jimmy were going with him.

19

December 1941

Ever since the train had dropped him in Seattle earlier in the week, Tolt's gut had felt as heavy as a rock. November had ended with no Japanese ambush; instead, Kurusu, the Japanese envoy who had flown on the Clipper with him and Sumiko, was still negotiating in D.C. Japan was deploying no weapons except diplomacy.

Maybe the previous winter Takeda really had been tasked with analyzing the feasibility of attacking the U.S. Navy at Pearl Harbor. That didn't mean Japan's government had decided to invoke his plan, however. Hadn't Jimmy's Captain Fisher told Tolt that he was likely being fed disinformation? He kept berating himself at what an idiot he had been in failing to enlist Sumiko to devise a plan. With her help, maybe they could have figured out a way to verify whether Takeda was for real. But what had Tolt done? He had persuaded a dear friend to stake his life on this matter. His friend's life had been sacrificed, as had the life of the woman Tolt loved, and now another friend was exiled from her homeland and her family. And for what? What if they had died for some propaganda scam? Sure, Jimmy would be safe, but everyone else he loved was down the drain. Some hero.

Perhaps Ronnie Jr. had been right all along. Tolt was so used to being admired by those who knew him that he insisted on being heard. Maybe he was devious in getting people to heed him. Had Tolt actually manipulated an innocent man into sacrificing his life based on Tolt's flawed interpretation of events?

Tolt clutched the telephone receiver close to his ear, asking in a loud voice, "Any news?" It was his third call to Jimmy that week.

"Nice to talk to you, too!" Jimmy replied. "Must be rolling in some serious change to run up these long-distance charges. You just got home and it's Saturday night. Don't you have anything better to do?"

Static came over the line. When it abated, Tolt asked, "Foster — has he said anything more to you?"

"Man, ain't you even going to make some kinda small chat? Yeah, Foster... me and him, we talk strategy all the day long." Jimmy laughed. "As it happens, yesterday he says he wants me to teach his mess crew to make dumplings for when he's out at sea. Tomorrow morning, 8:00 sharp, I'm gonna be down at the Harbor. Be sure to tell Ping to think of me playing teacher on the *West Virginia!*"

The pressure of it all was maddening, and he blurted to Jimmy, "For months now, I've been all biggity about that Takeda, telling every U.S. government official I can find that he's getting one over on us with his plans to attack Pearl Harbor. But fact is, they've got more access to intelligence than some conk buster like yours truly. It turns out, it weren't nothing but a bunch of hot air on Takeda's part. Some gum beater, that's all I am. All my two-bit talk got me or anyone else was the death of one of my best buddies and the murder of my girl."

Apart from the hissing of static, for a moment there was silence. "How long we known each other?" Jimmy asked.

"I don't know, going on twenty years? A lifetime? Something like that."

"Yeah, something like that. An' in that time, you ain't never acted the biggity fool. Lord knows, if anyone wanted to, anyone had a right to, it's you. What with the way your granddaddy brought you up, with servants, horseback riding, fencing and such."

Jimmy was picking up a head of steam. "Hell, most Whites ain't had what you had. But you've always called things for what they were. Didn't get big-headed about yourself. So, when you tell me that some Jap stormbuzzard's been bragging to you on how he's the Man, fixing to plan an attack on Pearl Harbor, I believe you."

Tolt knew that if they were together, Jimmy'd be slamming his hand on the table for emphasis. "It may not have happened yet, but the key word is '*yet*.' The U.S. government best not be thinking 'we solid.' And you... you best not be blowing your top, thinking you're no good."

Tolt went to bed feeling somewhat comforted by his buddy's faith in him. The rest of the world might not give him the time of day, but Jimmy he could rely on.

Sunday came, but even at mid-morning, the day still felt like dusk. Dark clouds pregnant with icy rain seemed almost to press against the Our House living room's windows. Despite Jimmy's encouragement the night before, Tolt was feeling low. That morning he persuaded his grandfather to take a Sunday off from church services.The prospect of facing the First AME congregants with speculation as to the reasons for his return to Seattle, had seemed too much. Instead of going to church, he, along with Bill and Sumiko, were gathered in the living room to read the Sunday papers and listen to the radio. As the mantel clock struck half past 11, the announcer's fruity voice came on, "And you've been listening to Sammy Kaye's Sunday Serenade on NBC Red Network. Next up, the University of Chicago Roundtable, where we'll be discussing "Canada: A Neighbor at War."

After taking another sip of coffee, Tolt let out a sigh of relaxation, leaning back in his favorite overstuffed armchair. Sumiko and his grandfather sat on the couch, across from him, with a low table between the chair and couch on which sat the coffee pot and a plate towering with morning rolls. Outside was icy, dark and wet. Staying home was a good decision.

The University of Chicago program began, but then suddenly, there was an interruption. A different announcer's voice broke in. In staccato tones, the man said, "From the NBC newsroom in New York, President Roosevelt says in a statement that the Japanese have attacked Pearl Harbor, Hawaii from the air." Then he reiterated, "This bulletin came to you from the NBC newsroom in New York."

"...For two years..." resumed the fruity voice of the regular broadcast.

Tolt lunged upright in his chair, sloshing some coffee onto his pant legs. "What? Did you hear that?"

Bill suggested, "Try the other station. See if one of the other stations has anything more."

Sumiko's face appeared frozen from shock, and her fingers glared white where she was clutching her own coffee cup. Tolt rotated the dial, and caught a voice saying, "Go ahead, New York."

An announcer came on. "The Japanese have attacked Pearl Harbor Hawaii by air, President Roosevelt has just announced. The attack also was made on all military and naval activities on the principal island of O-ha-u."

Tolt jumped up, shaking his head. "Doesn't even know how to say the name right! O-ha-u?" He looked around at Sumiko and his grandfather. "But it's happening! By air. Just as Takeda said it would." He looked around, his face turning fearful. "My God, what wouldn't I give to know where he is right now! What's next?"

Tolt sat on the edge of the coffee table and fiddled with the radio, but the only announcements coming on merely repeated what they had previously heard. Sumiko set down her cup, and wrapped her hands around her arms, seeming to retreat into the sofa. Tolt paced up and down the room, muttering to himself. "It's happening. It's finally happening! But what's the scale of the thing? Have we put up any defense?"

He stopped, then pivoted toward Sumiko and his grandfather as he gripped the back of his chair with tight fingers. "Jimmy. What about Jimmy?" Tolt's eyes widened in fear. "Last night he said he was supposed to be on one of the battleships. One of the ships in the Harbor." Tolt bent over, pain coursing through him. "Oh, God. Not Jimmy."

"Now, son, hold up. We don't know nothing for certain just yet. Let's bide our time until more is known."

Pounding steps could be heard on the stairs leading from the basement, then Ping came rushing into the living room, his eyes wild and his face red. "Did you hear? Those devils have attacked!"

Sato also came bursting in from the entry hall of the hotel. "Is it true? Have we really been attacked?" A curtain of anguish furled down over his face.

Bill stood and placed his hand on Sato's arm. "I'm afraid so. Sounds like we may be in for a spell of hellfire such as our country hasn't seen since — well, since eighty years ago, when it almost came apart."

Sato pulled his cap off his head, wringing it between his hands as his eyebrows twisted themselves in a parallel demonstration of tense anxiety. Bill walked over to Ping and said something in his ear, then went over to the fireplace, adding a log to the fire.

"Come on, friend. I need you to help. More coffee, and some food," Ping said to Sato as he gestured toward the door. Mechanically, without saying a word, Sato walked out of the room. Ping followed, shutting the door behind him.

Sumiko and Tolt looked at each other, then Tolt asked his grandfather, "Ping inviting Sato to the kitchen? To help him? Now I've seen everything."

Bill turned his back to the fire, facing Sumiko and Tolt, then answered in a somber voice. "This may turn bad for our Japanese friends. It's too early to tell, of course, but I asked Ping to keep Sato indoors with him... until we know more."

Tolt nodded. He and Sumiko exchanged anxious glances. Time seemed to inch along with aching slowness. Intermittently, brief announcements blared out from the radio, but bore no substantial news as to the scope of what was going on so many thousands of miles across the Pacific. Ping brought plates of sandwiches and refreshed the pot of coffee. The sandwiches remained untouched, but all replenished their coffee cups. Finally, another announcement blared out of the radio. "We now take you to Honolulu. One moment please."

The three of them froze, and a crackly faint voice came over the radio, "ONe, two, three, four. Hello NBC, hello NBC, this is KGU in Honolulu, Hawaii. I am speaking from the roof of the Advertisers Publishing Company Building. We have witnessed this morning the severe bombing of Pearl Harbor by enemy planes, undoubtedly Japanese."

The voice paused. Tolt, Sumiko and Bill all leaned towards the radio, as if willing it to resume.

"The city of Honolulu has also been attacked, and considerable damage done. This battle has been going on for nearly three hours. One of the bombs dropped within fifty feet of KGU tower! It is no joke, it is a real war. There has been fierce fighting going on in the air and sea. We cannot estimate deaths nor how much damage has been done, but it has been a very severe attack."

The door opened again and the tall form of Bill's dear friend John Gayton walked in, still wearing his overcoat and holding his hat. Normally Gayton wore his thick hair combed into a smooth halo above his broad forehead, but today his silver locks bore a more mane-like appearance, as if he had been running his fingers through them. Bill greeted him, then stood to help remove his coat. "Friends should be together on a day as sad as this one, shouldn't they? Sit down and join us, have some coffee."

Mr. Gayton observed Sumiko, whose eyes were tearing up, and Tolt who had retaken his seat and lowered his head to his hands. Gayton walked over to Tolt, placing a hand on his shoulder, "Son, I heard the news as I was coming from church. Tell us. What's going on?"

Tolt looked up at him, tears running down his cheeks. "I wish I knew, sir." He shook his head.

"Your Papa told me some... well, some about what you have been trying to do. Trying to warn folks. Is this thing unfolding as you predicted?"

Tolt swallowed, trying to clear his voice, but anguish made it thick. "From what little said so far, yes. It sounds like the kind of combined air and sea surprise attack Takeda warned of. We don't know the scale, but I'm afraid... I'm afraid that at the center of the attack is the Harbor. And Jimmy was supposed to be there this morning. I'm... Oh God, if only I had done more. If I had been smarter about this damned thing!"

Tears were now flooding his face, his nose was dripping and his voice choking. Tolt extended a hand in Sumiko's direction. "If I had consulted you, followed your idea... maybe Tak would still be here."

Sumiko rushed over and knelt alongside his chair. "No! Don't say that."

He rubbed his face roughly with his handkerchief. "I'm a fool. Everyone around me has suffered by my efforts to beat this thing. And at the end of the day, bombs are raining down in Honolulu and their suffering was all for nothing."

"Well, Tolt, I have to take exception there." Mr. Gayton sat down, on the adjacent armchair, his body angled towards Tolt, with an expression on his face both serious and compassionate. "When you were a little fellow, remember when I first told you about the Chevalier de Saint-Georges? Do you remember how his story ended?"

Wordless, Tolt shook his head.

Mr. Gayton raised his eyebrows. "Penniless, dead at fifty-three of an untreated infection after years of being falsely accused and imprisoned." He nodded for emphasis. "But does that make his accomplishments — his composing, his conducting, his skill at the violin, at fencing, in defending his country — all of that, are they less commendable because his worth wasn't fully appreciated at the time? A hundred years on, he still impressed you as a hero, didn't he?"

Tolt nodded. Mr. Gayton continued, his voice sober. "How many times have your Papa and I told you, if we Colored folks depend on whether others listen to us to judge whether we're right, we're going to be sorely disappointed? That's a lesson your grandpa and I know first-hand, and all too well. Our people can never rely on recognition — by history, by people in power — to determine our worth."

He looked at Tolt with compassion gleaming in his eyes. "Now, let me ask you this." He paused, adding weight to each question. "Did you try? Did you try to the best of your ability try to discover what Japan had up its sleeve? Did you tell people in positions of responsibility what you knew? Warn of the danger?"

Tolt nodded, tears again seeping from the corners of his eyes. "Doing so, did you put your reputation, your safety, others' safety at risk?"

Thinking of Diana, of Tak, Tolt's face crumbled, as he nodded again.

"Well, son, truth to tell, I'm not sure what more you could ask of yourself. *I* couldn't ask more of you, and I don't think your grandfather could either."

Bill nodded in agreement. "Fact is, we're proud of you," Mr. Gayton said. "Real proud. And you ought to be proud of yourself. People have died today; Lord knows it will be a sad figure once the tally is published. But *you,* you have a clean conscience. You did all you could to prevent today from happening. I'm not sure that's something many of us can ever say. And to me, that makes you a hero."

At this, Tolt broke down totally, shoulders heaving, as Sumiko, Mr. Gayton and Bill all placed their hands on his back, seeking without avail to ease his sorrow.

The next morning finally came. Tolt walked out to the front step to retrieve the newspaper. Huge headlines glared out from where the paper lay:

BLACKOUT TONIGHT
RADIO STATIONS TO BE SILENT

+2,000 DEAD IN	WAKE GUAM BLASTED
HAWAII ATTACK	WAR DECLARED BY U.S.

The death toll struck him like a slam from a heavy saber. The contest was over, and he had lost. The day before, Mr. Gayton's words had momentarily eased his agony, but the facts were clear:

he had failed to prevent Japan from surprising the U.S. forces and now, thousands were dead. Likely among them, his oldest and closest friend.

Sunday evening, they had stayed up late, listening to broadcast after broadcast of the developing news. The President had called an emergency cabinet meeting. Manila had been bombed. No, it hadn't — just American bases in the Philippines. War had been declared. Japan was on the move elsewhere in Asia: Hong Kong, Malaya, the Dutch East Indies. But despite all the words, all the bulletins, little had come through as to the scale of the death toll, of those injured in the attack. Seeing that figure now on the cover of Monday's newspaper, thinking of Jimmy, made his heart ache.

He picked up the paper, scanning the articles on the front page, as he turned to go back inside. He saw casualties were listed in a narrow column: was Jimmy's name among them?

Re-entering Our House, Tolt read the names on the casualty list in the paper. Tears blurred his eyes. *James Johnson, Messman Third Class, of Seattle, WA, at Pearl Harbor.* Oh, God.

Around him all felt cold and dark, with only the newspaper column vivid before his eyes. The phone at the entryway desk began to ring, its sound jarring. Bill answered, then handed the receiver to Tolt, who asked, "Who is it?" Bill shook his head and shrugged his shoulders.

Tolt swallowed, trying to hold in his tears. He took the receiver from his grandfather but didn't place it to his ear. Holding it between them so both of them could hear, he said, "Tolt Gross, here."

"Gross, Fulton here. ONI. Met last summer when you came to see Senator Smith."

"Yes?" Tolt doubted the Lieutenant Commander who had rejected his warning was calling to offer a mea culpa.

"Well, Gross, no sense beating around the bush. We've been

caught flatfooted. In view of yesterday's events, it's imperative we assess where things stand, figure out what's next."

Tolt said nothing.

After a pause, Fulton said, "Fact is, we need your help."

"What do you mean?"

"No one at ONI — hell, no one in the Navy for that matter, has had the interaction you've had with the frontline folks involved in Jap planning. What we need is *you*. To debrief us, tell us everything that Jap officer told you, what you make of it, how you assess the situation based on your wider knowledge of the situation in Asia. I've told the powers-that-be that you're the one to help us make sense of this thing. First thing is to figure out if a follow-on attack is in the wings."

Fulton finished, but Tolt still said nothing.

"Can I send a car to collect you?" Fulton finally asked.

So many images flashed through Tolt's mind: Diana grinning up at him on the dance floor the night he asked her to marry him; Quentin on the Bund with champagne welcoming him to Shanghai; Tak juggling glassware when his sister wasn't looking; Sumiko choosing the winning line-up at the Canidrome; Jimmy wolfing down pancakes at Our House while Mr. Planter recounted how all the tires to Ronnie's Packard had gone flat, and the cops nabbed him with a trunkful of bootleg liquor; Tak telling him how to save Sumiko; Sumiko, abandoning all — family, friends, country — and trusting him to make a new life; Jimmy, believing him when no one in Hawaii would. Jimmy, now gone. Just like Diana and Tak. So much lost. All because no one in power was willing to believe him. To believe a Black man. His grandfather looked at him, waiting for his answer. Slowly Tolt, spoke into the phone. "That would be fine."

"Good!" Fulton replied, the tone of heartiness in his voice tinged with a strong tone of relief. "Glad to know we'll have your help. See you soon, Gross."

Tolt hung up the phone and Bill straightened up from the hunched position he had assumed, trying to hear the call. The two looked at one another. "Guess that's about as close to an 'I'm sorry' as you're gonna get from those damned fools."

Tolt nodded. "Yep. Guess it is. Would have been a hell of a lot better if they had listened the first time." He pointed to the column of the paper listing casualties. "Then maybe he'd still be with us."

Bill put his arms around Tolt, who leaned on his grandfather's shoulder, finally letting the burning tears of agony flow.

POSTSCRIPT

IT WASN'T ENOUGH, of course. Later, after Japan surrendered and the war concluded, Tolt would look back with pride at the work he did with the ONI. In those first desperate weeks after the attack, it felt like American forces were looking through a swirling kaleidoscope and no pattern nor plan could be detected. He had worked feverishly with Fulton and others to assess the situation, to consider what other offensive plans Japan had in the works and how robust it was likely to be in pursuing them.

Like so much else involved in being a Negro in America, his role wasn't given a formal position, a formal title, but Tolt knew that his insights, his analysis had mattered. It didn't make up for all that had been lost through the hubris he had encountered before December 7, however. In the war's darkest moments, he seethed. Others talked of service to country, of sacrifice. He was still furious, and would remain so, at the sacrifice of those he loved and the senseless losses borne by those in Honolulu on that terrible day.

His service and his efforts were for Jimmy. For Diana. For Tak. They embodied the best ideals — of devotion and loyalty — that America was supposed to cherish. Supposed to. And Shanghai? Well, ten years on, that was now but a chimera. That dazzling neon-bathed cosmopolis, blending peoples from around the world, engrossed in dealing, toiling, scheming, cabareting, eating, dancing, and drinking their way through life... it had disappeared. An asbestos fire curtain of civil war and Communist victory descended on the stage that was Shanghai, extinguishing all the light. It was gone. But God, while the show lasted, it had been great. The best.

And on balance, Tolt felt Mr. Gayton's assessment of the life of Chevalier de Saint-Georges now applied to his own: tragedy and loss did not cancel out what he had achieved. He had ventured to play on a world stage, he had risked peril, and his performance had been one of daring bravura. Of that, he was now sure.

Acknowledgements

IN THE MONTHS following the September 11, 2001 attacks, U.S. media reported about people who sought to sound the alarm in the run-up to the tragedy. Their warnings were dismissed or ignored. Reading such articles made me curious: had there ever been a parallel in American history? I began to research the Pearl Harbor attack, learning of a similar dynamic in the countdown to December 7: people had provided specific cautions regarding an attack by Japan, but the outsider status of these individuals led the warnings to be rejected.

Around the same time 2002-03 period, the *Seattle Times* published an 1895 photo of a house belonging to Robert Moran, a prominent early settler, and recounting how Moran arrived in Seattle at age 18 with only a dime in his pocket. His first meals were given to him on credit by William Gross (sometimes spelled Grose), a Black man who owned a restaurant near the wharf. Moran was well known to me, but Gross's name I had never encountered. I discovered he was a successful businessman in early Seattle (restauranteur, real estate developer) and learned of other African Americans who played significant roles in Seattle's early development.

The Seattle history I learned growing up focused on White experiences (with occasional references to the Native people displaced by White settlers). Considering the experiences of these Black early Seattleites made me ponder: In addition to the ill-effects experienced by the marginalized, how does such diminishment harm society as a whole? The run-up to the Pearl Harbor attack seemed to offer a chance to explore those questions.

In 2004, my husband and I relocated our then young family (sons ages 8 and 3) to Shanghai. For over a decade we lived and thrived there, inhabiting an Art Deco style apartment on "Tifeng" Road (now Wulumuqi Road North), bracketed to the north by a little church that appeared transported from an English village, and to the south by the site of the former Model Dairy Farm. On my way to work, I cycled past the Paramount Ballroom and the gorgeous Edington House apartment building where Shanghai author Eileen Chang had lived. At that time, a number of expatriates resided in Shanghai who loved its old architecture and stories of pre-World War ll life. They wrote and gave frequent talks or walking tours about their findings. Michelle Garnaut, who had five years earlier flouted conventional wisdom by launching a fine-dining restaurant on the Bund, opened her establishment's doors to author talks, and then, a founded a Literary Festival, creating a delightful haven in which to hear about Old Shanghai.

I wanted to write a story that captured the sense of possibility that pre-World War ll Shanghai offered, a sense that in many ways was also present in the early years of Shanghai's twenty-first century incarnation. *Rumors from Shanghai* is my attempt to depict that world and the question of how society as a whole suffers as a result of our prejudices.

And now, to those who helped me in pursuing these aims (with responsibility for any deficiencies being mine alone):

The passion for and deep knowledge of pre-War Shanghai shared by Tess Johnston, Tina Kanagaratnam, Patrick Cranley, Peter Hiibbard and Duncan Hewitt in their walking tours, lectures and book talks were wonderful inspiration. Regarding life amongst the Chinese elite of pre-War Shanghai, our friend

John Hu kindly shared tales of his experience growing up in fairytale-like affluence as the oldest son of a wealthy Shanghai cigarette factory owner. A tricky part of historical fiction is getting the facts to align with the story you want to tell. Paul French's encyclopedic knowledge of all things old Shanghai was invaluable in figuring out how to move characters around the map amid rising US-Japanese tensions. When I had questions about dog racing in the pre-War period, John Slusar was generous in responding to the queries of someone he had never met.

In writing *Rumors from Shanghai*, I was honored by the encouragement from, and experiences shared by, modern day Black Americans with first-hand experience in China and elsewhere in Asia, including Bayo Callender, Muriel Tillinghast and Katherine Bostick. I'm particularly indebted to the generosity of Jamilia Grier who shared probing insights into identity, including how the opportunity to excel in China can offer a welcome escape from the skepticism African Americans still encounter in elite professional and business circles at home. Muguette Guenneguez, with an international story stretching across three continents, generously read an early draft of the manuscript. The path and experiences of these amazing women would make a compelling stories; I hope someday we will have a chance to read them.

I appreciate the support offered by various authors, including the opportunity to study at Hugo House, with skilled teachers and writers Nancy Rawles and Waverly Fitzgerald. My writing group has offered support in all aspects of the author journey: Bruce Funkhouser for slogging through an early draft and sharing home-truths; Joanna Richey for help preparing to query and pitch; Meg Diaz for her acute design sense and impeccable taste; and Judy Taylor for her above-and-beyond generosity in providing editing support. I am thankful to Graham Earnshaw of Earnshaw Books for believing in Tolt's story and helping bring it to these pages. Alex Britton's talents realized the evocative cover design. With her wise insights on publishing and vital life lessons, Kate Spelman always demonstrates her knack for being a true friend. Over the years, several of my assistants in my 'day job' provided help at key points: Cynthia Kawano, for insights into early Japanese-American identity in the Pacific Northwest and for introducing me to Monica Sone's memoir; Rita Xiong and Sylvia Chan for aiding in recovery from document corruption disasters!

Friends carry us along our journey. My thanks to the "Senatorettes," whose Friday after-work ministrations over cocktails at Shanghai's Senator Saloon always nurtured my spirits: Rebecca Catching, Brigitte Elie, Karen Eryou, Heather Kaye, Sarah Kochling, and Crystyl Mo. Thanks to Carmela Conroy for assistance with pre-war Japanese naming conventions and to Tess Johnston and Helen Zia for their encouragement.

Finally, I owe so much to my 'guys': Ken, Jack and Ryan, who over the years endured Saturday mornings when I disappeared to write, listened to me ponder frustrations, accompanied me on old Shanghai walks and talks, and generally cheered me on.

We say it 'takes a village' to raise a child, but arguably the saying applies to writers as well. I'm deeply thankful to the entire village that took the time to help me as I wrote this book. I hope they and you enjoy it.

RESOURCES

While the story of Tolt Gross is fictional, I have drawn on historical events, places and people to create the 1940-41 world that Tolt inhabits. For those wishing to read more about the period, places and some of the people who inspired this story, below is a list of resources.

Early Seattle:

Hobbs, Richard S., *The Cayton Legacy: An African American Family*. Washington State University Press, 2002.

Sone, Monica, *Nisei Daughter*. University of Washington Press, 1979 (originally published 1953 as an Atlantic Monthly Press Book by Little, Brown and Company).

Taylor, Quintard, *The Forging of a Black Community: Seattle's Central District from 1870 through the Civil Rights Era*. University of Washington Press, 1994.

Memoirs of Pre-War Asia:

Angulo, Diana Hutchins (Tess Johnston and Jeananne A. Hauswald, eds.), *Peking Sun Shanghai Moon: Images from a Past Era*. Old China Hand Press (Hong Kong), 2008.

Blair, Margaret, *Gudao, Lone Islet: The War Years in Shanghai – A Childhood Memoir*. AuthorHouseUK, 2017.

Gaan, Margaret, *Last Moments of a World*. W.W. Norton and Company Inc., 1978. (The incident in which Diana persuades the postal service to open mail bags heading for Hong Kong is taken from Gaan's memoir.)

Smith, Mabel Waln, *Springtime in Shanghai*. George G. Harrap & Co. Ltd., 1957.

Sansom, Katharine, *Living in Tokyo*. Harcourt, Brace & Company, 1937.

Black Westerners and Pre-World War II Asia:

Chen, Percy, *China Called Me: My Life Inside the Chinese Revolution*. Little, Brown and Company, 1979.

Clayton, Buck, *Buck Clayton's Jazz World*. Oxford University Press, 1986.

Gallicchio, Marc, *The African American Encounter with Japan & China*. The University of North Carolina Press, 2000.

Hughes, Langston, *I Wonder as I Wander: An Autobiographical Journey*. Hill and Wang, 1993 (originally published by Rinehart & Company,1956).

Koerner, Brendan I., *Piano Demon: The globetrotting, gin-soaked, too-short life of Teddy Weatherford*. The Atavist, 2011.

Pash, Sidney, "W.E.B. Du Bois: From Japanophile to Apologist," Japan Women's University Journal of American and English Literature (March 2016): 21-36.

Pre- and War-Era Japan:

Grew, Joseph C. *Ten Years in Japan: A Contemporary Record Drawn From the Diaries and Private and Official Papers of Joseph G. Grew, United States Ambassador to Japan, 1932-1942*. Simon and Schuster, 1944.

Havens, Thomas R.H., *Valley of Darkness: The Japanese People and World War Two*. University Press of America, 1986.

Helm, Leslie, *Yokohama Yankee: My Family's Five Generations as Outsiders in Japan*. Chin Music Press Inc., 2013.

Ienaga, Saburo, *The Pacific War, 1931-1945*. Random House (English Translation), 1978.

Moore, Frederick, *With Japan's leaders: An intimate record of fourteen years as counsellor to the Japanese government, ending December 7, 1941*. C. Scribner's Sons, 1942.

Pre- and War-Era Shanghai:

Field, Andrew David, *Shanghai's Dancing World: Cabaret Culture and Urban Politics, 1919-1954*. The Chinese University of Hong Kong, 2010.

French, Paul, *City of Devils: The Two Men Who Ruled the Underworld of Old Shanghai*. Picador, 2018.

French, Paul, *The Old Shanghai A-Z*. Hong Kong University Press, 2010.

Fu, Poshek, *Passivity, Resistance, and Collaboration: Intellectual Choices in Occupied Shanghai, 1937-1945*. Stanford University Press, 1993.

Hibbard, Peter (foreword), *All About Shanghai And Environs: The 1934-35 Standard Guide Book*. Earnshaw Books, 2008 (originally published by The University Press, 1934).

Johnston, Tess and Erh, Deke, *Frenchtown Shanghai*. Old China Hand Press, 2000.

Johnston, Tess and Erh, Deke, *Shanghai Art Deco*. Old China Hand Press, 2006.

Pan, Ling, *In Search of Old Shanghai*. Joint Publishing (H.K.) Co., Ltd., 1982.

Sergeant, Harriet, *Shanghai*. John Murray (Publishers) Ltd., 1991.

Pearl Harbor:

Goldstein, Donald M. and Dillon, Katherine V., eds., *The Pearl Harbor Papers: Inside the Japanese Plans*. Brassey's (US), 1993.

Hoyt, Edwin P., *Japan's War: The Great Pacific Conflict*. De Capo Press Inc., 1986.

Prange, Gordon, *At Dawn We Slept: The Untold Story of Pearl Harbor*. McGraw-Hill, 1981.

Toland, John, *The Rising Sun: The Decline and Fall of the Japanese Empire, 1936–1945 (vol. 1)*. Random House, 1970.

About The Author

Amy Sommers is a Sinophile and lifelong history fan. As a fluent Mandarin-speaking China-focused lawyer, in 2004 she moved to Shanghai with her husband and two young sons. Living and working in Shanghai during a period of intense legal, economic and social change, she became intrigued by the city's pre-World War II incarnation, one that served as both a mecca and a refuge for people from all over the world to reinvent themselves. Her debut novel "Rumors from Shanghai" explores the delights of a reinvented life and the dilemma of whether to risk it to avert a society-wide tragedy.